Praise for
FICTION RIVER

"[Fiction River] is one of the best and most exciting publications in the field today."

—Keith West, *Adventures Fantastic*

"Fiction River is off to an auspicious start. It's a worthy heir to the original anthology series of the 60s and 70s. ... It's certainly the top anthology of the year to date."

—*Amazing Stories* on *Fiction River: Unnatural Worlds*

"Editor Dean Wesley Smith has compiled an outstanding volume of time travel stories, no two alike. I highly recommend it."

—*Adventures Fantastic* on *Fiction River: Time Streams*

"A sugary Christmas treat for those who love romance."

—*Publisher's Weekly* on *Fiction River: Christmas Ghosts*

"*Fiction River [Special Edition]: Crime* edited by Kristine Kathryn Rusch leads off with strong new tales by three familiar EQMM contributors: Doug Allyn with a gangster whodunnit, Steve Hockensmith with a con game story, and Brendan DuBois with a fresh variation on the old brothers-who-took-different-paths ploy. A sampling of other contents, including experimental short-shorts by Melissa Yi and M. Elizabeth Castle and a clever turn on the greedy-relatives-want-inheritance by Kate Wilhelm, suggest high quality throughout."

—*Ellery Queen Mystery Magazine*

FICTION RIVER

Year Two

Fantasy Adrift
Edited by Kristine Kathryn Rusch

Universe Between
Edited by Dean Wesley Smith

Fantastic Detectives
Edited by Kristine Kathryn Rusch

Past Crime
Edited by Kristine Kathryn Rusch

Pulse Pounders
Edited by Kevin J. Anderson

Risk Takers
Edited by Dean Wesley Smith

FICTION RIVER
PAST CRIME

Edited by

KRISTINE KATHRYN RUSCH

Series Editors

DEAN WESLEY SMITH & KRISTINE KATHRYN RUSCH

Fiction River: Past Crime

Contents

A Reader's World

Dean Wesley Smith

Fiction River exists now because this new world of publishing and reading exists.

For a very long time, more decades than I want to think about, actually, the publishing of books never took into account the desires of readers. Editors and almost all publishers were based in New York, inside an echo chamber with almost no feedback from actual readers. Publishers in that echo chamber were deathly afraid to try new things, let new and unique voices free to tell stories they wanted to tell.

As I heard many editor or publisher say during those decades: "It wouldn't sell."

Yet they never once asked readers what would or wouldn't sell outside their publisher's bubble.

So during those decades, almost everything published had to be similar to things done before. Everything had to be easily classified so it could be easily sold to distributors and chains, and put on certain shelves in certain places in bookstores.

Then along came the electronic bookstore, with unlimited shelf space that allowed readers to easily access any book, either in hardback, paper, or electronic formats.

Suddenly, readers took back control of publishing. Readers who lived outside that publishing bubble and, surprise, bought books no one thought would sell inside the bubble.

And that freed up innovative publishers (such as WMG Publishing, who started outside the bubble) to focus on trusting their readers to be willing to try new and different types of stories, as long as the quality of the storytelling was high.

Many major publishers still inside the bubble have not switched yet to this new world of selling directly to readers and trusting them. But they will, or they will perish because readers now control.

Readers are smart. They know what they want and can find it just fine, thank you very much.

Fiction River is a result of trusting readers.

Fiction River trusts readers to enjoy a crime story beside a science fiction story beside a fantasy story. And sometimes have all those elements in the same story. *Fiction River* trusts readers to find a volume they want to read when they want to read it, which is why all *Fiction River* volumes are still completely in print in all forms for any reader to find when they want to read it.

Every volume of *Fiction River* is unique. The series name is the same and the quality we guarantee of storytelling is high in every volume, but that's where the similarities from volume to volume end. I edited a science fiction volume of stories focusing on moons. Kerrie L. Hughes edited a fantastic volume of urban fantasy stories called *Fiction River: Hex in the City*. Kevin J. Anderson has just finished editing a volume of fast-paced stories that cover varied genres called *Fiction River: Pulse Pounders*.

Now in this volume, Edgar Award-nominated writer Kristine Kathryn Rusch challenged professional writers to give her stories about crimes in the past that are now not crimes. And the professional writers came through.

This volume almost vibrates with the contained power of professional writers given the freedom to explore topics and crimes in the past that make each writer passionate. Trust me, this will be a volume of stories you won't soon forget.

This volume would not exist without the change in publishing, without the freedom now given to innovative publishers and writers to take chances, explore topics that no publisher ten years ago would have allowed.

This volume would not exist without readers taking back control of reading.

Thank you.

—Dean Wesley Smith
Lincoln City, Oregon
April 7, 2014

Looking Backward

Kristine Kathryn Rusch

Whenever I come up with an idea for an anthology, I have a vision of what I want in that volume. I never get exactly what I imagined.

I'm not complaining. What I imagine is what *I* would write for the anthology. That's the problem with being both a writer and an editor.

I could be petulant and send brilliant stories back, with a "it's not right for me," and maybe I would if I were editing only one anthology in the next five years.

But *Past Crimes* marks my fourth solo volume of 2014, and my fifth solo volume since we started *Fiction River*. (For those of you who don't know, Kristine Grayson is one of my romance pen names.) I have other solo volumes of *Fiction River* lined up for 2015, and I'm scheming ways to slide in some special editions and non-*Fiction River* anthologies. So I know that I'll have more than enough chances to get that volume I envision—if I push hard enough.

But I don't like to push. I like to be surprised.

The volume you hold in your hands is not the volume I imagined when I came up with the title for this anthology. It's better. The story quality here is so high that I had trouble choosing my final table of contents. The stories that I couldn't take were just as good; I simply ran out of room.

Now that publishing has changed so that I can edit without working for someone else or writing a goofy proposal to sell a by-guess-and-by-golly who-the-hell-knows anthology to a big publisher, the editing bug has bitten me hard. I've missed editing. Not the nightmare of dealing with a boss who had a different vision for the magazine than I did and not the strangeness of trying to get writers to commit to write for an as-yet-unsold volume of something or other that might never come out, but the pure joy of finding stories that I love and sharing them with readers.

I especially love asking truly gifted writers to give me stories on a particular topic and then seeing what they come up with.

Some editors write long requirements for their anthologies. No murders with knives, but murders with guns are okay; no dripping intestines, but blood spatter is fine—that sort of thing.

I think that stifles creativity. I want to inspire writers to think about a topic they've never contemplated before or, at least, contemplated in this way.

Hence *Past Crime*.

In March, *Fiction River* released its first special, also edited by me, called *Crime*. I didn't title it *Mysteries* because I like crime stories. Something has gone horribly wrong, but it might be something as small as a traffic ticket. That whole for-want-of-a-nail thing…

The crime volume covered past and present. Someday, I'll do a science fiction volume called *Future Crime*. We just don't have it on the schedule yet.

Past Crime, however…that phrase evoked something concrete for me, the historical mystery writer, the woman with a B.A. in History, the writer who likes thinking about things that are and aren't any more.

I wanted stories about crimes that no longer exist. Crimes that aren't crimes any longer. Now, that led some writers who tried to write for this volume to tie themselves into pretzels. They felt that they couldn't write about murder (people still kill each other!) or serial killers (they still exist) or pickpockets or, or, or…

And that wasn't my intent.

The end result could be a murder, but the precipitating event had to be based on some historical attitude or law that no longer exists. The obvious one for Americans is Prohibition. Once upon a time, it was illegal to sell alcohol in these United States, and that led to all kinds of mayhem, as M. Elizabeth Castle's "Blood and Lightning on the Newport Highway" so beautifully shows.

But her story also contains murder and all sorts of crimes that still exist, none of which would have happened without the Volstead Act.

I'll be honest: I did fudge with one story. It captured its time period so beautifully that I decided to include it. The paranoia of the moment made the world a different place, and I was willing to overlook a rule to include the piece. And no, I won't tell you which story that is.

This volume contains all kinds of crimes that no longer exist in the U.S., such as slavery, pretending to be someone of a different race, and carrying a gun in the West. But some of the other crimes happen in cultures incredibly different from our own. Richard Quarry's Egyptian tale shows us a world long gone as does Lisa Silverthorne's dark investigation of 18th century England.

Some crimes aren't that distant from us. Drinking in the Stonewall Bar in New York City in 1969 was illegal because Stonewall was a gay bar. The only reason it remained open was because of the protection the owners paid. That's 45 years ago—close enough for some of us to remember, for others of us to touch.

As I went through the volume to put together my final table of contents, I was struck by how very powerful these stories are. Each author managed to capture a different moment in time, and a different attitude toward the world. They also managed to take us on a journey into the darker side of that period, and make us empathize with people long dead who actually had to live in these circumstances.

History doesn't live in dry textbooks. The best history lives in fiction. And some of the best fiction is, in my not-so-humble opinion, in this volume. Enjoy!

—Kristine Kathryn Rusch
Lincoln City, Oregon
April 7, 2014

Dory Crowe's story, "Stolen in Passing," provides the perfect opening to Past Crime. *Not only does the story have a crime that is no longer a crime, it also features legal behavior that is now criminal. In other words, by using this particular moment in history, Dory turns everything we know about legality and justice on its head.*

Dory is one of four pseudonymous writing Crowes. This is the second time a Crowe has appeared in Fiction River. *The previous Crowe story appeared in* Crime. *Crowe stories have appeared under various guises in both Daw Books and Level Best Books' Best New England Crime anthologies. Dory's first novel,* Dark Secrets, *a contemporary companion to "Stolen in Passing" will appear in 2015.*

The Cape Cod house in this story actually exists, including the room that factors so deeply in the story's action. Dory rediscovered the room at the age of twelve, proving to herself and the family that the myths and legends about the home were true all along.

Stolen in Passing

Dory Crowe

Wee Hours of Hallowe'en Morning 1857
Cape Cod, Massachusetts

"Open up. Please, dear God, open the door. Let me in."

The commotion rose through the fog of a running dream—two sharp knocks followed five rhythmic raps and the stage-whispered plea. Never in her life had Marie-France hoped to hear that dear, sweet voice again—never.

The sound flowed like ice water into her heart. It sent chills to the very soles of her feet.

How had he found her?

Why, oh why, had he come?

* * *

"I ain't gots no choice." He stood in the moonlight streaming at odd angles through the bull's-eye glass in the kitchen ell windows. The stiff flat brim of the black-tarred seaman's hat he'd been so proud to wear twisted between his long, calloused fingers. His bellbottomed trousers and striped shirt hung in filthy tatters off his lanky frame. He smelled like a swamp. He bowed his nappy head, while his eyes peered directly into hers. "They's after me, hard."

"How hard?" The ice water began to freeze.

"I done lit out three week gone. They come on board my whaler. We's docked in New Bedford. The Cap'n seen 'em coming. He tol' the bo'sun and him and me rows away in a longboat. I catched me a packet to Boston. Storm fetched us up at Monomoy. I dunno how, but when we gets to Chatham, them slave catchers is right behind."

"How close?"

He shrugged.

"Jethro." She placed two fingers at his throat, lifted his chin and stared into those deep brown eyes, so like her own. "How, close?"

A tear rolled down one cocoa-colored cheek. He shivered. "Right behind."

The ice cracked. Hot anger welled into every fiber of her being.

"And you brought them here?" She let his head drop. "To me!"

His chin sunk to his chest. A tear splashed onto one wide pine floorboard, then another. "I gots no place else to go."

She could think of a thousand places: to the Quaker Meetinghouse in Bass River; to Walker's Farm; to the woods, for the love of God. She stiffened her back and pointed her own chin at the door. "You must leave."

The hat spun round and round. "Where can I go?"

His eyes pleaded. "What can I do?"

"How can you put me out?" His voice cracked.

"I'm a married woman," she whispered, barely able to bring the words to her mouth. "I have a son."

"And well you should remember that before entertaining strange colored men in my kitchen in the middle of the night." Mother Thomas strode into the kitchen from the keeping room, pulling around her shoulders the Paisley shawl she wore everywhere—day or night, dead of winter or high noon summer. In the best of times, her granite face, drawn and pinched and lined with woe, would scare the bark off a tree. "What is the meaning of this? Who is this man?"

Jethro's mouth opened, but Marie-France got there first. "A runaway."

Mother Thomas' eyebrows rose and disappeared under her nightcap. "A runaway? Here? In my kitchen?"

Marie-France nodded.

Jethro bowed his head and held his hat up under his chin. "I's sorry, ma'am."

"And well you should be!" Mother Thomas tightened the shawl around herself. "Do you have any idea what can happen to God-fearing people if a runaway is caught in their home?"

"He was just going." Behind the folds of her nightgown, Marie-France waved Jethro toward the door.

"Yes, ma'am, I's gonna take my leave." He took one step backward.

Relief flooded through Marie-France like hot soup on a cold night. She would send him to Walker Farm. They'd know what to do. They'd—

A hound bayed in the distance. Out the window, where moon-light bathed the open marshlands in silver grey, yellow torchlight bounced and drew closer.

Jethro's bare foot took root on the planking. His hat froze in mid-twist.

Blood pounded in Marie-France's temples, behind her eyes.

Mother Thomas sprang to the door. She threw it open and waved her arms the way she herded chickens into their coop. "Shoo, now, shoo."

"No!" Marie-France drew the door shut. "The dog, he will find him."

Mother Thomas's hands took a stance on her hips. "He can't stay here."

Marie-France threw the latch. "He cannot go. Not now."

The baying grew louder, the torchlight ever nearer.

"Mama?" Asa Frank, dragging a small square of well-loved blanket in one hand and rubbing his eyes with the other, toddled into the kitchen from the keeping room. "Doggie."

Marie-France scooped her son into her arms and grabbed Jethro by the wrist. "Come with me." Without as much as a backward glance, she said, "Send them away."

They hurried through the dim glow of banked embers in the keeping room hearth to the darkness of the front parlor. Marie-France felt her way past the brick fireplace to the feathered closet door. She threw it open and began pulling coats off their pegs and hats off the single high shelf.

"Help me," she whispered to Jethro.

"Do what?"

She piled coats onto the red velvet sofa and tossed hats on its matching chair. "Lift up this shelf."

Jethro, a head taller and stronger by miles, lifted the shelf with ease.

"Remove it."

He tilted the single board and pulled it out of the closet. "Now what?"

"Give it to me."

She hugged the shelf to her breast. "On the right, one of the pegs pulls down."

The rattle of a chain told her he'd found it. "Pull toward you."

Warm air, scented with dust and lavender and basil, rushed into the parlor.

"Step up where it widens and squeeze inside." She pushed Jethro up into the narrow space between the bricks and the back of the closet. "*Dépêche-toi.*"

Harsh male voices joined the baying of the dog.

Jethro all but disappeared, leaving visible only the wide open whites of his eyes.

Marie-France slammed the closet sidewall shut, reset the latch-peg in its hole and higgledy-piggledy hurled coats and hats onto pegs. The shelf in one arm and Asa Frank in the other, she inched her way out of the parlor and up the narrow front staircase.

* * *

Marie-France tucked Asa Frank into the small trundle bed pulled out beside her four-poster in the back bedroom running the width of the house. His thumb went immediately into his mouth. She stroked his baby-fine, flaxen curls and kissed his forehead.

"Go to sleep. *Dors-toi bien, mon petit choux.*"

His eyes had barely closed, when a fist pounded at the kitchen door and a gruff Southern voice shouted, "Wake up in there."

Marie-France sat cross-legged on the end of her bed, where she had a view of the kitchen stoop bathed in moonlight and the backs of two men in long dusters. She kept to the shadows, where they could not see into her darkened room, clutching her bed quilt under her chin and praying the men would go away. Her prayers, as so many times before, went unanswered.

A second, smoother, more familiar Southern voice joined the first. It stopped Marie-France's heart. "We know y'all are in there. We can see the smoke from your fire." The fists pounded again, harder, longer. "Open up or we'll break this door down."

The window sash at the top of the back staircase drew down and Mother Thomas' head poked out. "Who's making all that racket in the middle of the night?"

A Yankee voice answered. "Heman Howes, Missus Thomas. These gentlemen have tracked a runaway slave right to your door."

"A runaway? At my door?" Mother Thomas sounded even more surprised than she had in the kitchen.

"Yes'am, Missus Thomas."

"Well, go catch the thief, then, and let decent folk sleep." The sash began to rattle back into place.

"The trail ends at your door, ma'am," the smooth Southern voice said. "We need to search inside."

The sash crashed back down. "You most certainly do not! My husband will return from the General Court in Boston this morning. I will not have strange men in my house in his absence. If you are truly Southern gentlemen, you will understand; if not, you are no gentlemen. Until then, you *do* need to leave my property."

The sash slammed shut and almost immediately the door from the stairwell opened into Marie-France's bedroom. Mother Thomas tiptoed to the end of the bed.

"Are they going?" she whispered.

Marie-France shook her head and put a finger to her lips.

Asa Frank stirred, rolled over and fell back asleep.

"We can't wait all night. What if that damned maroon's already skedaddled?" the smooth voice said.

"My bitch is never wrong. He's inside this house, I tell you," said the gruff voice.

A large man Marie-France recognized from the blacksmith's shop inserted himself between the Southerners and the door. "There's always a first time, and I'm not letting two ruffians from Louisiana break down our first selectman's back door."

"Ruffians," said the smooth voice with an oily menace Marie-France knew all too well. "You're the constable, duly sworn, and we have a warrant. Y'all must enforce the law of the land."

"What I *must* do is seek the counsel of our first selectman when he gets here in the morning. If you so much as crack the glass in one window of this house, the law of *my land* says I arrest you both on as many charges beyond trespass and breaking and entering as Judge Walker can find."

Heman Howes ushered the two protesting Southerners away from the stoop. They stopped at the garden gate and looked back at the house. A patch of moonlight fell on their upturned faces. One wore a jagged scar from eyebrow to chin. Marie-France knew that scar. She had prayed she would never see it again.

Her breath caught in her throat. Her heart pounded.

The bedroom swirled.

A black abyss reached up and sucked her down.

* * *

Cool morning light played against Marie-France's eyelids. A warm hand caressed her brow. She snuggled deeper into the comfort of her feather bed and dreamed. Asa lay next to her, spooned in their marriage bed. He ran his fingers through her hair and blew in her ear. The cock crowed and she willed it away. A crow cawed and another answered. A hound dog bayed.

Marie-France's eyes flew open.

Mother Thomas scowled down at her. "'Bout time you rejoined the living."

"I had the most terrible nightmare."

"'Twas a real nightmare all right." Mother Thomas shook her head. "And it's not over yet."

Marie-France's heart skipped a beat. She pushed herself upright. "They are—?" She swallowed.

Mother Thomas peered out the window. "Constable Howes took the scar-faced one with him to meet Father Thomas' train in Yarmouth. The man with the dog," she shuddered, "he's been here all night, prancing round the property like he owns the place—which he may if we're hiding a runaway here. Lets his dog loose to sniff the ground." She stared hard at Marie-France. "Blasted beast always tracks back to the kitchen door. Where on earth did you hide that fellow? I've been all over this house and can't find a trace. I hope you got him away."

"Would that I had. I put him in the drying space."

Mother Thomas' eyes grew wide. "In *my* drying space? With my herbs and flowers?"

"You haven't opened that space since Asa Frank was born. I removed the shelf. He could have escaped," although she doubted it.

"If he's still there, he's quiet as a mouse."

"He has nowhere else to go," *and neither do I*. Marie-France shivered.

Asa Frank lay on his back in his trundle bed, forefinger curled around his button nose, thumb secure in his mouth. She turned from her son and, taking her mother-in-law's hand in hers, heaved a prodigious sigh. "There is something I must tell you. I should have—" The words, so long repressed, tried to hide down her throat.

Mother Thomas' squeezed her hands. "Come now, girl. It can't be as bad as all that."

"It is worse. Worse than you can imagine."

Mother Thomas' raised a skeptical eyebrow. "It won't seem so bad once you get it out."

*　*　*

Marie-France took a deep breath and hoped Mother Thomas was right. "Jethro, the man in the drying space, he is my brother, my half brother."

Mother Thomas stiffened. Her hands lost their grip.

"His father is my mother's husband. My father was her owner." She hung her head, not risking what she might find in Mother Thomas' eyes. She took a deep breath and found the courage to go on. "My father was a good man, but he had no luck. He died and left his wife with more debt than dollars. She had no love for my mother." The next words tasted worse than bitter almond. "He meant for us to be free." She dared a glance at her mother-in-law. The blood, drained completely away, left her face the color of skimmed milk. "The condition of the child follows the mother—"

Mother Thomas gasped. Her hands slid completely away.

Marie-France dropped one hand to the trundle bed and smoothed Asa Frank's hair.

"Then my grandchild—" Mother Thomas' hands covered her mouth. "My God. This can't be right."

"Right has nothing to do with it. It is the law."

"But how—"

"Jethro and I escaped the night before the estate sale. We made our way north, to New Bedford."

"Where my Asa met you."

Marie-France raised her head. She nodded. "We fell in love."

"Did Asa know…you're not French?"

"Oh, but I am French. You've seen me reading my father's copy of *Le Comte de Monte Cristo.* It is all that he left me," she said. "The family of my father were sugar planters on *Saint-Domingue,* before the slave revolt named it Haiti. They escaped to *Louisiane* with their lives and little else. My mother was the natural daughter of her first owner. He was the younger son of a count who lost his head to the guillotine."

"And you let us believe—" recrimination strained Mother Thomas' voice.

Marie-France hung her head. "I love your son. He loves me. He went to California to seek a fortune to buy my freedom, and that of the son he has never seen." A tear escaped down her cheek. "Never in my life did I dream—. I am so sorry."

"Why didn't he come to us? We are not as rich as some, but Father Thomas is not a poor man. He could have bought your freedom."

"And if my father's widow, out of spite, would not sell and demanded my return and claimed my son as a lagniappe?" Marie-France shook her head. "Would Father Thomas have broken his precious law and let us escape to Canada?"

Mother Thomas' face turned as hard as the granite of her native New Hampshire and as white as the sheets on the bed. Her lips pinched so tightly they disappeared. One muscle twitched at her jaw.

The hound bayed at the rattle of an approaching carriage.

Mother Thomas leapt to the window. "My God, Father Thomas must have caught the earliest train. Constable Howes has brought him and that scar-faced man home in his dray."

The black abyss worked at the edge of Marie-France's mind. She pushed it back. "He must not see me."

"What?"

"He knows who I am." As fast as she could without waking him, Marie-France pulled Asa Frank from his bed and held him to her chest. All the air oozed out of her lungs. "We must hide."

Mother Thomas turned in a circle, eyeing first Marie-France and her child, then the scene out the window.

Heavy male voices joined the welcoming barks of the dog.

"Please," Marie-France begged.

Mother Thomas took one last look out the window. She turned her back on the men and crossed her arms over her bosom. "Yes, you must hide. Where did you put that closet shelf?"

* * *

The sidewall of the closet pulled shut and the drying space went as dark as a grave. The space rose along the backs of six chimney flues from the plain plank flooring to the underside of the attic floorboards two stories over their heads, where it widened as the flues merged into a single, central chimney. Where she stood, Marie-France had barely room to stand next to Jethro. She could feel him breathing, smell the stench of his fear over the lingering lavender and basil—now dried to dust. Wood scraped on wood and the chain rattled as Mother Thomas replaced the peg and the shelf and stuffed the closet full of coats and hats on the other side.

"Be more quiet than mice," she whispered. "They're at the kitchen door. I'll be back as soon as I can." At full volume she said, "Come, Asa Frank, your grandpa is home."

Hard as she tried, Marie-France could hear nothing but two breaths, hers and her brother's. She dared not speak.

Dared not cough, or worse, sneeze, despite the tickle in her nose and throat.

Jethro's hand found hers and they waited.

"I will not," Mother Thomas' voice rose to full dudgeon, "have that smelly beast in my house. It's bad enough you would let strangers poke into every nook and cranny. Since when is the word of the wife of a first selectman not enough for the likes of these, these, these—"

"Officers of the law," the deep mellow voice Father Thomas used so well in court filled in. "They are doing their duty under the law, Mother. We must obey the law."

"But not the dog!"

"Gentlemen, you can see my dilemma. I grant you have a warrant to search for your fugitive, but I see nothing here about a dog. I would bar your hound rather than face the wrath of my wife. Search, if you must. I will help you."

"Yes, Seth Thomas, you do that. And while you're at it, make sure they don't steal the silver. Your grandson and I will wait in the parlor until they are gone. Come along, little man."

The parlor door clicked open and soon the sounds of hands slapping against knees and thighs and each other accompanied Mother Thomas' version of patty cake and Asa Frank's giggles.

Heavy boots trod through the rest of the first floor of the house as the men opened doors and drawers and Father Thomas kept repeating, "Really, gentlemen, no man could hide in something that small."

"You stay here. Make sure he don't escape," said the scarfaced man.

"You there, stay where I can see you," Mother Thomas directed from the parlor. "I won't have you alone in my house."

Marie-France listened to the sound of footsteps, easily distinguishing the tread of Scarface's heavy boots from the soft leather of

Father Thomas' city shoes, as they moved up the back stairs and on into the attic. Dirt from the underside of the attic floorboards rained down into the drying room. It coated Jethro and Marie-France's heads and faces and seeped down the collar of Marie-France's nightgown. She dared not brush it away. She hardly dared breathe.

Finally, after searching the bedrooms, steps descended the front staircase.

"What's this?" said Scarface. Door hinges creaked and Marie-France imagined that scarred face poking into the closet under the stairs. Only a thin wall of plaster and lath separated him from the drying room. She held her breath.

"Dead storage." Father Thomas' voice betrayed his exasperation. "Next you'll want to check the root cellar and crawl under the house."

"Damned right we will."

The front parlor door opened and patty cake came to a halt.

"Satisfied?" Mother Thomas said. "Look at your boots. You'll not trod over my carpet in those."

"I have to search this room."

"Take off your boots then, man. You heard my wife."

One boot after the other fell to the floor in the front hallway.

"Ma'am," Scarface said.

Hard as she tired, Marie-France couldn't hear the fall of his stocking feet on the carpet.

"What's in here?" The closet door opened.

"Coats, hats," Mother Thomas said so calmly Marie-France gave a silent prayer of thanks. "Did I hear something about crawling under the house. I warn you, there are snakes and who knows what else down there. I won't be responsible, if you are bitten or skunked."

"I've been through worse, but I thank you for your concern, Ma'am." Scarface's voice dripped sarcasm. Marie-France wanted nothing more than to spit in his eye.

The closet door closed. "Where's this cellar?"

"This way," Father Thomas said.

"And take your friend with you. Wouldn't want you to be all alone in the dark with the spiders and such."

Marie-France kept herself from shuddering at the thought of spiders. They made her skin itch.

The closet door opened and Mother Thomas whispered. "If they crawl under the chimney, they can get into the drying space. You must be very, very quiet and pray they don't squeeze between the chimney stones. I'll keep that dog out, if I can."

The door closed and the silence of midnight fell upon them. Jethro squeezed her hand. She rested her head on his chest and let tears drip down her cheeks.

* * *

"Can't see a guldarned thing with no more light than from yonder hatchway," Dogman said from somewhere under Marie-France's feet.

"You should have brought lanterns, not torches," Scarface said.

"You think that old bat would let any flame under her house?"

"Her husband might."

"He wouldn't even let my dog—Did you feel that?"

"What?"

"Something slithered over my hand. Let's get out of here."

"I thought sure that nigger'd lead us to his sister. She's so light, she could be passing for white. You told me that dog of yours is never wrong. That griffe has to be here somewhere. We've searched everyplace else."

"Hate to admit it, but like that constable said, there's always a first time. That sambo done slipped out on us again. I say take the dog to the harbor and see if we can pick up his trail. If not, we come back and try again."

"He'll be long gone by then."

"He's long gone already."

"Ow!"

"What"

"Something bit my nose."

Marie-France almost laughed. She hoped whatever it was would leave an even nastier scar on that ugly face.

"You ready to go now?"

"Okay, okay. But if that dog of yours can't find a new scent, we're coming back."

* * *

It seemed forever—long after the sounds of men crawling on elbows and belly had ceased and the crawlspace hatch had thumped into place—before Mother Thomas opened the closet door. "You two all right in there?"

"Who are you talking to, Mother?"

The closet door slammed shut. "Nobody, dear."

Father Thomas' voice grew nearer. "I heard your voice."

The closet door opened.

"I was muttering to myself, looking for something for Asa Frank's costume. Can't have the boy miss his first real Hallowe'en."

"Don't know as I approve of all these newfangled customs. Although, if the village children do come this way dressed as horribles, I've got a treat in store."

"You?"

He chuckled. "It was riding Heman Howes' dray gave me the idea. He sold me a barrel of his best strawberry wine—just a small one, mind you. I'll greet the children at the north gate and drive them around to the south, where I'll give them all a draft of strawberry wine before sending them on their way."

"Do you suppose there'll be many?"

"Who knows. If word of my wine gets round, I should expect a mob."

The tickle, plaguing Marie-France since she squeezed into the drying space, erupted in a sneeze.

"What in the world?"

Wood scraped on wood.

Marie-France fumbled for the chain. It slipped through her fingers as Father Thomas pulled the peg on the other side. A ray of weak sunlight, blinding after hours in the total dark, streamed into their hiding place.

"Who's in there? Come out this instant."

Jethro pushed Marie-France aside. He put a finger to his lips. "I's comin." He squeezed between the chimney bricks and the closet wall. "I's comin."

Marie-France wedged herself in the deepest shadow against the far chimney flue. She pinched her nose and held her breath.

"Mother," anger deepened Father Thomas' voice to a growl, "what is the meaning of this?"

"I can explain, but you'd best sit down."

* * *

"And that's why we had to hide this man." Mother Thomas finished her story, leaving out Jethro's kinship to Marie-France.

"I don't understand. Why would Marie-France take such a risk? And where is she now?"

"Mama in dah," Asa Frank babbled. Suddenly his small pink hand appeared in the narrow slit between brick and wood at the bottom of the drying space opening. "Come out, Mama."

Her son's first two sentences, and they had betrayed her.

"Daughter, if you're in there, you had best come out and explain yourself."

Father Thomas spoke no dire ultimatum, but Marie-France heard both the disappointment and the anger. She squeezed herself into the closet, then stood barefoot on the parlor carpet in her nightdress. Not since the death of her father had she felt so hopeless.

Mother Thomas rose from her seat on the red velvet side chair and stood between Marie-France and her husband. "Before you get all high and mighty with your precious rule of law, I think you must hear all the facts." She pointed to the sofa. "You will all sit down while I explain."

Marie-France held a squirmy Asa Frank on her lap. He needed a diaper change. Jethro sat beside them in clothes which smelled hardly better. This time, Mother Thomas told the full story.

"My God!" Father Thomas rose from the ladder back chair. "It's not enough the South's stranglehold on government forces an abomination like the Fugitive Slave Act through Congress, that doughface Buchanan bends over backwards to please men who hold others in bondage and that our highest court issues appalling rulings like Dred Scott. Now their damned fugitive law reaches into the bosom of my family." He paced, head down, hands nestled in the small of his frock coat. "Once I would have bought freedom for you all, much as the thought of paying one penny to a slaveholder disgusts me."

Marie-France started to protest, but Father Thomas raised his hand for silence. "Moot point, since the *Central America* sank in September with all the banks' gold."

He stopped pacing and slammed his fist into his open palm. "No. Enough. I never thought to speak these words, but that starry-eyed muckraker Thoreau is right, when a law is unjust, civil disobedience is the only recourse."

He stared straight at Marie-France. "Are you sure this scar-faced man would recognize you?"

"He was the auctioneer for my father's estate," Marie-France said.

"Then how shall we keep you safe and get your brother away?"

Marie-France hugged Asa Frank to her breast. "Judge Walker will know."

Mother Thomas rose and took her husband's hand. "Yes, Father, you must go to him at once."

* * *

All day they hunkered behind drawn blinds, ears pricked for the first bay of a hound or Father Thomas' return. He arrived an hour before sunset. Judge Walker and three young men barely old enough to shave came behind in the old jurist's buggy. The young men followed Father Thomas and Jethro upstairs, while Mother Thomas led Judge Walker to the parlor.

He sat in the red velvet chair. Mother Thomas plied him with tea and her special sweet honey cakes. He nibbled and sipped before speaking.

"Mr. Thomas has explained your circumstances. I have advised him never to tell another soul. I advise you the same. It is sound advice and, if it weren't for that blasted slave catcher, it would be enough." The judge sighed. "But it is not, and I think you know the truth of what I must say."

Marie-France nodded. A stone the size of an anvil lodged in the pit of her stomach.

"My grandsons will take care of your brother. Each one, dressed in part of his clothing, will create a false trail for that hound from hell. We'll scrub the boy down and paint him up with cayenne pepper. It'll sting, but it will throw the dog off for the hour or so we'll need. Dressed as a horrible in one of your old sheets," he nodded to Mother Thomas, "we'll get him away on a fishing smack bound for the Grand Banks. It will land him in Canada."

Marie-France breathed. "Will that succeed?"

"As well as anything." There was a twinkle in the judge's eye. "Don't you worry, we've done this before."

"And Marie-France?" Mother Thomas asked.

The judge drained his teacup and waved off Mother Thomas' offer of more.

"Alas, it's too dangerous to send them together. The dog already has his scent. There's no point in giving it hers as well. If they were caught—. We have to consider the child."

"But surely the slave catcher will some day give up and leave," Mother Thomas said.

"This one, perhaps. But there may be others." The judge's blue eyes bore down on Marie-France. "How badly do they want you back?"

Marie-France shrugged. "It's been nearly three years and they're still looking. I guess that tells the tale."

"Indeed. It says you have two choices. Leave for Canada with your child or without him, but leave you must, and the sooner the better. Just not tonight."

"My husband is on his way home from California. I received a letter only last week. We expect him any day." She couldn't face Mother Thomas. She lowered her voice to a whisper. "We already planned to go to Canada."

"Well," the judge rose and handed his teacup to Mother Thomas, "that's settled then. Get word to me when you're ready. In the meantime, keep to the house until you hear this slave catcher has gone. Even then, you should avoid going abroad where a stranger may recognize you. No point in taking chances when you're so close to an escape." He bowed to Mother Thomas. "Wonderful cakes. If you don't mind, I'd like the recipe for Mrs. Walker."

* * *

"Jethro's away to Barnstable." Father Thomas flung himself onto the red velvet chair and stretched out his legs. His cheeks were flushed from wine. "The boys are leading that dog on a merry chase to the docks in Harwichport. Judge Walker will stop here to let us know that the *Northern Star* is safely away."

"I won't feel safe until he does," Marie-France said.

"Nor I," said Mother Thomas.

"Too bad the horribles have drunk all the wine. The judge could join us in a toast to breaking the law." Father Thomas sighed. "This business makes criminals of us all."

"What's that?" Mother Thomas rose from the ladder back chair. "Did you hear that?"

Marie-France had heard the knock at the kitchen door. She couldn't move.

"There it is again. Surely, it can't be the judge, not this soon," said Mother Thomas.

Father Thomas jumped to his feet. "I'll go. Get the closet ready. If it's them, you hide." He left the parlor door ajar.

Mother Thomas sprang to the crack and put her ear to it.

Marie-France threw coats and hats on the couch and thanked God the shelf remained propped on the floor. She put her hand on the peg and waited.

Father Thomas' voice was loud enough for Marie-France to make out a word or two—*Central America*, lost, reward." She thought she heard another man, not one of the slave catchers, and a woman.

"…into the parlor." Father Thomas pushed open the door.

In stepped a very pregnant, red-headed woman in a thin cotton dress and a blue-black man.

Father Thomas swept the coats off the couch. "Have a seat, Mother." He joined her on the couch and took her hands in his. "These people have brought news of our Asa. Very bad news indeed."

Marie-France listened to Moses DaSilva's story in an agonized fog. With each sentence she felt her heart sink, until it could have oozed out her toes. She willed herself not to faint.

"That's the last I seen of him, standing on the deck of the *Central America* all awash and me rowing away to the *Brig Marine*. Rosie, here, has something for you."

The woman pulled a silver sewing bird out of her purse and handed it to Marie-France. "He give me this for his wife." She pulled a visiting card out and handed it to Father Thomas. He read the message on the back aloud.

"Please pay this brave woman whatever you can. I have entrusted this bird and my fortune to fate and her good graces. Tell Marie-France I love her. Asa."

Mother Thomas began to rock and keen.

"I'm afraid I can't offer much in the way of money. The loss of the gold on the *Central America* has all but ruined me. But I will do everything I can to help you both." Father Thomas stood and shook Moses' hand. "Anything."

Marie-France examined the silver bird, running her fingers over the spring-loaded beak, the c-clamp and the green velvet pincushion. For all she adored Asa, she cursed him for sending such a useless token and, in one more Southern storm, for dashing all her hopes for a free life together in Canada.

* * *

In the cold light of another morning, Mother Thomas stirred a pot of pumpkin soup at the kitchen stove. "Are you sure?"

Marie-France spooned a mouthful of mush into Asa-Frank. "Judge Walker is right, I cannot stay."

She had clamped the sewing bird to the edge of the oaken table, a reminder of all she had lost. She would leave it behind—with her son.

"You must tell anyone who asks that I have gone in search of my husband, in the vain hope he fetched up on some Southern shore and was not lost at sea.

"It was too late for me to sail with my brother. I will take another ship north, to Saint Pierre or Miquelon and then on to Paris, where my father had family. Perhaps there I will meet my compatriot Alexandre Dumas and introduce myself as the Countess of Monte Cristo." She forced a laugh and fed more mush into Asa Frank. "I cannot take my son. He will be safe here in my absence. One day I may return," but she knew she could not. She had not the courage of Peggy Garner, could never kill her own child to save him from slavery. But she could sacrifice her own happiness, as she must.

Mother Thomas sniffled and brushed at her eyes with the back of her hand.

"I only wish you to speak well of me, to give him my father's copy of *Le Comte de Monte-Cristo* and this." Marie-France pulled an envelope sealed with wax from her coat pocket. "When he is old enough, if ever the day comes that he can enjoy the full and free life which all of us want, when anyone among us would be content to have the status of his mother or the color of his skin changed and stand in his place."

A knock at the door made her heart skip a beat. How had she been so careless, sitting with her back to the windows where anyone could look in?

Judge Walker poked in his head. "Are you ready?"

Life returned to Marie-France's limbs. She rose and placed a kiss on the top of Asa Frank's head.

"As ready as ever I will be."

She took one last look at the sewing bird, slid the envelope onto the table and turned her back on the country that had long since turned its back on her.

One of the great things about crimes in the past is that they can take us any-where through the eyes of people we might never have otherwise understood. Leah Cutter makes a habit of writing about places and people not normally seen in tra-ditionally published American fiction. Her first three novels, Paper Mage, Caves of Buda, *and* The Jaguar and the Wolf, *take place in Tang Dynasty China, World War II Budapest, and the Viking Era. Her most recent novel,* When The Moon Over Kualina Mountain Comes, *is set in a fantasy world of her own design.*

She's published a lot of short fiction, most recently in Alfred Hitchcock's Mystery Magazine *and in* Fiction River. *Her previous* Fiction River *stories, pub-lished in* Unnatural Worlds *and* Hex in the City, *are fantasy but "New World Gambles" is set firmly in a real place and time: Vancouver B.C. during the build-ing of the Canadian Pacific Railroad. Leah explores something I've never seen in mystery fiction before—the Chinese-Canadian Tong.*

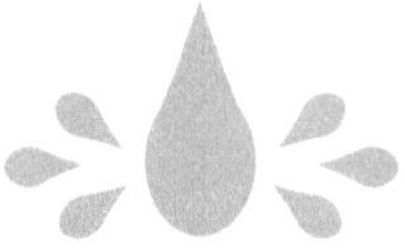

New World Gambles

Leah Cutter

"Place your bet, sir?" Mei Quon asked his patron. He kept his smile simple, doing his best to convey happiness and not the truth of how his empty stomach growled, or how his feet hurt from standing for so long, or how his back and neck screamed from staying bent over so his head was properly placed below that of his short patron.

He reminded himself how lucky he was to be here dressed in fine blue-cotton robes and not camped out in the wilderness someplace, swinging a heavy mallet and laying rails for the grand Canadian Pacific railroad. That here, in Victoria, Mei Quon might actually make his fortune and be able to pay back the horrendous sum of money it had taken to bring him to the New World.

Even if it meant working in a crooked *fan tan* parlor that stank of the opium being smoked next door and the despair of desperate men, instead of using the books and scrolls of a scholar.

"What do you think?" Old Ren asked, contemplating the top of the table in front of him. "You've been lucky so far, tonight." He leaned closer and whispered, "My good luck charm," his breath tainted with sour fish and cheap plum wine.

Mei Quon shivered and ignored the implied intimacy. He wasn't so broke that he had to whore himself out—always an option when there were only three women for every hundred men. All he ever agreed to was companionship: Enough for the lonely, fat, and old to get by on, enough to keep Mei Quon fed most days. It was a gamble. Too much insinuation would ruin his reputation. But he had to eat.

Instead of replying to Old Ren, though, Mei Quon studied the table.

The *fan tan* table was about four feet high, three feet wide, and eight feet long. A beautifully carved wooden spindle railing outlined the edge, separating the players from the table top. A simple red square, divided into four quadrants, was sewn into the center of the black cloth covering the table. Each quadrant represented a number—from one to four—that patrons could bet on. They could also bet on the corners—doubling their chances but lowering the percentage of their winnings.

It was a fool's game, without the strategy and tactics of something like classical *xiangqi*, which the westerns likened to chess. No skill was involved in *fan tan*, just luck.

But Mei Quon needed fools for patrons, who would tip him without expecting too much.

Who would never notice the look Mei Quon gave the *tan kun*, the man responsible for gathering the coins to be counted, who knew by weight the number in each handful.

The *tan kun* blinked twice, put his fistful of coins into the center of the square, then covered them immediately with a decorated gold bowl.

"Last call," Mei Quon whispered. "Put your marker on four."

Old Ren beamed at Mei Quon. Not only did he bet his winnings, he put down a playing card that indicated he was betting his entire purse.

Mei Quon knew better than to ask his patron about the wisdom of his bet. Old Ren didn't like to be questioned, and Mei Quon had worn his scarf high for a week to hide his fat lip the one time he had asked. The purse Old Ren carried to the game that night had been filled with twice the amount of money Old Ren generally had, but again, Mei Quon didn't ask any questions.

Maybe Mei Quon should have listened to his cousin and learned how to fight. He'd shot up since coming to the New World, and now stood almost a head above most of the men around him. He didn't just have to rely on his good lucks, charm, and manners anymore.

But as a scholar, he'd always believed that violence was never the answer.

Silence descended around the table as the *tan kun* lifted the bowl. Using a curved bamboo stick, he started dividing up the pile of coins, counting by four.

When the *tan kun* finished, whatever number of coins remained, indivisible by four, would be the winning number.

Old Ren had just bet on four. If two, the square on the table opposite of four, was the winner, as the *tan kun* had indicated by the number of times he'd blinked his eyes, Old Ren would lose everything.

And Mei Quon would make a percentage of what the house acquired. More money that he could apply against his debt.

The pile of bright gold coins in the center of the table—minted in the current dynasty, never in circulation, only used for the game—grew smaller. Mei Quon's stomach tightened. Maybe he could finally get rid of this stupid Old Ren, find a better patron, someone more free with their money. Who wasn't pushing for more than Mei Quon would give.

Mei Quon tried counting the number of coins remaining. He'd have to be clever about leaving Old Ren. Maybe he could disappear into his cousin's attic for a couple days.

The number had to come down to two.

If it was one or three, Old Ren wouldn't lose his purse—his bet would be returned to him. If it was four, Old Ren would make four times what was in his purse, and Mei Quon would never be welcomed back to that *fan tan* parlor again, though he'd just done what the *tan kun* had said.

Only a small pile of coins remained. Mei Quon caught his breath. Was it actually going to be four? He tried to catch the eye of the *tan kun*, but he wouldn't look up from his duty.

Damn it. If Old Ren won, Mei Quon would be stuck. And the old man was getting more lecherous.

The count was easy to make—it looked as though the *tan kun* had been wrong, and Old Ren would win.

"Raid!"

The door banged open. Police poured in.

Mei Quon started with everyone else. The *fan tan* parlor was in the basement. The room had been quiet. Why hadn't they heard the raid approaching? Whoever had been stationed on the ground floor should have warned them.

Time for questions later. Mei Quon turned and ran. Old Ren's querulous tones sounded behind him, making Mei Quon move faster. He vaulted over one patron who'd fallen and made it into the kitchen.

"Police raid!" Mei Quon shouted at the cooks in Cantonese.

They followed right behind him, out the back door and up the short set of steps into the narrow alley.

Mei Quon ran left in the cool night air. The others turned right.

Above Mei Quon, a warning whistle sounded. He sprinted, keeping his hands over his head, protecting it as he ran.

A heavy iron door slammed down behind him, blocking the alley. The police could force their way through, but it would take time, and Mei Quon would be long gone.

He stopped and leaned against a rough brick wall, trying to catch his breath. Why had the police only come through the front door? They knew there was a back alley. Generally, a second squad would have been waiting there. Also, why hadn't there been a warning? Had the lookout on the ground floor been bribed?

At least Old Ren hadn't won. But neither had Mei Quon. He was out his tip for the night. The *fan tan* parlor always served dinner at the end of gaming: tonight, Mei Quon wouldn't get fed, either.

Maybe he could beg a bowl of rice from his cousin.

Mei Quon made his way down the skinny lane, skirting the pile of sand left next to a doorstep—someone making improvements to their flat—and waving his hand over his nose as he passed by another sickly sweet opium den.

With a sigh of relief, Mei Quon stepped out of the small, dank alley, onto the main broad walk on Pandora Street. He took a deep breath of the cool night air and tightened his stomach. Maybe he could go another night without a proper meal—

"That's him!"

Before Mei Quon could turn around, something blunt and hard struck the back of his head and a colder darkness embraced him.

* * *

Mei Quon knew that opening his eyes would hurt. He kept them closed and took stock first. His wrists were twisted and tied behind his back. Hard, cold packed earth pushed up against his sore butt—he'd been dragged and thrown into some sort of storage room, in a basement somewhere, he'd bet. It smelled of dried onions and wet stone. His head wasn't actually being pounded on by hammers, but it felt that way.

With a wrenching pain, Mei Quon opened his eyes, blinking to keep the tears from blinding him. A pale outline of light came from above his head—a boarded-over window. He couldn't see the outline of a door, though he knew there must be one. Rough brick scratched his arms when he turned to the side and examined the far wall.

"Hey!" Mei Quon shouted. "Anyone there?" He spoke first in classic Mandarin, then repeated his words in Cantonese. It would be better to find out the worst of it, than to sit in the dark and let his fears build.

After taking a deep breath, Mei Quon forced himself up to his knees. Idiots hadn't tied his feet.

Or maybe they'd bricked over the door and there was no way out.

Mei Quon pushed down on his fears and staggered up, forcing himself to stand, though the movement made his head hurt worse. Where was he? He could be in any of the storerooms under Victoria's Chinatown.

"Hey!" he called again.

Shouting made Mei Quon's head ache, but he didn't know what else to do.

"Is anyone there?" he called, this time repeating the phrase three times, using Mandarin, Cantonese, and English. He stumbled forward, hitting wood instead of brick.

This had to be the door.

Before Mei Quon could kick at the hard wood and probably break his foot, he heard a jangle of keys on the other side. Mei Quon stepped back quickly into what he thought would be the center of the cell.

Light flooded the room. Mei Quon blinked against the sudden brightness.

"Boss wants to see you," came a rough voice, speaking Cantonese.

"Who?" Mei Quon asked, not moving.

"You heard me. Boss. Now move. If I have to drag you, I'll drop your head on every step," the man warned.

With an internal sigh, Mei Quon staggered into the light. His sight had cleared enough that he could see the other man—shorter than Mei Quon, but at least twice as big around, with powerful shoulders and a squat neck, like a bull. He wore a Western style cowboy hat over his partially shaved head and Western pants under his black, knee-length robe.

The hallway was roughly cut out of dirt, shored up with wooden beams, like a miner's tunnel. It smelled wetter here, as if water dripped behind the walls. Mei Quon had to duck his head to avoid hitting the crossbeams. The stairs were also cut into the dirt, shored up with wood.

Wafting down from the open square above Mei Quon's head came the stench of rotten potatoes and sour cabbage. Was he below a grocery store?

Mei Quon paused before pushing his head up. The stout man behind him gave him a hard shove. Mei Quon swallowed down all his complaints and kept going.

The room above was a storage room, at the back of some sort of shop. Wooden shelves lined the walls, heaped with produce: Leafy greens, dark carrots, Western potatoes, and Chinese cabbage.

A plain table had been set up in the center of the room—skinny and long, like an altar. A thin man sat behind it, with white whiskers dangling almost to his waist. Like in the paintings of old, his eyebrows had been shaved off and repainted further up his intelligent brow. He wore a black scholar's cap, square, with a long black tassel. White-silk plaques embroidered with lucky blue clouds and bats covered the collar, cuffs, and front of his cream-colored robe.

Mei Quon instinctively bowed low before this man.

"I am Ang Woo. Head of the *Chee Kung Tong*." The old man spoke in beautiful Mandarin, clear and precise.

Mei Quon contained his shiver. He had no idea Old Ren had been involved in a tong.

"You've caused a great deal of trouble," Ang Woo continued, his voice unsurprisingly strong.

"Sir?" Mei Quon asked.

"I need that money back," Ang Woo said. "Old Ren wasn't betting his own purse."

"I see," Mei Quon said, blinking. He had wondered where Old Ren had gotten his money, but he hadn't been about to question it. "I'm sorry, but the police raid—"

"Was very convenient, don't you agree?" Ang Woo asked. "Think about it. How often has that particular parlor been raided whenever there was a large pot at stake?"

Mei Quon thought back furiously. He'd known the parlor was crooked—they'd recruited him, after all.

But for them to also be working with the white, western police? Against their own people? That was revolting. It turned Mei Quon's stomach.

"Sir, I'm not sure how I can help," Mei Quon said honestly. He knew he'd likely get beaten for such an admission, but it was the truth.

He really was going to have to learn to fight with more than words and the pen.

"That's all right. I have a plan." Ang Woo gave Mei Quon a smile that chilled him more than the thought of being bricked in down in the cellar.

Still, Mei Quon knew he had to take this one last gamble, to declare, "all in"—*zai suoyou*. "Tell me how I can help."

* * *

A new lookout sat at the doorway to the *fan tan* parlor. Mei Quon breathed a quick thanks to Kang Ti, ruler of ten-thousand household ghosts and a patron of lost causes. It meant that he wouldn't be barred at the door because Old Ren had made a complaint against him, and could make it into the actual parlor, a first hurdle overcome.

He hoped that wasn't the end of his luck—he needed more throughout the night.

The *fan tan* parlor hadn't changed since three days before: Plain wood made up most of the walls, with a few black and red paper posters painted with white characters, describing how to play the game, the rules of the house, as well as a general blessing on all who came there.

The *tan kun* recognized Mei Quon, but the cashier was new and he took Mei Quon's purse without a question, issuing him a white pigeon playing card, indicating that he'd started with a kitty of one hundred Canadian dollars—more money than Mei Quon had ever held in his hands.

But he knew that if he'd tried to leave Victoria with the cash, he never would have made it to the pier alive. The tong wasn't very forgiving.

A game had just started. Mei Quon watched the first count, paying particular attention to the *tan kun*, but Mei Quon didn't see him pass along any signals. Either he didn't have a partner that night, or he'd changed his system.

At the next game, Mei Quon placed a small bet on one, with a red "dog's tongue" card: If he won, the house would pay out four times what he'd bet. If three—the number on the square opposite of one—was the remaining number after all the coins had been spread out and divided up, he'd lose everything.

Mei Quon maintained a passive expression when three turned out to be the remaining number of coins. He was going to have to win at some point, enough to threaten the house. But not right away. Ang Woo needed Mei Quon to play for an hour or more, betting the entire time.

Keeping the house occupied was a strategy Mei Quon recognized from chess, similar to harrying the king while mounting a surprise attack on his henchmen.

The head of the parlor, Bei Hai, came by while another count was being spread across the table. He wore a new, fine robe, made of black silk. Had he paid for it out of Old Ren's purse?

Bei Hai stared hard at Mei Quon and had a whispered word with the cashier, who handed over Mei Quon's purse.

Mei Quon kept his face impassive though his heart beat hard in his chest. They had to believe he'd just come back to gamble, to bet. They couldn't suspect there was anything more than that.

"Who's your new patron?" Bei Hai asked once the count was finished and Mei Quon collected his minor winnings, minus the house cut.

"Yi Chen," Mei Quon said carelessly, a made-up name that Ang Woo had given him. "You wouldn't know him. He works for the railroad."

Mei Quon turned and stared at Bei Hai, delighted that he was able to stand tall and look down on the other man.

"Why isn't he here with you?" Bei Hai asked.

"He'll be along shortly," Mei Quon assured him.

Bei Hai made a face, crossing his arms over his chest.

"What, my money isn't good enough on my own?" Mei Quon challenged.

"Of course it is," Bei Hai replied, slipping back into his place as a company man, hosting a game. "Please, enjoy yourself."

Mei Quon knew Bei Hai was also wishing him to lose all his money at the same time.

The next bet had Mei Quon sweating more. He won a corner, as did his neighbor, meaning the house would pay out double the amount, and they'd both bet heavily.

If the house lost too much, they'd close the table. And he needed to keep it open. Until he could make a sizeable bet.

Mei Quon was more cautious with his next bet, buying a twist, placing his money at the end of the two side with a red dog tongue, and breathed a sigh of relief when he won.

Little by little, Mei Quon's purse increased. Was the house working for him, instead of against him? He looked toward the front entrance once or twice. Bei Hai knew that he was waiting for his new "patron" so it was to be expected.

Finally, Mei Quon decided he'd taken enough time—and won enough money—to take a risk. Like Old Ren from three nights before, Mei Quon bet on four, placing his white pigeon card down on the side along with his marker.

Time to bet everything.

The *tan kun* slowly turned over the bowl and started counting. Mei Quon tried to keep his face impassive though the skin under his palms itched and his breath came short.

It was a huge amount of money. The house had to call and ask for "help."

Suddenly, down the stairs came the loud tromp of feet and the shout of, "Police!"

When the *tan kun* looked up, Mei Quon shot his hand out and dropped a dozen coins into the pile already sitting on the table.

Special coins that looked identical to the ones already there, but weighted differently.

"Cheater!" Mei Quon said in clear English, standing up as the police entered. "They're cheating!" he added, pointing at the *tan kun* then at Bei Hai.

The police looked from Mei Quon in his fine robe to the workers. "We were called in for a disturbance," the head one said, walking forward.

"They're cheating!" Mei Quon said again, pointing to the table. "Feel those coins. They're weighted!"

The policeman reached over the railing and picked up two coins, weighing them in his hand.

"This one is a featherweight compared to the other," he said, nodding at Mei Quon. "I'm surprised you were able to tell."

Mei Quon quickly repeated the words in Mandarin for those whose English wasn't as good. The other players around the table gasped and turned as one to face Bei Hai.

"Now, now, we don't want any violence. Why don't we all take a walk down to the station and settle this?" the policeman suggested.

Bei Hai stepped forward. "Good. We can see Officer Bradly, then."

"Seems Officer Bradly had to go on an extended family leave," the policeman said with a shrug. "You might be having to deal with me, now. Officer Karlson."

Bei Hai glared at Mei Quon, who merely shrugged.

"Seems like we should do as this good officer suggested," Mei Quon said. "Though you won't be able to meet my new patrons. The *Chee Kong Tong* and Ang Woo."

Bei Hai stiffened. He knew who he'd have to buy his freedom from.

Ang Woo would get his money back—Bei Hai would have to pay a lot to get out of jail this time, then even more to keep his *fan tan* parlor open, as his friendly policeman had just been replaced by Ang Woo's.

And for doing his part, Mei Quon was going to have new opportunities with the *Chee Kong Tong*. He'd learn how to fight, but maybe he'd be able to use his scholar abilities as well.

Particularly when Ang Woo insisted on going through the books of all the *fan tan* parlors under his protection.

Mei Quon's biggest gamble—coming to the New World—was finally paying off.

Now we move just a little south to Port Townsend, Washington, for a tale of sailing ships and the results of crime on the high seas—even though most of this story occurs on land. Sailing has inspired Jamie McNabb before. His story for Fiction River: Universe Between *also has a sailing motif, as do some of his novels, available through Soapbox Rising Press.*

Jamie spends his summers on his own boat and it shows in his sea-faring tales. So does his love for history. Both of those things give "The Bank Teller" its incredible strength.

The Bank Teller

Jamie McNabb

He stopped at the top of the hill above Port Townsend and set his suitcase down on the pavement. He stretched his back, worked his injured leg, and scanned back along the way he had come. Only three other people were on the street, and he had seen none of them down by the harbor. No one had followed him up the hill.

It was a bright summer afternoon, and the air away from downtown smelled of trees and flowers, rather than horse dung and cooking grease. Off to the southeast, out in Port Townsend Bay, two full-rigged ships, a steamer, and three lumber schooners rode at anchor. A tug was heading to the southwest.

It amused him to think how readily he had identified the rigs. How quickly he had learned the seaman's trade. He'd actually enjoyed that part of it, the learning and the work itself.

Farther out, to the east and northeast, lay Admiralty Inlet, the northernmost end of Puget Sound, lumberyard to the world. He felt an odd sense of pride in that and a much odder sense of having come home.

After five years.

When he'd left, it had been the 19th century, and now it was the 20th. A line crossed. The equator, too. He'd become a shellback.

With yet another line waiting for him to cross.

But all in good time.

He turned his back on the water, on the way he had come. He picked up his suitcase and walked on.

He'd bought his suitcase used at a pawnshop in Portland, Oregon, but he'd bought his shoes new in Seattle. They were good shoes, heavy and durable, and he could smell the new smell rising off of them. But they were too new to be comfortable. His feet hurt, and because of it, his injured leg was acting up and his limp was becoming more noticeable with every step.

The limp was neither here nor there, but he had no wish to become memorable, no wish to be identifiable as a man with a limp.

He wondered how much farther he would have to go before he reached the New Bedford House.

* * *

Ten minutes later he was standing in front of the New Bedford, identified as such by a small sign hanging above the steps leading up to the front porch. The building was a large, three-story house with a mansard roof. The siding was white, and the trim was gray. There was a fussy yard, complete with flower beds and a kitchen garden.

He climbed the steps. An engraved brass plaque next to the front door announced the New Bedford to be a gentlemen's boarding house. He rang the bell.

＊ ＊ ＊

The door was opened by Mrs. Cornelia Abbott, the owner. She was a stout woman in her middle fifties. Her eyes were keen and quick and pale blue.

They sat in the parlor, which was at the front of the house. He was glad to be off his feet, to give his leg a chance to rest.

The furniture was old but in good condition. The cloth upholstery was worn but not threadbare. The room was clean and in good order. An oil portrait of a sea captain hung over the fireplace. A brass plate identified the subject as Captain Ezekiel Makepeace Abbott, 1847—1893.

A slip of a girl brought tea and disappeared wordlessly back into the recesses of the house.

The tea was strong, and the conversation dispensed with the business at hand in short order. He wanted a room; she had one to let. He wanted quiet; she insisted on it. He never drank to excess; she evicted drunks without hesitation.

She ran the most respectable boarding house in Port Townsend; he insisted on nothing less. It was comparatively expensive; he could afford it.

She took him into her office. It was a compact, overcrowded room that had probably once been the sea captain's study. It smelled of paper and furniture polish. She sat him at a table and put the register in front of him. She provided pen and ink.

"Please sign the book," she said.

"It would be my pleasure," he said, and picked up the pen.

He studied the empty, waiting line.

What name should he give her?

Not his own, surely, although that was likely to be safe enough. *Likely...*

In the end, he gave her the name they had given him five years ago: Johan Schmidt. He'd gone by Smitty, mostly. Sometimes John. Sometimes Jack. The names had followed him around the world. They had carried him from one life into another. It was only fitting that they should carry him back.

But he wasn't that stupid.

Five years couldn't be stripped away, erased as though they had never happened.

That said, however, it might be possible to achieve some measure of balance. Barely. Now that he had returned to Port Townsend.

He signed his name as *Johan Schmidt*. He added his arrival date: July 15, 1901.

She read the line and seemed quite satisfied. "An educated hand, Mr. Schmidt," she said, and gave him a slight nod. "Welcome to the New Bedford."

"Thank you for allowing me to stay," Schmidt said, and counted out his rent.

Mrs. Abbott said, "Breakfast is at six thirty, and supper at six o'clock. We ring a gong fifteen minutes ahead. Late arrivals may eat in the kitchen."

She handed him a receipt, a key to the front door, and a key to his room.

* * *

Schmidt's room was at the front and provided a good view of the street and the bay and a snowcapped mountain off in the distance to the east, but not of the Strait of Juan de Fuca.

The room was large. It had a bed, a wardrobe, a washstand with a blue-and-white enameled pitcher and basin, a shaving mirror on the wall above the washstand, a table and chair, a nightstand next to the bed, a kerosene lamp, a box of matches, and a red-and-blue rug. A coat hook had been fastened to the wall next to the door.

He unpacked his suitcase and took off his shoes. He locked the door and hung his jacket and hat on the hook.

With those tasks out of the way, he lay down on the bed. It was neither too hard nor too soft, neither too large nor too small. It was just right. He felt like Goldilocks.

He did, however, choose to leave his revolver, a short-barreled Colt, secured in its shoulder holster, readily available.

He closed his eyes and allowed his mind to wander.

He'd bought his gun, his shoes, and his suit in Seattle before coming over on a steamer. He liked Seattle, what he'd seen of it. He imagined that someday he might settle there.

In the meantime, he had work to do. Apropos of which, he wondered what sort of people his fellow lodgers were…

* * *

The gong woke Schmidt out of a sound sleep.

He pulled on his suit coat and went down to dinner.

The dining-room table was piled with food, while around it were crowded five men and Mrs. Abbott, who sat—Where else?—at the head of the table. She had a small brass bell within easy reach. She'd changed into a more elaborate dress and tidied her hair.

There was an empty chair at the foot, not directly opposite her, which would have never done, but to her right. She waved him toward it.

Mrs. Abbott introduced him and offered only that he was newly arrived in town. The names of the five men as well as the men themselves blurred into a haze that was neither effusive nor aloof.

Schmidt hoped he would be able to remember the names when called upon.

Mrs. Abbott led her guests in saying grace, which they did with their heads respectfully, if not reverently, bowed. At the *Amen* the man across the table from Schmidt crossed himself in the Roman Catholic manner, left shoulder then right, rather than in the Orthodox Christian manner, right shoulder then left.

At Mrs. Abbott's instruction, the plates of food began to make the rounds.

* * *

After dinner, Schmidt went out onto the front porch. The weather had remained fine, and the evening air was balmy but held the first chill of the approaching night. It reminded him of San Francisco.

A man walked over and stood next to him, the one who'd crossed himself. He was thin and neatly dressed to the point of being prim. He had ink stains on the fingers of his right hand.

"Evening," the man said.

"Evening," Schmidt said, and scrambled for the man's name. Charles McNeill. No, that wasn't it. *Clayton* McNeill. Yes, that was it. Clayton. "Beautiful evening, isn't it, Mr. McNeill?"

"Yes, it is," McNeill said. He looked from side to side, then asked, "I don't mean to pry, but what's your line of work?"

"Bookkeeper," Schmidt said, and told himself to roll with the conversation. He'd known there would be questions, and here they were.

"You have the look of a sailor."

Schmidt smiled as warmly as he could—jovial, friendly, unthreatening. "I was a sailor."

"Recently?"

Schmidt laughed, a little self-consciously. "Until a few days ago, yes."

"Ship's purser, I'd say."

"Correct again." Schmidt smiled as though he were enjoying the conversation immensely. He wasn't. "You're very astute."

"No, not really. What with your limp and all, it pretty much had to be purser, cook, or sailmaker. But your hands aren't beat up enough for you to have been a sailmaker, and you don't have the look of a cook. So that left purser."

There was, evidently, no possibility of hiding the limp. Schmidt said, "Process of elimination, then?"

"Something like that. Were you always a purser?"

"No, only after I acquired the limp."

"How was that? If you don't mind my asking."

"I fell down a companionway ladder."

"You were lucky," McNeill said.

"So I've been told," Schmidt answered. It was hard for him to keep his voice relaxed, but five years at sea, and several bucko mates, had taught him that, too.

"You any good? With numbers, I mean."

"Good enough to make a living at it."

"Looking for work?"

"Depends," Schmidt said.

McNeill handed him a business card. It identified him as a bookkeeper with the Olympic Lumbermen's Bank of Commerce. "Come by tomorrow morning. Eleven o'clock or thereabouts. The bank's looking for a teller."

"Thanks," Schmidt said, and pocketed the card. It was more, much more, than he could have hoped for.

"Don't forget," McNeill said. "Eleven." He nodded and walked out to the street. He turned and walked off to the southwest.

Schmidt followed but turned in the opposite direction, to the northeast, toward Morgan Hill, toward the corner of Grant and Madison.

* * *

The house that occupied the north corner of Grant and Madison was a mansion by Port Townsend standards. It had three floors, dozens of windows, trim so ornate that it made the New Bedford look like the country cousin, and an observation turret. The house was everything that local fashion demanded. And it was ablaze with light. It shouted wealth and influence and power.

It was the home of Captain Douglas Victor Hansen, sea captain and ship owner, and it made the man who went by the name of Johan Schmidt feel small and powerless and easily crushed.

* * *

The next morning at eleven o'clock, Schmidt presented himself to Clayton McNeill at the Olympic Lumbermen's bank. McNeill handed him over to George Lindauer, the head teller, and by two o'clock that afternoon, Schmidt had the job.

He had nothing to do now but work at his new job and watch and wait.

* * *

Olympic Lumbermen's was down on the flat, on the inboard side of Water Street. It was not far from several of the town's landmarks: the Union Wharf, the Paris Opera House, the infamous Blue Star Saloon, and the notorious Gloucester Arms Residential Hotel. The bank was directly across from the worst Shanghaiing den of the lot: the Mariner's Rest, which was owned by none other than Captain Douglas Victor Hansen.

However, regardless of which place a footloose man picked, he stood a good chance of paying for his lodging or his meal or his entertainment with a fit of sudden unconsciousness and a voyage to the Orient.

And sooner or later, everyone, from the owners to the stable boys, came through the bank. Schmidt remembered their names and where they worked, and he never failed to smile and ask how they were doing. Everyone agreed that the bank's new teller was a real gentleman. It was just plain too bad about his limp, though, the poor man.

The poor man made notes.

He read the shipping columns, the society columns, the business pages, and the shipping registers. He read current issues and he read back issues. Page by page, he gleaned that the resident of the house at Grant and Madison was active in his church, was shrewdly expanding his business holdings, was a major contributor to the Port Townsend Policeman's Trust, and was also a major contributor to the current mayor's political campaigns and favored causes.

The jewel in the crown, however, was the information that two years ago, he had retired from his career afloat in order to devote his full energies to the betterment of his community.

Schmidt recorded the comings and goings, the schedules. He wrote down arrival and departure times, especially those of Captain Hansen, but also those of two particular runners: Jimmy "Shanghai Rooster" Gibson and Harry "No Ears" Pederson.

Jimmy "Shanghai Rooster" Gibson worked as a bartender for Big Mike Gamble, who owned the Blue Star Saloon. Big Mike was Port

Townsend's so-called King of the Crimps. Like Hansen, he, too, was a stalwart contributor to the Port Townsend Policeman's Trust. As it turned out, Big Mike was Hansen's only serious competition.

Harry "No Ears" Pederson occupied a rung much farther down the social ladder from the one occupied by Jimmy "Shanghai Rooster" Gibson. Nevertheless, No Ears fell within Big Mike's orbit. He filled in at the Blue Star's bar, swept the place out, and did "odd jobs."

The days went by, the pages of Schmidt's notebook filled up, and the picture grew from a vague sketch to a roughed-in landscape.

On September 5, 1901, the arrival of the four-masted bark *Susan B. Shattuck* ended Schmidt's wait.

* * *

The *Susan B. Shattuck* was a hellship, always had been. Five years ago Douglas Victor Hansen had been her proud owner and courageous captain. But he'd seen the handwriting on the wall—the irreversible advent of steam—and had sold out to his chief mate. Hansen's chief mate, then her new captain, had soon gone bankrupt and had sold her to her current pair of owners: Captain Lars "Blockhead" Burgess and his chief mate, Bully Johnson.

And through all the changes, nothing about her had changed, except that she had grown older and more tattered. She never sailed with a full crew, she fed her hands starvation rations, and she made do with worn-out equipment. Occasionally, she paid her men what she owed them. Usually, she shorted them or refused to pay at all. Her sails were no better than rags, her rigging was frayed and rotten, her plates were rusted beneath her paint, and her captain and chief mate were, now as then, sadists.

She had been Johan Schmidt's first ship, Douglas Victor Hansen his first captain.

The man whose name would become Schmidt had not volunteered.

And now there she was, anchored in the bay, her captain and mate hungry for a crew; desperate for men to haul, and lift, and hoist, and pull; greedy for men to bully, and starve, and beat, and kick, and maim, and cripple, and murder.

"I kill at least one man every trip…or more," Bully Johnson was said to have once bragged, right there in a Port Townsend saloon. "It discourages the rest of them from starting something I'll have to finish."

Yes, Schmidt thought, they'd need a crew, and therein lay the great opportunity for an enterprising soul such as himself.

However, to help meet that demand, Schmidt would have to recruit a crew of his own. Two men. First one, and then another. He decided to begin with No Ears. Given his relationship with Big Mike and given the rivalry between Big Mike and Hansen, No Ears seemed like a logical choice.

* * *

Harry "No Ears" Pederson wasn't a hard man to find, especially on a Friday night. On Friday nights, he was usually working behind the bar at the Blue Star Saloon, where he did his best to persuade likely sailors to sign articles without a moment's delay.

Schmidt approached him, and they arranged to talk after closing.

* * *

They talked across a battered table in the barroom, amid the stench of spilled beer and vomit.

"To what do I owe the pleasure?" No Ears asked.

"I need to hire a couple of runners. One night's work. Good money."

No Ears shook his head. "Big Mike wouldn't like that. The town's lousy with crimps as it is."

"I'm trying to do a favor for one of the bank's customers," Schmidt said. "Two guys. One night. There'd be absolutely no threat to Mr. Gamble's interests."

"I don't know," No Ears drawled out. "Why not ask him? Directly like?"

"This has to be done *quietly*. You understand? Too many cooks?"

No Ears nodded. "I get it. Big Mike ain't one to *help*. He likes to run the show."

"Exactly."

"And it won't crowd him?"

"Not at all."

"I see," No Ears said. "Somebody wants somebody out of the way, and somebody else has offered to lend a hand."

Schmidt smiled a conspiratorial smile. "Something like that."

No Ears nodded. "Okay. I know a guy who might be willing to help out."

They agreed to meet again in twenty-four hours on the pier behind the Blue Star Saloon.

* * *

Schmidt was the first to arrive. The pier was dark, lit only by the wash of light from the windows across the back of the Blue Star Saloon. The heft of the Colt in its shoulder holster reassured him. He had, after all, no desire to "volunteer" again.

Two men stepped out of the gloom between the saloon and the next building. The one on the left was No Ears. He introduced the one on the right.

"This here's Charley Ludlow," he said.

Charley was tall, broad through the shoulders and fat through the gut. He smelled like a chamber pot that hasn't been emptied in several days.

"Glad to meet you," Schmidt said.

The two men moved apart.

It was a move that Schmidt had seen many times.

"I tried to tell you Big Mike don't hold with unwelcome competition," No Ears said.

"Yeah," Charley said. He was twitching with anticipation. "He told us to make sure you don't never forget it, neither."

"He said as how a sea voyage might help you remember," No Ears said.

The two men continued to move apart.

Schmidt unbuttoned his suit coat. "No need for that," he said. "I'll go my way, and you can go yours."

"Too late," No Ears said.

"Too bad," Schmidt said, and drew the Colt.

He backed up, sliding his feet behind him, feeling the planking to make sure he didn't trip and go over backwards.

The two men were on opposite sides of him and much, much closer than he would have liked. He ought to have put his back to a wall sooner, but he hadn't.

He'd made a mistake, and now that mistake was going to cost him his life.

Maybe.

Schmidt cocked the Colt. "One of you dies," he said.

"Not a chance," Charley said.

And then they were on him.

Schmidt fired, but it came too late. The shot went wide, and a blow hurled the Colt from his hand.

No Ears scooped it up, while Charley kicked Schmidt's legs out from under him.

Schmidt went down.

They kicked him in the stomach, in the ribs, and then in the stomach again.

Charley cocked his foot back.

"Hold on," No Ears said. "Mike told us not to kill him. He ain't no good dead."

"Yeah, right," Charley said, and landed a blow to Schmidt's head with the side of his boot rather than with the toe.

Schmidt's head snapped to one side. His vision darkened and blurred.

Then came a shot. The flash lit up the pier, the buildings, and the two men. Schmidt saw them as though they were being reflected in funhouse mirrors. The sound slammed off the buildings, tremendous, overpoweringly loud. It rolled like thunder out over the scummy water.

A startled yelp.

Not his.

Then came another shot, deep and loud.

"I got four more in this one and six more in this one."

The sound of drumming boots answered the newcomer's challenge.

The sound faded around the nearest corner.

Schmidt tried to get up but a sharp, hot pain in his ribs stopped him.

A figure knelt down beside him.

"What a miserable way to spend Saturday night. Well, Sunday morning, I suppose," the figure said. It was Clayton McNeill.

"I agree," Schmidt managed to say. "What are you doing here?"

"Saving your miserable hide."

"Thanks," Schmidt said. He could feel himself weakening, suddenly. His body was giving up its hold on consciousness, edging him toward an exhausted collapse. "My revolver. Where is it?"

"Not here."

"I remember No Ears making a grab for it," Schmidt said. "He must have made off with it." And then he could say no more. The effort had become too great.

"All right," Clayton said. "Let's get you home, you damn fool. Didn't you learn anything aboard ship?"

* * *

Schmidt had learned a great deal aboard ship. One of the things he had learned was how to tell the difference between being helped and being taken advantage of. Clayton McNeill was helping.

He sat Schmidt on his bed, pulled his shoes off, took his jacket off, and removed his empty shoulder holster.

"Your shirt's a goner," he said, stating the fact.

"I have others."

"I should hope so, a prosperous bank teller like you."

Clayton cleaned the dirt out of the cut over Schmidt's left eye and washed away as much of the blood as made sense. The rest could wait. They got Schmidt under the covers.

Schmidt asked, "What were you doing down there?"

McNeill made a wry face. "I haven't always been a bookkeeper."

"That's no answer."

McNeill thought for a long time, then he said, "You've been leaving a trail a blind man could follow."

"Trail?"

McNeill arched an eyebrow. "Yes, a *trail*. What you're planning to do, you can't do alone. The rub is you'll need the sort of help you can't hire, not around here, anyway."

"What am I planning to do?"

"Send someone on a sea voyage."

"How do you know that?"

"Hansen isn't dead yet."

"What are you going to do?"

McNeill thought again, scratched his jaw. "I'd like to throw in with you if you'll have me."

"What have you got against Hansen?"

"Enough."

"Once we cross that line, there'll be no going back."

"What makes you think I haven't already crossed it?"

The room fell silent and the first full light of Sunday morning streamed in through Schmidt's window.

* * *

The dinner gong—dinner was served on Sundays—woke the man that Hansen and his mate had signed on as Schmidt. The midday light was bright, and the air drifting in through his window smelled of fir trees and coastal pines.

Schmidt cleaned up as best he could, shaved carefully, changed his shirt, and went down to the kitchen. He was far too late to be seated in the dining room. The cook took pity on him and gave him more than a late-comer's due.

As he ate, he thought back through the mistakes he had made, reviewed the lessons he had learned in the *Shattuck*'s forecastle and on her decks. They were good lessons, ones he vowed never to ignore again. Over his coffee, he decided to retrieve his Colt.

But before he could accomplish that laudable task, he had two items to buy. One of which he should have bought the moment he'd landed in Seattle. In truth it had been his vanity and not his desire for anonymity that had stopped him.

* * *

The Quimper Mercantile and Chandlery was open for business on Sundays.

It was the task of a few minutes to purchase a derringer, a box of cartridges, and an ebony-wood cane. The cane wasn't a belaying pin, but it would do for the likes of Harry "No Ears" Pederson.

* * *

No Ears was a man of neither regular employment nor regular habits, but he did have one fixed point in his routine. On Sundays, when he could afford to, he ate supper at Mrs. Chang's Chowder and Oyster Bar. After which, he would cross back over to the Blue Star and do whatever Big Mike had in store for him.

Today, however, No Ears cut around the rear of Chang's and headed for the Northern Lights Hotel, the best brothel in Port Townsend. His route took him down Sherman's Alley, which had a sharp dogleg that sheltered it from Water Street.

Schmidt sprang from a gap between the buildings and surged up behind No Ears. Before No Ears could swing around, Schmidt brought his ebony-wood cane down and across onto the man's thigh. He brought it down hard and fast.

No Ears yelled and collapsed into the slurry of horse-dung and mud that served as the alley's pavement. His eyes were wild, his face twisted in pain. He was gasping and moaning. His breath was foul with the stench of clam chowder and decaying teeth.

Schmidt planted the heel of his shoe on the man's neck, hard enough to mean business. "Where's my revolver?" Schmidt asked.

"I sold it."

Schmidt twisted his heel. "No, you didn't. You'd keep a gun like that." He lifted the cane, readying it. "Where's my gun?"

"Honest. I sold it."

Schmidt drew his new derringer and cocked it. He aimed it at the other man's face.

"To whom?"

"A guy. He came into the Blue Star and we got to talking about guns. You know how it is. I sold it to him."

"Who is he?"

"I don't know. Logger, I guess."

"I want my gun back." Schmidt pressed harder with his heel. He increased the pressure until No Ears squealed like a pig and started coughing. "Find it."

No Ears nodded as vigorously as he could with the side of his face pressed into a pile of horse dung. "Yes, sir. As soon as I can."

"Sooner than that, my friend. Much sooner," Schmidt said, and stepped away, releasing him.

No Ears didn't say a word, but rubbed his neck and scrambled off down the alley.

Schmidt watched him until he disappeared around a corner, then Schmidt turned and headed for Water Street. He had nothing to do until he showed up for work on Monday morning.

* * *

Shortly before the bank opened its doors on Monday morning, Clayton McNeill came over to Schmidt's teller's cage. He was carrying a neatly folded newspaper.

"You have any interest in the *Susan B. Shattuck*?"

"What about her?" Schmidt asked.

McNeill handed him the paper. "Interesting piece about her," he said, and moved away.

The shipping column reported the *Shattuck* was scheduled to sail on Wednesday morning for Suva. Her cargo consisted of lumber and balks of timber.

Which meant that every crimp in Port Townsend, including Hansen, would be scouring Water Street on Tuesday night. The beer and the hard stuff, together with the chloral hydrate and the laudanum, would be flowing like the runoff from a monsoon.

Under those conditions, two extra men were hardly likely to attract attention.

* * *

After supper on Tuesday, Mr. Schmidt and Mr. McNeill joined Mrs. Abbott and Mr. Kearney, a schoolteacher, for a game of whist. At nine o'clock, they excused themselves and went to their rooms. By half past nine, they were on Water Street, and by ten o'clock, they were crouched among the pilings beneath the Mariner's Rest, Hansen's boarding house. They had their guns drawn. Schmidt held his derringer in his left hand, his cane at the ready in his right.

Sooner or later, unaware of what he was doing, Hansen would come to them.

All they had to do was wait…in the dark and the cold—wait and listen to the raucous voices filtering down from the rooming house above them, listen to the gentle thud of a rowboat as it rocked against Hansen's neatly ordered dock.

* * *

Their wait was over before Schmidt's leg had stiffened in the cold.

At ten thirty, Hansen and two of his runners descended the stairs that led down from a trapdoor in one of the back-rooms. Hansen was in the lead, dressed in a business suit and a derby hat.

His two runners were half dragging and half carrying a man between them. He was Harry "No Ears" Pederson. His hands were tied behind his back, and he looked decidedly the worse for what-ever it was he'd been drinking. He was mumbling semi-coherently about how he'd get even with them someday.

"Shut up," one of the runners said, and thumped No Ears on the back of the head with a sap.

No Ears let out a long, agonized sigh and sagged.

"Now look at what you've done," the second runner said.

"Shut up, the two of you," Hansen said. "Get him into the boat and be quick about it. Burgess is waiting."

The first runner said, "Yeah, Burgess and Burgess's money."

"With lots more where that's coming from," the second run-ner said.

The first runner pointed at No Ears. "And lots more where *that* came from."

The three of them shared a hearty laugh and manhandled No Ears toward the boat. They set him down, and the first runner climbed into the boat.

They had No Ears straddled between the boat and the dock when Schmidt and McNeill charged out of the gloom.

Their attack was fast, but it wasn't instantaneous. Hansen had time to turn, his face wide with shock. He thrust his hand beneath his suit jacket.

McNeill shouldered the second runner, the one who'd stayed on the dock, into Hansen, throwing him backwards.

The runner bounced off his boss, stumbled, caught his foot on the bullrail, and pitched over the edge. He hit his head on the boat's gunwale and ended up flailing in the filth-choked water, stunned and disoriented.

No Ears dropped onto the planking like a sack of weevil-infested flour. He lay there, breathing but otherwise inert.

By this time, Hansen's gun had cleared. For all the good it did him.

Schmidt brought his ebony cane down on Hansen's forearm, a vicious, snapping blow.

Hansen's hand jerked open and his gun—a nickel-plated showpiece—flew into the water. His mouth opened in a startled gasp.

"Hurts, doesn't it?" Schmidt said.

The first runner, the one in the boat, had his gun out. It was a small-caliber pocket pistol, also nickel-plated, more a piece of jewelry than anything else. He fired several times, but because he was panicked and because the boat was rocking, the shots went wild. The slugs hit pilings and joists and the mud at the edge of the water.

McNeill leveled his gun at the man's forehead.

"That's enough, Sammy. Behave or I'll blow your head off."

Sammy nodded.

"Ditch the gun."

Sammy looked pained. "Aw, gee, Mr. McNeill, I just bought it. Took me months to save up for it."

"Too bad," McNeill said. "Do it."

Sammy gazed lovingly at his gun, but then he dropped it overboard.

Hansen said, "You here to get a little of your own back, are you, Clay?"

"Call it a down payment," McNeill said.

"I had a hunch you'd turn on me someday."

"You should have paid it more heed."

The drumming of heavy boots sounded from the planks over their heads. Sammy's shots had attracted someone's attention.

Schmidt said, "We're running out of time."

* * *

Five minutes later, No Ears was fumbling his way back toward Water Street and freedom. Out on the water, Hansen and his two runners sat tied up in the rowboat, while McNeill and Schmidt rowed away from the pier.

The minutes ticked silently by.

When they were no scant distance out in the bay, Schmidt and McNeill stopped rowing.

McNeill drew his gun and trained it on the three captives.

"This where you're gonna kill us?" Hansen asked.

"No," Schmidt said. "This is where I'm gonna offer to buy you boys a drink." Schmidt produced a pint bottle and pulled the cork. "You can drink it," he said, "or we can force it down your throats. Your choice."

The three men drank, round after round until they'd drained the bottle. Then, thanks to the chloral hydrate, they passed out, making an irregular heap. They looked like nothing quite so much as a pile of garbage.

Schmidt and McNeill gripped their oars and resumed rowing.

Ahead of them lay the *Susan B. Shattuck*. She was tall, and graceful, and outmoded, and stunningly beautiful in the starlight.

* * *

By the time the bank opened on Wednesday morning, the *Shattuck* was a memory.

By the time the bank opened on Thursday morning, the news had spread up and down Water Street that Captain Hansen and two of his goons had gone missing. The police said that it was too early to declare him missing. Like as not, he'd taken the steamer over to Seattle. His employees said otherwise.

Shortly before closing on Friday, Harry "No Ears" Pederson presented himself at Schmidt's window.

"Good afternoon, Mr. Pederson," Schmidt said. He smiled warmly. "May I help you?"

"Hello, Mr. Schmidt," No Ears said. "I wanted to thank you for what you done for me. I'd have been halfway to China by now if it hadn't been for you."

"Thanks, but I don't have the vaguest idea what you're talking about."

No Ears wasn't stupid. "Then I must have you confused with somebody else."

"I'm sure of it," Schmidt said.

No Ears set a box about the size of book on the counter. He slid it across toward Schmidt. "I believe this belongs to you."

"What have we here?" Schmidt asked, and carefully opened the box. Inside, nestled in a wrapping of oiled brown paper, was his Colt revolver. It had been cleaned to a bright shine and freshly oiled. "Thank you very much, Mr. Pederson. I won't forget."

"Are we square?"

"Yes, we're square."

Pederson nodded and hurried from the bank.

Schmidt placed the box in a drawer.

McNeill approached and said, "He returned your revolver?"

"He did."

"That was considerate of him."

"I suspect it's because he isn't on his way to Suva."

"Come on, Smitty. He would have had to have hocked his shoelaces to buy it back. How'd you convince him to do it?"

Schmidt said, "Well, I haven't always been a banker."

An Education for Thursday

Dean Wesley Smith

ONE

Angela stopped her trusted grey mare she called Betsy at the small shack that had the sign *Delamar Marshal's Office* hanging from the front eave. Made from twisted lumber and covered in black paper in places, the office looked like a good wind could knock it down, except the back half that had been made out of stone and more than likely was a cell.

At the edge of town, she had passed the standard signs warning that anyone staying in Delamar, Idaho, needed to check their weapons with the marshal. That rule was standard for all western towns, and she had expected it.

No guns allowed.

That was the law. Even in a small mining town like Delamar. In fact, she knew of no town in the west that allowed guns in the town limits. Everyone carried them between towns, but never in town. The gun laws were strictly enforced.

If she had just been going on through town, up the hot and dusty sage-covered valley toward Silver City, four miles farther, she wouldn't have bothered.

And no one would have cared, since the only wagon trail in this narrow valley was also the main street for Delamar. Everyone had to pass through this small twenty-building mining town to get from Murphy to Silver City, the main town and county seat, at least coming in from the Oregon side.

But she planned on spending a few nights in the big Delamar Hotel tucked against the hill ahead. Staying in that hotel was the point of this trip.

Right now she didn't want to even look at the big hotel. She would soon enough, and teach a few men a few lessons in the process, if everything worked as planned.

She took a handkerchief from her light riding jacket pocket and wiped the dust and sweat from her face. She wore a wide-brimmed blue-cloth hat that kept the sun from her face and matched her light blue-cloth riding jacket.

She dismounted and took the moment to stretch as much as a lady was allowed such movements in public in 1880.

She looked exactly the part of a fine woman traveling, although it was rare for a fine woman to travel alone. But it was done.

She had ridden all day from her small camp spot down on the Snake River, only stopping twice to rest. Now it was late in the hot summer afternoon and she was looking forward to a bath, a good dinner, and a soft bed.

The Delamar Hotel was known for all three.

They were even known for having drinks with ice, since they stored ice in large blocks from the cold winters in a deep root cellar accessed from their basement. An iced-tea with actual ice chips would taste very good right now.

She didn't plan to be in this tiny mining town for long. She couldn't imagine how anyone actually lived here, considering that the town was nothing more than some buildings tucked in the bottom of a very narrow valley between tall mountains. Even the miners who worked the mines either camped in tents or lived in bunkhouses near the big mines.

She would be here just long enough to do what she needed to do, and then, before the feeling of being trapped closed in, she would be gone. But while here, she was going to enjoy herself as much as she could for a woman of her pretend higher position in society.

Actually, she was a land owner and fairly rich in her own right, but not high-class at all. She loved working with horses, not something a fine lady did. But for this coming lesson, she needed to play the part of a lady of high society. She could do that. She had been coached well.

Around her, the dusty trail from the summer's heat seemed to radiate between the wooden buildings. She could see the big Delamar mine across the road and up the valley slightly, its tailings covering a vast amount of ground and almost blocking the stream bed in one place, showing how really large the mine actually was.

Back down the valley, she had passed a gold stamp mill, its boilers kicking off clouds of steam into the hot afternoon air and smelling like sulfur matches. Clearly the mines in this area were still working strong.

She pulled her saddle rifle from its leather sling on the side of Betsy and opened the chamber, making sure it wasn't ready to fire, and headed toward the front door of the sheriff's building. The small caliber rifle was exactly the type of protection a fine lady would carry on her horse between towns.

She had a Colt revolver in her satchel on Betsy, but that one she wasn't turning in, no matter what the law said.

Before she could step up onto the narrow wooden porch in front of the door, a man wearing a star on his long duster coat came out. Beyond him she could see an almost empty office and a clean old wooden desk and the stone cell beyond. That small room was no doubt very hot and she had no idea why the marshal wore a long duster coat and a wide cowboy-style hat. But he didn't even seem to be sweating.

She was just glad she wasn't going to have to go inside. More than likely the marshal had seen her coming through cracks in the wooden planks that were the walls of the office shack.

He looked almost too young for the job of sheriff, with long brown hair that was pulled back and dark eyes that seemed to see everything.

He nodded to her and tipped his hat.

"Marshal," she said. "I would like to check my rifle. I'll be staying at the hotel for a few days."

"Nice to have you in town, Miss…?"

"Lehman," she said, giving him her fake last name and making sure he was clear from the tone of her voice that asking her was out of line, as she should have done for someone of her stature. She needed to play this part perfectly. Actually her real name was Buchtel, but on this trip she had grown used to Lehman and kind of liked it.

The marshal nodded, his dark eyes almost smiling at her only for a moment before looking away. She knew that what he saw was a spoiled, young woman who was out of her element.

That's what she wanted him to see.

She handed him her rifle.

He handed her a piece of paper with the number ten scribbled on it.

"Have a nice stay, Miss Lehman," he said.

"I hope to," she said. "A stable for my horse?"

"Beyond the hotel two buildings, against the hill."

She nodded. "Thank you, marshal."

With that she turned away and took Betsy's lead and started walking up the hot, dusty main street toward the Delamar Hotel.

Behind her she could feel him watching her walk away.

Her plan was in motion, the bait tossed out.

Now for a hot bath, a nice dinner, and a night's sleep.

If she was allowed to sleep the entire night. Since she said she was staying both nights, she had a hunch she would be able to sleep, at least on the first night.

It would take that long for the word to get out that she was here.

TWO

After she got Betsy settled into the stable and made sure she would be brushed down and fed and watered in the correct way, Angela went back to the big hotel.

The Delamar Hotel was everything she had heard. Two stories tall, it stretched for what seemed an obscene distance along the main road like a wall protecting the road from the mountain. A long covered porch with white narrow posts and decorative trim ran the entire front of the building. Chairs were placed at various places along the porch, all empty.

She figured a hundred men could stand on that porch and not even begin to fill it.

Over the porch was a covered second-floor balcony with chairs set along at intervals in the shade. No one was using the upper deck as she approached.

The side of the hotel was white-painted boards and the windows on the second floor were tall and almost all up and wide open. As she climbed the two steps onto the wide front porch, she could see that all the windows on the main floor were also slid open and the big main double door was braced open, clearly allowing whatever breeze that came along the valley to blow through.

The insides were as plush as any hotel she had seen in San Francisco or New York, which stunned her a little. This far up in the dusty mountains in a small mining town was not a place she would expect to find this kind of hotel.

Polished dark maple wood and thick area carpets made the room feel cooler than outside, even with all the tall, brown drapes pulled back and the light streaming in.

A huge river-stone fireplace was to the left of the big, main foyer with thick, overstuffed couches and chairs around it. And a grand, polished-maple staircase led up on the right of the foyer.

This hotel must have cost a fortune to build way up here in the mountains like this.

Even though the valley was dusty, nothing inside the hotel seemed to have any dust on it at all. She wasn't sure how that was possible. They must have someone cleaning night and day during the summer months when the windows were open.

A smiling man in a dark suit stood behind a long, polished-wood front desk. A nameplate sitting near the book gave the man's name as Stanley. Two ornate lamps with long brown shades framed the long desk and gave it a soft brown glow.

Behind Stanley was a wall of square wooden boxes, clearly for room keys and guest mail. Most of the boxes still had keys in them, which surprised her. The summer was the season for this hotel. In the winter it was impossible to get into this valley.

She asked for the largest suite and registered, paying in cash ahead for two days, signing her name to the big book on the desk. She put her home town as Boston and signed Andrea Lehman as if she had signed it her entire life.

Stanley asked if he could take her bag to her room, but she said it wouldn't be a bother for her to carry it. It was light. She wanted to take no chance he would notice the Colt revolver hidden inside.

"Dinner in the dining room to the left is serving for another hour," he said.

"I will wash up first and would like to have a bath after dinner," she said. "Would that be possible?"

"Most assuredly," he said, nodding. "It will be drawn and heated when you return."

"Thank you," she said, giving him her best smile. "But not too warm on a day like this."

He smiled and nodded.

Then she turned and slowly went up the stairs, studying the details of the big room and the ornate wooden staircase as she went as any woman of class would do.

At the top of the stairs, the wide, carpeted hallway stretched in two directions, lit by oil lamps on the walls. It would have been a very stuffy and hot corridor if the window at one end wasn't wide open and a door at the other was open. As it was, there was a nice breeze in the corridor that seemed to keep the insects clear as well.

The suite she had asked for was right beside the end of the hall with the door. A small deck with a few chairs were outside the door and an exterior staircase leading down. She looked at the deck and stairs, making sure she knew how to get down it if she had to.

She had known that this was the room she wanted. It was the farthest from the main desk and had easy access.

Plus a woman of her pretend means would ask for this suite. So it played along in the charade.

The suite was basically two large rooms and a smaller room off to the back side.

The main room had a fireplace with an area rug that filled most of the room. Couches and overstuffed chairs circled around the fireplace. The room looked comfortable and would be wonderful on a winter evening with the fireplace going. Two big windows in the room were open, heavy brown drapes pulled back, showing only the steep, sagebrush-covered hillside behind the hotel.

Considering this was the second floor, it wasn't that far to the ground. But far enough she didn't need to worry about anyone coming in that way, at least not without a ladder.

The bedroom had a large ornate maple bed in the middle of an area rug with a dozen pillows and a large comforter over a feather-filled mattress. The bedroom also had two windows open to the steep hillside behind.

The third smaller room contained a claw-foot bathtub, a sink, and a toilet. She knew that the hotel had indoor plumbing in the top suites, so it didn't surprise her, but it pleased her. She missed her bath features from home.

She knew that most of the rooms here in the hotel shared a bath and toilet between every ten rooms. But even that was amazing for a hotel this far up in the mountains.

The small room with running water made the suite worth the price.

The small room had a high window that was also open and allowed a cross-breeze through the three rooms, but didn't allow anyone to see in.

It wasn't late enough in the day to really start cooling down yet, but she knew this valley would get downright chilly later in the evening.

She used a damp cloth and the cool water in the big ceramic pitcher on a wooden side table in the bedroom to wash down. The suite had running cold water in the big sink next to the tub, but Candace, her coach on the ways of being a lady, had told her that a woman of her means would use the water and a fresh cloth to freshen up instead of just running water in a sink.

Angela still splashed water on her face from the sink to start with before using the cloth. The cool well water felt great and got her head completely clear.

Within fifteen minutes, she had changed behind a changing screen in the bedroom from her riding clothes into more eve-ning-like clothes and had hid the Colt revolver she carried in her satchel under the mattress in the middle of the bed. She didn't think anyone turning down the bed would find it there or report the break in the law if they did.

A few minutes later, she was being seated in the dining room that smelled of a wonderful pot roast and potatoes even with the windows open to allow a cross breeze.

There were only three other customers in the dining area, all three older men sitting together at a table to the right of the large dining room. They were intent on their conversation and didn't seem to notice her.

She asked for the table away from them on the left with her back to the wall, and then after ordering the night's special of pot roast, asked the friendly waitress named Bonnie for a glass of iced tea, with ice if possible.

Bonnie was a tall, thin woman with a large, friendly smile. Her pale skin seemed to have avoided any of the sun and she had her long brown hair pulled back and tied.

Bonnie didn't seem to be much older than Angela, but Angela felt as if Bonnie was looking right through her.

"I do have ice," Bonnie said. "It will take me just a moment to get it."

"Thank you," Angela said.

And with that, Angela sat alone, pretending to be someone she wasn't, alone in a hotel a long ways from home, waiting.

And doing her best to stay calm now that she was actually here.

THREE

The first night in the Delamar Hotel went as Angela had hoped it would. A wonderful dinner with some great conversation with Bonnie, the waitress. Then a warm bath that felt great after a long day of riding.

Then, with her hand on the revolver under her pillow and the door bolted, she slept soundly through the night as the cool air washed over her.

Bonnie was there in the dining room the next morning serving breakfast and the marshal was just finishing his breakfast as she came in. The windows were still closed and the room felt cool and smelled of bacon and pancakes. The smell made her feel like she could live in this place.

The marshal tipped his hat to her as he went out, still wearing the long duster coat. More than likely he lived in this hotel in an area on the far side reserved for staff and long stays. He sure looked as if he could afford it.

"What's his story?" Angela asked Bonnie, indicating the marshal, as Bonnie came up with a glass of cool water to take her order.

"He's a strange one," she said, smiling. "Just took over the job here last month, since the town needed a marshal. The previous one retired I hear. I have a hunch this marshal won't be here long, moving up to larger cities."

"He does seem out of place," Angela nodded.

"A bit," Bonnie said, smiling.

The afternoon, Angela spent time in her room until it started getting stuffy from the heat. Then after a light lunch of cold cuts and breads with an iced-tea with actual ice again, she went to the shade of the second floor porch to sit and watch what little activity there was in the valley.

And that was very little.

Even in the summer, very little seemed to happen in this remote mountain valley. Noises came from the mine at times, and a few times men rode past, tipping their hats to her when they noticed her sitting in the shade.

But that was it.

Finally, she went back to her room to take a nap before dinner, then again had a wonderful beef meal with potatoes served by Bonnie yet again.

It seemed the woman was the only waitress. When Angela asked her about it, Bonnie shrugged. "Not much else to do in this valley but work."

After one day here, Angela certainly understood that.

After dinner, Angela went back to her room, changed into her riding clothes, put her riding hat beside the door on a stand there, packed what few personal belongings she had in her satchel, and put it beside her chair.

Then she took the Colt revolver from her hiding place, checked it to make sure it was loaded and ready. She closed the windows and pulled the drapes closed in all three rooms.

Then she turned down all but one lamp and wrestled around a large overstuffed chair so it directly faced the door to the room, but wasn't too close. She made sure everything was ready, including a small pillow beside her left hand and a couple of washcloths near her.

Then she sat down with the gun on her lap to wait.

It was time for some revenge.

She had set herself up as a helpless victim, a young woman traveling alone, just as her friend Candice had been two months before. Candice had checked her only weapon as was required and had been defenseless when the two men came into her room and did unimaginable things to her.

Candace could not dare report the men or tell anyone, for that matter, since as a lady of the time, that would sully her name and her husband, who she met two days later in Boise, and from there went on to their home in San Francisco.

And in this small mining town, there was no one Candace could have told that wouldn't have caused her more troubles than she had already endured.

Candice had never told her husband what had happened, but had confided in Angela one day in tears. Angela worked with her and her husband, making sure their horses were cared for correctly, as well as ranching her own estate in the hills above San Francisco with forty head of horses.

Angela had shot a horse thief one night and buried his body before anyone could find it. She had managed to survive that. Since the man had hurt one of her horses enough that Angela had had to put it down, the guy dying seemed like clear justice to her, and she never once lost an ounce of sleep over the man's death.

She thought of him as nothing more than an animal that needed to be put down.

When she heard Candice's story and over a few days helped get Candice back on her feet and moving again, Angela decided that the only justice the two men who did that to Candice would get would be the same thing she had done to the horse thief.

Six feet down in hard ground.

They were animals, nothing more.

Angela had convinced Candice of her plan and gotten coaching and descriptions of the two men. Candice thought both had been miners in the Delamar Mine.

Delamar was a very small place. Everyone knew a lady from Boston was staying a second night in the hotel, alone. Who knew how many times these two men had gotten away with such unspeakable acts against unarmed and defenseless women.

They would never do it again if Angela had anything to say about it.

All she had to do was wait.

FOUR

Just over two hours later, as night had settled completely on the deep valley, Angela heard the lock on her door rattle gently. Then a key was inserted and it was opened slightly.

If she had been asleep, she never would have heard it.

She wondered where they had gotten a key to her door. Or how they had even gotten into the hotel without being seen.

A thin knife came through the slit in the door and flicked back the security bolt.

The man leading into the room wore dark clothes and had the same white scar on his face that Candice had described exactly.

Angela could smell the man's sweat, mixed with a sour smell of whiskey. The guy had clearly not bathed for a very long time.

The man behind the first one was short, with a thin, red beard.

Again, he matched the same description of the second man that had attacked Candice.

And he smelled worse than the first one, if that was possible.

Angela had lured the two animals out of their hole.

Angela shuddered at thinking what her friend Candice had gone through that night, alone here in this desolate place.

And then Candace had not been able to tell anyone.

The thought of that just made Angela want to shoot both men where they stood.

The first man was turned slightly to his friend as he came in the room.

The red-bearded man eased the door closed behind them before they both turned, expecting her to be asleep in her bed, defenseless and unarmed.

As Candace had been, because she followed the law of this stupid little town and checked her gun, her only defense against these animals.

"Gentlemen?" Angela asked. "May I help you?"

Her voice, and then the sight of the Colt leveled at them jerked both men back into the closed door as if pulled by the same rope.

"Uhh, we must have the wrong room," the first man said.

"Oh, I don't think so," Angela said, remaining seated. "You planned on doing to me what you did to that woman three months ago."

"What woman?" the second man asked, his voice almost squeaking.

"Lying will get you a lot of pain," she said, shaking her head, but not letting the gun move.

"We were just having a little fun is all," the first guy said. "No harm and she didn't seem to mind."

"She didn't hardly cry at all," the red-bearded man said. "We thought she liked it."

Angela almost shot both of them right there. She wanted to be sick just thinking about what her friend had endured.

But Angela forced herself to take a deep breath and stay calm. A quick death would be far, far too easy for these two.

"On the ground, both of you," she said.

"Hey, I don't think so," the first guy with the scar said, stepping toward her. "Never seen a woman who could even hit a barn with one of those. You sure it's even loaded?"

The guy was dumber than he looked, and that was going some.

With a quick movement, Angela took the small pillow off the arm of the chair beside her and put it over the barrel to muffle the sound and shot the idiot in the leg before he had moved two steps toward her.

The sound of the shot was still louder than she had expected and practiced with, but she doubted anyone heard, since the hotel had so few guests and she was on the far end from where the marshal would have a room.

The smell of gunpowder filled the room as the guy went down swearing, holding his now useless kneecap. He would never walk on that leg again.

The bleeding wasn't bad, but bone had splattered against the wall near the door. He would lose that leg, she had no doubt.

"On the ground," she said to the red-bearded guy who had clearly just pissed in his already filthy pants as he stared at his hurt friend.

The smell in the room was already bad from the unwashed men and now it got much, much worse. She wished she could stand and go open a window, but she didn't dare.

The shot guy was swearing, and the sound was getting louder and louder, so she tossed a washcloth to the guy who was slowly lowering himself to the floor, whimpering.

"Stuff that in your friend's mouth before I shoot him again for being so loud. Then stick the other in your mouth."

The guy did that.

"You go to take that cloth out and I shoot you in the hand, understand?" she said to both of them. "And who knows, since I'm a woman I might miss and shoot off your nose or something in the process."

The guy with the red beard nodded, the other guy just looked at her with deep anger glaring out of his beady rat-like eyes.

Then, as the guy with the red beard was lying on the floor, she put the pillow over the barrel of the Colt again, and shot him in the knee as well.

The shot blew his knee apart, also splattering bone against the wall.

Now they were both bleeding onto the large area carpet. More than likely it was being ruined, which made her feel bad.

"Now that is some fine shooting," a deep voice said from behind her.

She instantly swung around to face the marshal standing there in the doorway to her bedroom, smiling. He still had on his hat and long duster.

As her gun aimed at him, he laughed and raised his hands. "I'm unarmed, as you are supposed to be," he said.

He indicated the two on the floor. "Looks like it was a good thing you broke that law."

Angela glanced at the two on the floor, then back at the marshal.

"I knew about your friend's run-in with these two," the marshal said, "and have been trying to pin something on them since I got here, without luck. I heard what they said to you, though, about what they did, so that's as good as a confession in my book."

Then he waved his hand in front of his face. "They do smell, don't they?"

"How did you know?" she asked, frowning at the man. "Candace said she hadn't told anyone. And now did you get in here?"

"Climbed up a ladder into your bedroom window," Bonnie the waitress said, smiling as she stepped into the room beside the marshal. "Damn hard to do and keep quiet, let me tell you."

Angela just stared at Bonnie, not knowing what to say.

Bonnie went on. "I'm the one who brought the marshal here to come after these men. I'm a friend of Candace's in San Francisco and she confided in me right after she got home. I contacted the marshal and we came here a month ago to see what we could do. Candace sent me a telegram that I got the day before you arrived that you were coming."

"Candice wanted us to keep an eye on you and help," the marshal said. "Which is why we climbed in here as you were confronting the two. We saw them coming in the back way."

Bonnie nodded. "Candice said you wanted revenge for what they did to her. Seems you got that just fine so far. Brave setting yourself up as bait like that."

Angela didn't know what to say, so she kept quiet. She couldn't believe the marshal had known of her plan and let her go through with it. But it was nice of Candice to worry about her.

The marshal glanced at Bonnie. "You want to bandage their knees, stop the bleeding?"

"Not really," Bonnie said, waving her hand at the smell that was filling the room as both hurt men emptied their bowls into their already soiled pants. "I think those two got exactly what was coming to them."

"I agree," the marshal said.

Angela shook her head, not believing that the marshal was agreeing with what she had done, then glanced back at the two animals on the floor.

The first one she had shot seemed to be slowly losing consciousness, more than likely from the pain, since he didn't seem to be bleeding that much. The other one had his eyes smashed shut, but didn't seem to be bleeding that badly either.

They both smelled worse than a latrine that had some whiskey dumped in it.

The marshal turned and picked up her rifle from where he clearly had leaned it on the other side of the door and came forward and handed it to her as she stood.

"Your horse is at the bottom of the side stairs and there's enough moonlight to ride back down the valley if you take it slow and easy."

"What are you going to do with these two?" she asked.

The marshal glanced at Bonnie, who shook her head.

"I'm going back to my room," he said, "see if I can get some sleep."

"Mind if I join you?" Bonnie asked, smiling at the marshal in a way that told Angela they had been a couple for a very long time.

"If someone reports this," the marshal said, "I'll come and toss these two in jail, I suppose, until the Doc can get to them when he comes down from Silver City on Saturday. I think they'll spend a lot of time in jail after that, from the confession they gave."

"This is only Thursday," Angela said, starting to understand.

"Yeah, hope they can hold on that long," the marshal said, shrugging. "Got to be painful. I just don't have anything that's going to help them in that little cell and building I call an office."

Angela laughed, picked up her satchel, and tucked the Colt down inside it. Then, with the rifle in her hand, she moved in a wide circle around the pool of blood and piss that was soaking into the thick area rug, and put on her travel hat.

She pulled the door open, then glanced back at the marshal and Bonnie. "See you in San Francisco?"

"You'll see me," Bonnie said, smiling. "Tell Candice I said all is well when you get there."

"I will," Angela said. "And thank you."

Then Angela glanced down at the two animals she had shot, both sprawled on the carpet.

"For Candice," she said.

And then with a quick step forward, she kicked the red-bearded one in the face, hearing his nose shatter under her boot.

She smiled at the marshal and Bonnie. "That felt good. Just a little bit more of a lesson."

Both laughed softly, shaking their heads.

Bonnie tucked her arm in the marshal's and said to Angela, "Safe journey."

Angela nodded to them, then looked both ways down the empty hallway and headed for the staircase. Betsy was saddled and waiting below.

She had taught the two animals who had attacked Candice a lesson, if they lived to remember it. If they didn't, they would die a very painful death.

And she had learned a lesson as well. She had learned that there were good people in the world that sometimes believed in justice as well.

She had no idea where they came from, but she was glad to know they were out there.

Our final story set in the west returns us to Canada and the train motif. The story itself is a bit of a bridge between the American West tales and what's to come, since the echoes in this tale are of the First World War.

"The Curious Case of the Ha'Penny Detective" marks Lee Allred's third appearance in Fiction River. *His work has also appeared in* Time Streams *and* Universe Between. *He'll also act as guest editor for our next special edition,* Valor. *These days, Lee spends most of his time scripting comics for Marvel and DC, but he also finds time to write short fiction, for which we are very grateful.*

He says this story has two inspirations. He writes,

"My good friend and great writer, the late K.D. Wentworth, belonged to a local Baker Street Irregulars group. The conceit of BSI, I gather, is that Conan Doyle's fictional character is actually a real, historical person—and all of the ramifications that implies. I also have on my shelf a book entitled Rivals of Sherlock Holmes, *reprinting exploits of other contemporary fictitious detectives in* The Strand *and other Victorian-era magazines."*

Leave it to Lee to make a connection here. He adds puckishly, "If Doyle's detective is real, then his rivals, too, must be. And all that implies as well..."

The Curious Case
of the Ha'Penny Detective

Lee Allred

April 25, 1923
Canadian Pacific Railway
Somewhere West of Moosejaw

Samuel Drennan had just lit the last cigarette from his second pack of the day when a porter rapped softly on his door. Acrid blue smoke filled the first-class rail coach compartment. The porter's experienced knock carried easily past the rhythmic clack-clack-clacking of the rails beneath, each rap hitting in the pause between clacks.

Drennan set aside his homemade wooden travel lapdesk, its whorled white pine surface polished smooth with age and use. It had begun life as the top of a packing crate in a rear-area AEF hospital, the day Samuel Drennan had come to terms with what was left of his life and his body.

He moved stiffly, more from the hours spent watching the flat, featureless Manitoba prairie flash past than from the jagged shrapnel of Belleau Wood still there in his shoulder long after it had sliced off his left arm. He readjusted his black leather eye patch, making sure it covered as best it could the gaping horror show beneath. The stub of his left arm had to make do with a folded sleeve pinned cuff-to-shoulder.

"Yes?" Drennan called, preferring if possible not to stand to walk even the short distance across the compartment. The sway of the car, the jostle of the rail clacks was pain enough.

The porter—a white, red-haired Canadian Scotsman, the back of Drennan's mind noted, rather than the Negro his America upbringing still expected despite Drennan spending the past five years in London—opened the door apologetically. It was well past midnight.

"Begging your pardon, Mr. Drennan, but the gentleman insisted I give you this." The porter handed him a small white calling card with the individual's name printed in graceful italics. Upon the back of the card was penned in firm angular strokes: "Amenable to a short interview. Your servant." and the block initials E.N.

Drennan turned the card over a couple times as he stared at it. His eye narrowed. "Is this a joke?" he demanded of the porter, his gravelly smoker's voice all the more harsh from unbidden anger.

The porter blinked. "Oh, no, sir! It's him himself, it is. We've been keeping it quiet, all of us porters, so as not to let him get mobbed by the other passengers. But he's very much aboard this train."

The porter added. "He said to tell you he'll be awaiting your company in the club car."

"The dining car's closed this late at night," Drennan said half-inattentively, his mind racing at what an interview like this could mean for himself and his paper.

"Yes, sir." The porter's head bobbed. "That's why we took the liberty of making it available to you, so you'd have some privacy, along with some refreshments."

Drennan set the card down and dug a finger in the silken lining of his vest pocket and extracted a folded Canadian bank note. He pressed it into the porter's palm. "See that it remains private." He dug out a second, larger bank note. "And divide up among the rest of the boys for helping keep things this quiet."

"Yes, sir!" The porter grinned.

Drennan cocked his head in the direction of the club car. "And tell *him* I'll be there straightaway."

The porter left, still grinning at the size of the second banknote. Drennan was already on his feet, too excited to even wince in pain.

Old Man Carruthers had sent Drennan all the way from London to try to salvage Carruthers' failing Vancouver daily newspaper. Drennan's failing career, too, if it came to that. With a scoop like this…

Drennan splashed cold water on his face, ran the back of his hand across his jaw to feel his stubble. He'd shaved earlier in the evening when the train had pulled to a stop at a station. It'd have to do. Attempting to shave one-armed on a swaying train was a bad idea.

His hair slicked back with Brilliantine, Drennan straightened his tie and slipped on his suit jacket in a smooth one-arm-and-a-shrug movement.

He checked the small white card just once more before leaving, half-expecting the name to have evaporated like a hospital bed fever dream.

The name was still there:

Major Sir Elihu Nevins, GCB, CBE, DSO

Elihu Nevins, faithful companion and biographer of the most famous man on the planet: Professor James Jonah Chase, the Ha'Penny Detective. Both Chase and Nevins had vanished completely from the public eye shortly before the Great War.

And Samuel Drennan, who so desperately needed a miracle in his life, had an exclusive.

* * *

Drennan didn't recognize Nevins at first. The old man sitting under the feeble glow of a single lamp in an otherwise darkened railway club car. Then the pieces clicked and Drennan could see beneath the deeply lined face the underlay of the young beefy army officer so ably depicted by artist Sidney Pagett in *The Strand*, *The Windsor*, and *Pearson's Magazine* the past forty years.

Drennan slid into the seat opposite Nevins.

The old man took Drennan's extended hand warmly, brushing off a proffered "Sir Nevins."

"Call me Elihu," he said. "My readers always did." He paused. "As did James, himself, of course."

Before Drennan could even ask Elihu the first question, the club car waiter was hovering, order pad in hand.

"I'll have a few slices of bread on a plate, an empty bowl, and a pitcher of milk," Elihu told the waiter.

Nevins ordered a liquid meal: a bottle of whisky and a shot glass.

The waiter hurried back with the items. Elihu began tearing the coarse brown prairie-wheat bread into small pieces and dropping them into the bowl. He poured milk over them.

"Bread and milk," Elihu said as he cleaned his spoon on his napkin. "An old man's dish, although my wife's people eat it at all ages. I find it soothes the nerves late at night when one can't sleep." He titled his head slightly at Drennan's as-of-yet unopened bottle of Canadian Club. "Perhaps you should try it."

Drennan felt his cheeks flush at the old man's disapproval. "I'm not a boozer, if that's what you think, it's just…"

Hating himself for his weakness, Drennan touched his arm stump with his good hand. "Shrapnel. The War." To the public, it was the Great War. To the men who'd been there, it was and always would be simply "The War," as if there were or could be no others. "Sometimes late at night, straight whisky's the only thing that cuts the pain."

Elihu nodded, relaxing a touch. "Picked up a bit of tin myself at Mafeking. Leg, though."

Drennan's turn to nod. *The Curious Case of the Ha'Penny Siege Gun*, Professor Chase's battle of wits against the beautiful Boer spy Eliza Brevoort during the siege of Mafeking. Its once-shocking blunt depiction of the battle now reminded Drennan of a Boy Scout outing.

Elihu gestured at the half loaf of bread and jug of milk still untouched. "Sure you won't try an alternative medication?"

Drennan smiled. " I prefer heartier meals."

"So did I when I was your age. I spent my days and nights gadflying about on the Empire's business. Very hard on the children. Sometimes after the job was finished and I would came home late of a night, I'd sit in the kitchen and fix me a bowl of bread and milk and wait for the children to pad down the stairs and tell me their problems, ask me their questions. And now you're here to ask yours."

Drennan's fingers strayed toward where his notebook and pencil lay hidden in his suit jacket. "You had children? How many?" The Ha'Penny chronicles had always been guardedly vague, even contradictory about Elihu's home life away from Professor Chase.

The old man smiled. "When they are small, even one can seem like dozens."

A twinge, and Drennan's hand was automatically reaching for the bottle. "You must feel right at home on this train, then." He poured two fingers into his glass. "Never seen so many brats and doting mothers aboard a train before. Curiously small ratio of fathers, though."

Or not so curious. Canada had lost its ample share of young men to the scythes of Verdun and the Somme.

Elihu chuckled. "You really don't know about this particular train, do you?"

Drennan shook his head. "All I know is Old Man—I mean, my employer—"

"I know your employer. Go ahead and call him the Old Man. Professor Chase and I always did, even in our twenties, when we'd toddle around Clubland together with Carruthers during my drinking days. He was an old crusty fussbudget even then, bless his heart."

The Chronicles had never mentioned this, but then Carruthers' publishing empire was bitter rivals with *The Strand* and *The Winsdor* which had published the Ha'Penny stories. "Yes. Well. All I know is the Old Man wanted me in Vancouver soonest. This was the only train available—and completely full at that. I know he had to pull some strings to get me—."

Elihu nodded. "I was the string he pulled. I'd booked a second compartment for conducting business affairs."

The old man took another bite of his bread and milk. "The rest of the train is completely full of Mormon families traveling to Alberta. The Mormons are opening a temple there this week. Mormons across all Canada are heading to it."

"To do whatever it is they do in them," Drennan finished. "All that secret wife-swapping marriage sealing stuff and underground grottos."

Elihu chuckled at the reference to the Ha'Penny Detective's first published adventure, *The Scarlet Scripture*. The battle against the bloody-handed Danite 'Avenging Angels' had climaxed with a thrilling boat chase and shootout deep under the Salt Lake Mormon temple in a vast labyrinth of underground grottos. "I'm afraid that particular case was nearly all the fevered imagination of some nameless scribbler at *The Windsor*."

This time Drennan's notebook did emerge from his jacket pocket. "So that case never actually happened?" He'd always wondered about that. The tone and the writing style read so differently from the rest of the Chronicles. Even the title was different. The rest were all entitled *The Curious Case of the Ha'Penny* whatever.

"Oh, there was indeed a man found shot on the dock berthing a ship chartered for Mormon emigrants. And his killer was later found with a torn page of Mormon scripture on his person, but it proved a simple quarrel among sailors over gambling debts and the scripture was part of a wad of torn pages covering a hole in the sole of the man's boot, not a fantastic conspiracy by a Mormon vigilante group."

Drennan quickly penciled notes in shorthand. "So why then—?"

Elihu set his spoon down. "You have to understand. The British Empire in 1881 was a completely different world than our modern 1923. What we take as commonplace today would have been scandalous if not dangerous back then. Jazz music and flapper skirt lengths, for example."

Drennan shook a cigarette from a pack and stuck it in his mouth. "I can imagine what old Queen Victoria would have thought."

"I *know* what she thought about Mormon polygamy. The fact that her British subjects were converting in the tens of thousands and leaving Utah to practice it alarmed her greatly."

Drennan fished out his Ronson Wonderlite lighter and lit up. The acrid calming smoke in his lungs was a welcome friend. "I can imagine."

"And Diogenes Chase—"

Drennan nodded. "Professor Chase's father," he supplied.

"—and his Clubland friends who for all intents and purposes *ran* the British Isles were also alarmed. Not over the polygamy aspect, but over the sheer manpower leaving the Empire. Those adventurous and hearty enough to set out for the unknown, just the sort you want to keep. Or at least send to our own overseas Dominions."

Drennan examined the tip of his burning cigarette. "So you're telling me—"

"That *The Scarlet Scripture* was indeed a conspiracy, but one by the British government: a concerted effort against Mormonism waged in the pages of Fleet Street."

"So why tell me now, after all these years?"

Elihu pushed back his empty bowl. The push brought the sodden mess and its cloying smell closer to Drennan's nose. "Times change. What is seen as a heinous crime today may not be one tomorrow. Mormonism today is at worst a mere curiosity, hardly a threat to the Empire. Time to make amends."

He stood suddenly. "Time, too, to excuse myself for a moment. I'm afraid I suffer from the usual complaints of old age." He slipped from the table and toddled towards the washroom.

✱ ✱ ✱

Drennan set his cigarette down and took another fiery shot of Canadian Club—and this time not because of any painful twinge in his shoulder.

So many of the other famous real-life consulting detectives and adventuring heroes during their golden age in Fleet Street magazines had also started their caseloads battling Mormons. Maybe not all them, maybe not Miss Loveday Brooke or Martin Hewitt or Dr. Halifax, but enough of them—the Purple Sage, the Crime Doctor, and of course Conan Doyle's detective, chief rival of the Ha'Penny Detective—that an obvious pattern emerged once you knew.

Drennan frowned.

The key virtue of the often poorly written consulting detective stories was their credibility. Unlike the wildly exaggerated American Old West stories of the Penny Dreadfuls, these criminal cases actually took place and could be verified by the newspaper stories of the day. Many of the same Ha'Penny Detective cases depicted by Sidney Paget in *The Strand* used the same Paget engravings in *The Illustrated London News* for the factual reportings of the case.

To call into question the truth of any of the Ha'Penny Chronicles was to call into question not only the entire canon—but by extension, the truth of contemporary newspaper accounts. Of Truth itself.

And Drennan's business was Truth.

To throw Truth away for a temporary political convenience. It chilled the blood of a man like Drennan.

Because without Truth, without men like Drennan who had seen real Truth firsthand in the trenches of Verdun and the shell craters of Belleau Wood, had breathed in the choking chlorine gas of Truth, had lived with the squelching trench mud of Truth in their boots for months on end, had screamed in the burning flames of Truth, and had spent the rest of their shattered lives fighting to bring that Truth to others, the War to End All Wars would be but the first of many.

* * *

Elihu returned from the washroom, the lilac scent of its milled soap fresh on his hands.

Drennan no longer looked at Elihu with the same admiring eye as the secondary hero in stories that had filled his childhood imagination nor as the man a grown Drennan had tried in some degree to emulate, both before and after Belleau Wood. Now Drennan wondered if he could even trust the old man.

Elihu, who'd spent a lifetime observing the smallest of clues, actually smiled at Drennan's expression. "I'll wager you're now wondering exactly how far you can believe me or any of the stories I wrote." He had the gall to pat Drennan on the hand. "I wouldn't have expected anything less from Old Man Carruthers' chosen successor."

Chosen—? Drennan nearly lost the cigarette dangling languidly from his mouth.

All the knock-down drag-out arguments he'd had with the Old Man. Drennan had barely been hanging on to his job as a reporter— and lucky at that, given the Old Man's oft stated opinion about the quality of Drennan's writing. To even joke about Drennan being made—

Elihu smiled. "Ah. Hasn't told you, has he? You must have thought you were being banished to Siberia, him bundling you off to faraway Vancouver."

The old man poured himself a glass of milk from the burbling jug. "Carruthers is my age, remember. Can't travel the way he used to. He's sending you to do in his place what he himself would do if he could. Hardly banishment."

"But—"

"And all those strings he pulled getting you on this train weren't so much about getting you to Vancouver, but getting you aboard this *particular* train. So I could look you over."

Elihu dabbed his mouth with his napkin. "This interview isn't of me by you, but the other way 'round. I'm to interview you for the Old Man's job as publisher and pass along my judgment."

* * *

Drennan lit up another cigarette, totally unconscious of doing so. "I just don't buy it. I know what the Old Man thinks of my writing: the same thing the unadoring public thought when I tried my hand at a novel: I stink."

Elihu shook his head. "The newspaper business isn't about how pretty words are strung together. If it was, poets would be reporting the news and reporters would be getting *them* their coffee."

Drennan felt his cheeks flush yet again. That's exactly how he'd gotten his foot in the door of the Carruthers Syndicate: fetching tea and delivering typed copy in one of their London offices for a couple shillings a day after he'd discovered just how hungry a starving novelist could get.

"You've two much more important qualities," Elihu said. "The ability to lead others and the ability to make good decisions under stress." He added: "You and your men wouldn't have survived Belleau Wood otherwise."

"Okay, okay," Drennan growled. "So I'm some sort of *wunderkind*. Why are you sitting here telling me this and not the Old Man?"

He sipped at his milk. "Because it involves one final quality Carruthers isn't qualified to judge and I am: whether or not you can handle the Ha'Penny Detective secret."

* * *

Drennan stubbed out his cigarette butt. "You just told me the Ha'Penny secret. It's all fake. Just a pack of lies." His voice sounded bitter even to himself. He hadn't realized what great stock he'd put into the truth to all those stories.

"No," Elihu gently answered. "I told you our first case didn't happen as written. Something neither I nor James ever let happen again. That is why I took over the writing, poor at it as I was."

Drennan thrummed his finger tips on the starched linen tablecloth. Elihu's words had the verisimilitude of Truth, but then so had *The Scarlet Scripture*, at least to his mind.

Elihu watched the thrumming fingers. "You're still troubled by *Scarlet*? Surely, you couldn't have believed any of that, outside of what I told you happened, was actually real? Not one single thing described about Utah or the Mormons was true—seemingly purposely so, in fact. We should know. Diogenes sent us both to Utah afterwards to make an actual field report on the 'menace.' A précis of which, I might add, *The Windsor* had in hand when they wrote that ridiculous first story anyway."

Now that Drennan thought about it, of course it couldn't have been true. Gigantic limestone caves under a desert floor? Secret society of seven-foot tall bearded patriarchs unkillable by handgun fire? Camel-pulled Conestoga wagons? Riders atop white buffaloes ranging bareback across the Plains?

At the very least the Ha'Penny account of the Mormon's Utah contradicted the equally thought-to-be-true Conan Doyle account of Chase's chief rival, an account even Drennan knew to be a blatant cribbed copy of Robert Louis Stevenson's work of fiction, *The Dynamiters*—right down to character names.

Drennan's fingers stopped. "So I'm supposed to start playing hide-and-seek with some clue you've hidden in your stories, and that's supposed to make me a great newspaper man?"

He stared at Elihu."I'll tell you the only Ha'Penny Secret I'm interested in. Where's Professor James Jonah Chase now? Why did he—and you—vanish over ten years ago? *That's* what will make me a newspaper man and sell papers. Not some hide-and-seek game of clues within clues."

Elihu shook his head sadly. "If that's what you truly believe, I cannot help either you or my friend Carruthers."

The old man took out his gold pocket watch and opened it. A photo portrait of Professor Chase nestled inside its concave inner surface, just as the Chronicles described. "If I told you today that James lost both his legs at Second Ypres, or that he was listed as missing in action after vanishing after an artillery barrage like Kipling's son Jack, or that he eloped with Miss Eliza Brevoort, or that he simply grew old and retired—if I told you any one of those possible outcomes today, yes, you would sell papers tomorrow.

"But what of the next day and the day after and the all the years after that?"

Elihu snapped the watch shut. "The Ha'Penny Secret isn't something so short term as sales or a momentary scoop. Quite the opposite in fact." He bit his lip as if he'd said too much.

Somewhat mollified, Drennan asked, "So what is the Ha'Penny Secret then?"

Elihu spread his hands. "I'm afraid that your finding it out is part of the test. I can tell you this. That it's in plain sight in the Chronicles, provided of course you use James Chase's method of deduction."

Unlike the other consulting detectives of his day, Professor Chase had eschewed the meticulous gathering of clues at the scene of a crime. Instead, Chase had focused his concentrations on what *wasn't* there. Indeed, much of the appeal of the Chronicles for its readers was the repeated ritual of Chase leaving the crime scene and retiring to a hearty English meal of Yorkshire pudding or steak and kidney pie, pausing during his trencherments to pose his companion the awaited question: 'Elihu, what am I missing?' and then going on from there to speedily solve the unsolvable crime.

"So it's somewhere in one of your one hundred and twenty-seven cases?"

Elihu frowned. "Did I say anything about cases? I said it was in the Chronicles as a whole, provided you use the Ha'Penny method."

Which meant it was something that *wasn't* in the Chronicles, as evidenced by what else was in. An elegant deductive method in fiction. Utterly impossible in real life.

"This interview is complete," Elihu said. "You should have enough now, or at least by the time you leave this train to puzzle it out."

Elihu stood to leave, then half-turned. "As one wounded veteran to another, I'll give you one last question. Ask it wisely."

How to ask what wasn't in the Chronicles in a single Homeric question. Drennan could rule out details of any case, Elihu had said as much. But what else was the Chronicles beside those cases.

Then Drennan immediately knew. The Chronicles weren't about the individual cases. They were about the persons and the lives of James Jonah Chase and his good friend Elihu.

"What," he asked, phrasing the question carefully, "is the greatest thing about your friend, Professor Chase, missing within the Chronicles?"

Elihu relaxed slightly as if Drennan had taken the right tack. "His great love and knowledge of the arts, of music, of writing, of the intangible things that impinge upon the heart and soul.

He didn't want to let his personal preferences on such matters known, however, for fear his readers would invariably assign his infallible deductive abilities towards his merely personal preferences of what was best and true."

Elihu made to leave. Drennan put out his arm to hold him for one last moment. "Elihu, one last question. Not for the 'Secret' but one thing in the Chronicles I've always wondered about over the years. A personal question about your private life."

The old man frowned. "I thought my reticence about the personal was made quite plain in the Chronicles."

"Yes, sir. This is just for my curiosity, not for publication," Drennan assured him. "Earlier tonight you mentioned your children. That presupposes a wife, but the Chronicles are unclear even about that. It's mentioned once that you lived with a wife named Sarah in a house in Mayfair."

Elihu nodded. "Yes, in *The Curious Case of the Ha'Penny Quartet*."

"But then in *The Ha'Penny Invalid* it seems to read that your wife had died or perhaps otherwise left and that you'd remarried a girl named Mary."

Elihu said nothing.

Drennan hastily continued. "And then late in the Chronicles, *The Ha'Penny Autograph* refers to a third marriage—"

"An errant word inserted by a typesetter, not from me," Elihu said frostily.

Elihu fell silent for a moment, then answered finally: "For the sake of my friendship with Carruthers, I'll divulge this much: the account in *Quartet* is accurate. On the return leg of that 1887 trip abroad for Diogenes I mentioned, I met and fell in love with a sweet young Canadian girl named Sarah. We were married shortly before the events in *Quartet*. Sarah is very much alive and we have never parted—will never part. And that is all I have to say publicly about my marital affairs."

The old man walked out of the club car, leaving a thoughtful Samuel Drennan alone with his cigarettes and his bottle of Canadian Club.

* * *

Drennan spent much of the rest of the night poring over copies of the Chronicles borrowed from the porters, as well as a dog-eared copy from a passenger of Doyle's detective's first case.

In the first fictitious case of both canons, Drennan noted not just omission concerning but an emphasizing of a stated indifference toward the arts, literature, and even religion by both detectives. Armed, however, as Drennan was by Elihu's information, they both read now as if the authors had been playing games, cleverly working in allusions and near quotations of literary works in the pretense of denial.

He also paid closer attention to his fellow passengers during breakfast in the dining car, eavesdropping on their conversations. The Mormons would be leaving the train at the Calgary, Alberta stop. They were then to proceed by hired motor coaches to the small town of Cardston where their new temple had been built. Cardston apparently had been founded in the1880s as a refuge by Utah Mormon polygamists fleeing an American crackdown.

What puzzled him at first was that these already-married Mormon couples were getting re-married in their Mormon temple. Drennan actually pulled one of the Mormon fathers aside and asked him about it. The Mormon went on at length that a civil marriage was only to "death do you part" but what he termed a "temple marriage" was for "time and all eternity"—for forever in a Mormon's eyes.

Drennan spent the rest of the morning in his compartment, watching the Albertan prairie rush past, just as flat and featureless as Manitoba's the day before.

He chain-smoked his cigarettes and pondered the great Ha'Penny Secret.

* * *

When the train pulled into Cardston to disgorge passengers and to refuel, Drennan disembarked onto the platform with the rest of the crowd. Partly to see the spectacle of the now-harmless Mormon hordes heading off to their magic temple, grottoless though it might be. Mostly, however, to try to catch a final glimpse of Elihu Nivens. The porters had told him Nivens was leaving the train for "business affairs in Alberta."

Drennan was no further to figuring out Elihu's supposed secret than he'd been in the club car last night. The hope of inheriting the Old Man's job had faded into a dull disappointment. Still, there was always the chance that Elihu might let one last clue slip.

He saw Elihu in the crowd. The throng of mulling Mormons made reaching him impossible, so Drennan mounted the steps of the Pullman car to get a higher vantage point.

Elihu was carefully shepherding a woman his own advanced age. Drennan, trained in the thunder of constant artillery barrages, could read the word "Sarah" spoken on Elihu's lips. Elihu guided his wife of sixty years to a waiting contingent of apparent family and friends.

Two waiting women, slightly younger than Elihu, but not young enough to be daughters bussed Elihu on the cheeks. "Mary" and "Catherine" he lip-read.

Next to them, sat an elderly bearded man in a wheelchair. Thick blankets could not hide that both of the man's legs were missing at the knees. Even at this distance there was no chance of mistaking the small lapel ribbon of the Victoria Cross in the man's jacket. The woman pushing his wheelchair had a white leather gilt-edged eyepatch, exactly matching the one Sidney Paget depicted Miss Eliza Brevoort wearing in his illustrations.

As the Mormons began boarding their waiting motor coaches, Elihu and his three wives, and his great friend and companion, James Jonah Chase, once known as the Ha'Penny Detective began boarding as well.

• • •

No mention of Drennan's meeting with Elihu ever appeared in the Vancouver paper, nor of his sighting of Professor James Chase.

Six months later, however, after returning to London to take over the whole of the Carruthers Empire, an envelope arrived from Elihu's solicitor.

"Congratulations in learning the Ha'Penny Secret," the short hand-written note read. "Newspapers exist to chronicle the facts as they happen. The truths of the day if you will. But as for Truth, that is for each soul to discover on its own without the certainty of infallible experts or perfect knowledge."

The note was signed simply "Elihu."

"The Curious Case of the Ha'Penny Detective" looks at the impact the fictional has on the real. Richard Quarry takes us even farther back, to the time of King Tut's father, when most everything that happened seems absolutely fictional, and yet truly was real.

"The Horns of Hathor" marks Richard Quarry's first print publication, but his work has appeared online for a few years now. Like most writers, Richard has had a variety of jobs. He's been a caseworker, a drywall hanger, a juvenile corrections officer, and a sales rep for Social Studies textbooks. None of which directly influenced this story. Instead, the influences for "The Horns of Hathor" came from Richard's love of history and the King Tut exhibit's appearance in Seattle.

Richard writes, "The rich religious and mythological heritage of Egypt quite transported me. So I got some books to learn more and when Kris Rusch asked for a submission story for the Mystery Workshop, this piece…more or less put itself together."

The Horns of Hathor

Richard Quarry

In the fifth year of the reign of Amenhotep IV, when the Pharaoh changed his name to Akhenaten, declared himself the son of the self-created solar deity Aten, and decreed that henceforth no other gods would be worshipped throughout Egypt, Chenzira the Scribe was dispatched to the Temple of Karnak to stop the Festival of Opet.

Held in the second month of the Nile flood, when the silt-laden waters reached their height, the Festival brought tens of thousands—many tens of thousands—to Thebes to beseech the god Amun-Re for a bountiful harvest, that they might not starve to death in the coming year. For this reason, Grand Vizier Ramose urged the Pharaoh not to drive Amun-Re and his priests from Karnak until the Festival had been completed and the hordes returned to their villages.

Nefertiti, however, the unsurpassingly beautiful and equally unsurpassingly strong-willed queen, demanded that the Festival be cancelled at once, and the priests forced to worship the new god.

And so it was decreed.

Before leaving for Thebes, Chenzira, whose name meant "Born On A Journey," was transformed by royal decree into Second Prophet of the Temple of Karnak, the traditional title for the priest who carried on the actual administration of temple affairs, the High Priest attending to religious functions. The appointment was a great, indeed an unprecedented, honor for one of common birth.

Nevertheless, Chenzira did not celebrate. For the Second Prophet sent to cancel the Festival before him had suffered a grisly death. And messengers from Thebes reported that the killer was none other than the goddess Hathor herself.

* * *

The crowds poured out to surround the column before they arrived in sight of Thebes.

First came clouds of dust roiling above the desert, which General Nizam announced signaled the approach of thousands. He called for the soldiers marching along the road to spread out in defensive formation. Chenzira countermanded the order.

"Take the statues from the carts," he directed.

General Nizam looked at him dubiously. The Second Prophet squatted slightly and with a snicking sound called his leashed baboon, who clambered up into his arms and bared her formidable teeth that he might stroke her gums.

"The statues," he repeated.

General Nizam gave the order.

They'd debated this in camp the night before. Or not debated, exactly. Instead General Nizam and his close-ranked officers had pointed out that as pious followers of the god Aten for all several months of the new divinity's existence, they would hardly be fulfilling the spirit of the Pharaoh's directive if they marched into Thebes displaying statues of Amun-Re, not to mention his wife Mut and son Khonsu along with Isis, Hathor, Osiris, Horus, and even the dwarf god Bes, cat goddess Bastet, and pregnant hippopotamus goddess Taweret, all looted from smaller temples passed along the way.

"If you prefer," Chenzira replied, "we can approach the city behind the Dazzling Sun Disc of Aten, that the divine Pharaoh in all his bounty has given us to install in the Temple of Karnak."

"The choice is yours, Second Prophet," General Nizam said quickly, his senior officers nodding solemnly while a scribe noted the transaction on his writing tablet. "We merely wish to point out our great love for Aten."

"Very commendable. But we march behind Amun-Re."

He had previously sent messengers ahead to inform the priests at Karnak that despite all ill-founded rumors the Festival of Opet would not be cancelled. At which General Nizam, in one of his rare outbreaks of sincerity, intimated that Chenzira the Scribe would die with Nefertiti's voice ringing in his ears.

"Do you remember Inherka, who so displeased the queen?"

"I have been trying not to," replied Chenzira.

"How many days did that go on? And every single one of them Nefertiti came and—"

"Enough, General."

And sensing her master's unease, Panya, whose name means "Mouse," flashed her eyes at Nizam in a way that might strike one almost as flirtatious, did one not know baboons.

Now the mob from Thebes, vast beyond counting and armed with staves and stones, axes and adzes, swarmed shouting and gesticulating around the marching soldiers, until the dust was so thick a man could hardly see more than his own length before him. The soldiers kept on, eyes ahead and spears shouldered, every twentieth man or so carrying small statues, figurines, or stone disc carvings of some god other than the despised Aten.

Upon beholding the familiar gods the mob slowly quieted. Sullen, ominously hulking, the crowd, vast enough to chop, pound, and trample the soldiers into sticky red mud, parted along the roadway, and flanked the column all the way to Thebes. The smell of sun-heated dust, half-dried sweat, and half-dissipated rage dogged the soldiers' every step.

Chenzira, leading the column before a statue of Amun-Re so large it took six soldiers to bear it on a litter, felt like the smallest spark would set off a massacre. Trying to keep the stiffness from his fingers he stroked Panya, still cradled in his arms despite her fifty pound weight.

No attack was made, no stones thrown. But all the way the mob kept chanting:

"*Hathor. Hathor. Hathor.*"

* * *

Over the centuries the Temple of Karnak had become a sizeable city of its own, surrounded by high stone block walls over which could be seen the tops of still taller obelisks and colonnades, their gray stone faces heavily carved and colored with hieroglyphs and depictions of gods.

Passing by the Sacred Lake and the temple of Mut at the southern entrance, the Second Prophet's column was admitted through high wooden gates. Beyond the walls Chenzira could still hear the chant: "*Hathor. Hathor. Hathor.*"

Along with soldiers from the Pharaoh's first deputation, the High Priest and Karnak's own Second Prophet awaited them in a courtyard of dirt-packed brick, hardened by a millennium of use, at the head of ranks of priests in white linen kilts with broad pectorals of gold, jade, and amethyst worked into figures of the gods.

"Do you march under Aten's protection, or Amun-Re's?" demanded the High Priest. The soldiers bearing the statues and figurines rather sheepishly began placing them back upon the ox-driven wagons of the supply train.

Chenzira deposited Panya on the ground. "We are sent by the Pharaoh, with great love for all his devoted subjects."

"And now having cowered from the people all the way to our Temple," the High Priest went on, "do you seek to announce that despite your promises there shall be no Festival of Opet after all?"

"The Festival shall take place as I have said."

The High Priest, a wizened old man with surprisingly good teeth and an ostrich feather headdress set off by the sun disc of Re, quite entirely different from the sun disc of Aten, at least to the Pharaoh, harummphed.

"For all this professed love, Amenhotep prefers to send soldiers and scribes to this holy place rather than priests. But you shall need a great many more soldiers still if you deny the people their blessing for a bountiful harvest. Come then, Blasphemer. You and these others, since it can't be helped. Amun-Re's true Second Prophet will see to your needs."

With that he turned his back and hobbled off toward the complex of closely carved colonnades, starting to turn from gray to red-gold as the sun began to set, that framed the dark vastness of the main temple of Amun-Re, by the pavilion of Queen Hatshepsut. Some of the priests came forward, joined by an array of servants suddenly appearing from doors and alleys, to lead the oxen to pens along the outer wall that could be smelled but not seen past rows of storage sheds, kitchens, manufactories, and barracks.

Karnak's Second Prophet stepped forward and bowed. "You honor us, Prophet. I am Penmaat."

He was a tall man, narrow-featured, with shrewd eyes that retained a hint of humor despite his recent reversal. His pectoral featured gold and lapis segments shaped into the vulture wings of the goddess Nekhbet, in the center of which a golden scarab pushed a great red jewel representing Re through his nightly journey through Duat, the underworld.

Chenzira bowed in turn. "Greetings, Prophet. We have much to discuss. But first, if we may leave the matter of lodging to others, I would like to see this place where the Pharaoh's previous Second Prophet met his death. By the hand of Hathor, if I heard aright."

"Rather by her horns," Penmaat corrected. "The goddess appears to have been in a most vengeful mood."

* * *

The dead man's name had been Neferenphet. His blood did not show well on the ebony frame of the bed in which he'd been found. There had however been quite a lot of it, according to General Kamose, leader of the first expedition sent to cancel the Festival of Opet. Noting several dark splotches on the porous stonework of the chamber floor, Chenzira did not doubt his account.

"Here is what killed him," said Second Prophet Penmaat, picking a large golden object up from atop an ebony-and-ivory chest and handing it to Chenzira. "The helmet of Hathor."

Hoisting the artifact, Chenzira guessed its weight at seven or eight pounds. It consisted of a golden cow's head surmounted by a pair of golden horns curving around a solar disc, also of gold, bearing the image of a cobra.

Besides being goddess of love, dance, and a number of other things, Hathor was goddess of fertility, and in this guise generally depicted as a cow. Her head in this case came dotted with triple-lobed obsidian markings. The cobra, or *uraeus*, on the golden disc, seen worn upon the brow in depictions of Re, signified Hathor's role as Eye of Re, able to spit fire at the god's enemies.

From the base of the neck to the tip of the horns the artifact stretched almost two feet. Flecks of dried blood coated the horns, which unlike the solar disc and the cow head itself, looked to be covered with leaf rather than solid gold.

Chenzira turned the helmet back and forth. "Why would a goddess resort to such a tool as this, when she could slaughter a mortal in countless ways?"

"Perhaps to leave her mark," suggested Penmaat, "that her purpose not be mistaken."

"Perhaps."

"The helmet was not here before the Second Prophet, that is, Neferenphet," said General Kamose, recalling there were now two other, live, Second Prophets in the room, "retired for the evening."

"You stake your life on this?" asked Chenzira.

"I do, Prophet. I myself, along with two other officers, four reliable soldiers, and the scorpion charmer searched the chamber most thoroughly. We feared for the…for Neferenphet's safety, given the hostility of both mob and priests. Naturally we were most concerned for asps and scorpions. Yet besides the bedding, the chests, and the chamber pots, we also searched most diligently for any concealed cubbyhole that might hide an assassin, and tapped and pried along the joints of the entire chamber looking for secret passages. And at all times a watch was set in the corridor."

Chenzira looked toward the ceiling. The chamber lay on the upper floor of a building three stories high, and like most such rooms in this stifling land, included two roof vents to help circulate air. "Roof?"

Kamose looked uneasy. "We set a guard upon it, of course. A heavy one. Twelve men, under two officers. However—"

"Yes?"

"A party of four Hour Priests carried out their duties during the night."

Chenzira stared hard at the General, so hard that Panya, walking about unleashed in a vain search for insects along the close-set stones of the floor, sat and flashed her eyes. "You feared the priests, yet you let a party of them on the roof above the Second Prophet's head?"

Penmaat stepped forward. "He did so at my special request, Prophet. Given the height of the colonnades inside the Temple, this roof gives the best vantage for the Hour Priests to study the stars for what auguries the gods in their grace provide."

"Four men and an officer stayed close by the priests all night," Kamose added hurriedly. "Two more by the roof vents above this room. The rest patrolled the length of the roof. I also stationed men around the building throughout the night."

"Consider yourself fortunate," said Chenzira, "that you report to me rather than the queen, may we all be blessed in her infinite mercy. And after Neferenphet retired, who saw him then?"

Both Penmaat and General Kamose lowered their eyes.

"Well?"

Penmaat spoke first. "A dancer, Prophet, and her accompaniment."

"A dancer. And her accompaniment." Sighing, Chenzira looked sadly at Kamose. "Perhaps you will be fortunate. Perhaps Pharaoh, most glorious son of Aten, will decree a quick death."

"My lord, please." The General shrank in on himself until having been an inch taller than Chenzira, he now stood two inches shorter. "It could not have been them. They could not possibly have hidden such an object. I examined—that is, I considered them myself, because of our concerns about weapons. They wore nothing but, well, waist-belts. Along with bracelets and earrings, but nothing else."

"What, all of them?"

"All five, Prophet."

Chenzira turned toward Penmaat. "Is this the sort of entertainment usually featured in the Temple of Karnak?"

The man winced, embarrassed. "The Second Prophet, as he was, requested some such entertainment to be included during dinner. At that time the four musicians wore simple white robes, and the dancer herself a short kilt. Apparently when the Second Prophet asked them to, ah, play for him later in his chamber, he himself specified the garb they should bring."

"What of their instruments?"

"Two flutes and a lyre," said General Kamose. "One girl clapping to keep time. The soldiers in the hall heard music all the time the girls were inside the room. Then the four girls of the orchestra left, taking their instruments with them. The dancer stayed behind. Neferenphet came to the door to order wine."

"He was actually seen by the guard?"

"Yes. Then, and a little later when the wine came."

"Brought by who?"

"The officer of the watch. At that time Neferenphet ordered that he not be disturbed for the rest of the night. After a little more than two turns of the water clock, the dancer left. Still wearing no more than her waist belt. Following the orders they'd been given, the soldiers did not then disturb the, ah, Neferenphet. When his servant came in the morning, he found his master dead. Bearing numerous wounds caused by those."

He pointed at Hathor's horns.

"This dancer," asked Chenzira. "What is her name?"

"Imiu, Prophet."

"She killed him."

"But how, my lord? How did that"—Kamose pointed once more to the head of Hathor—"get into the room?"

"Where are these girls now?"

"I have been holding them, Prophet," said Penmaat, "in a storage room. Understand, however, that following whatever happened in this room, they left the Temple complex. When we discovered the Second Prophet dead, even though Hathor's rage seemed clear, I at once sent men into Thebes seeking the dancer and her company. However, my men failed to find them. Instead they themselves came to a side entrance that afternoon, asking if they would be granted an opportunity to perform again. Is this the act of murderers?"

"Another thing, Prophet," added General Kamose. "The amount of blood on the bed and the floor around it was copious indeed. Had the dancer killed Neferenphet, she must have been covered with it. Yet the officer of the watch, who would have looked her over most carefully—as you might imagine, Prophet, given her costume—reported no such marks."

Chenzira rubbed the sides of his temples, careful not to dislodge the wig that he, like most Egyptians above the peasant class, wore because lice were more easily managed with short hair, and the elaborate weaves favored by the wealthy or those aspiring to be so were better achieved in a wig than keeping long hair ruly in the searing heat.

"When did you search the room?" he asked General Kamose.

"Immediately before the Second Prophet retired. The scorpion charmer especially was most meticulous."

"And Neferenphet himself. How was he dressed when he came to this chamber?"

"In a light robe."

"Could he have hidden that beneath it?" Pointing toward the head of Hathor.

"Why would he?" And when Chenzira gave him a withering glance, Kamose thought hard, then replied, "No, Prophet. Perhaps if it were strapped tightly to his body... but even then, it is still too long. I would have noticed the bulge of his robe."

For a while Chenzira remained silent. Then bending, made the snicking sound. At once Panya came bounding into his arms, her leash trailing.

"Would you like to talk to the girls?" Penmaat asked.

"Not yet. I don't know what to ask them, and there is much else to be done. I understand the customary gifts of bread, cakes and beer given in Amun-Re's name have not been made to the people?"

"No, Prophet," replied Penmaat. "We were forbidden to do so by the Pharaoh's previous Second Prophet, then by General Kamose."

"Very well. The offerings will begin tomorrow."

"In whose name?" Penmaat asked delicately.

"In Amun-Re's," said Chenzira. "As the people expect. Now come, we have much to do. We need to plan how the offerings shall be distributed without riot breaking out. And I wish to check the temple storerooms."

"The storerooms, or the records?" asked Penmaat. "I assure you, our records here at Karnak are most meticulous."

"I'm sure," said Chenzira. "But records do not give as clear an idea as touch, taste and smell. Now let us get started. I shall dine late. Oh," he said suddenly to General Kamose, pausing as he started for the door. "You did search the room after you found the dead man in the morning, didn't you?"

"Most thoroughly, Prophet."

"And what did you find?"

"Just what is here now, except for the bedding, which has been burned. The head of Hathor, of course. These two chests, containing his clothes and what personal items you see."

"Nothing else?"

"Nothing, Prophet."

But the General sounded uneasy. So uneasy that Panya gave a little chitting hiss, the baboon's way of recognizing when some troop member has lost status.

But Chenzira let it go. "How much of the wine Neferenphet ordered had been drunk?"

Kamose furrowed his brows. "The cups stood empty, but perhaps a quarter of the jar was left. We had a servant drink it in case it had been poisoned, but the man showed no effects."

"So between the wine and his other presumed activities, Neferenphet would not have been in any great state of awareness by the time the girl left."

"So one might suppose, Prophet."

"Very well. To the storerooms, then."

"Prophet," said General Kamose. "Where will you sleep tonight? I must make my preparations."

"Why, right here," replied Chenzira. And when both men looked startled, he laughed. "If Hathor is indeed the killer, the goddess will find me in one place as well as another. If not, I have Panya here to guard me."

General Kamose, his head already held on by very thin thread indeed, displayed a strained composure. "A most estimable animal, Prophet. I have seldom seen one so well-behaved. But is she equal to the task?"

Chenzira chucked the ape under the chin and kissed her muzzle. Panya returned the kiss by lipping his face for vermin.

"Why baboons," said Chenzira, "like scribes, are under the protection of Thoth. And since Panya is a lighter sleeper than I am, she shall be quicker to call on him should need arise."

* * *

The next morning, having woken still alive, Chenzira the Scribe made further arrangements for the distribution of bread, cakes, and ale, then took Penmaat and General Kamose down to the *Wabet,* or Clean Place, where the embalmers plied their trade.

Normally mummification would be carried out in the necropolis across the Nile from Thebes. However, since the hostile crowds milling around Karnak made it unlikely that either the deceased Second Prophet's body or the soldiers bearing it would arrive intact, the High Priest had given his permission to prepare the body on Temple grounds.

At first the priest in charge of the embalming process refused Chenzira's directive.

"It is sacrilege to unwrap the bandages before forty days have passed," he boomed, his voice gaining resonance from the wooden jackal mask he wore in honor of the god Anubis, guardian of the Western World.

Only when Penmaat intervened, reminding the priest that Chenzira represented the word of Pharaoh, did the man relent.

"Prophet," asked Penmaat, as the linen was unwrapped from the corpse, "for what do you search?"

"I know not, Prophet," replied Chenzira. "The first task is to see all that may be seen. The rest we must leave in the hands of Thoth, god of knowledge."

General Kamose frowned at this reference to a proscribed god, then quickly wiped the disapproval from his face.

Aromatic candles flickered all around the underground chamber, and incense smoldered. Nevertheless Penmaat, Neferenphet's private retinue of four priests, and even General Kamose, who having survived battles in the stifling desert heat must have experienced a bad smell or two in his time, blanched.

Only the embalmers and Chenzira kept straight faces as the bandages came off. He had seen and smelled a number of unusual things working for the vizier Ramose, of whom it was said "he knows all that is, and all that is not." But even more he was a man of ambition, and you did not gain a reputation for being more useful than other men by acting just like them.

Inside the wrappings the corpse had been packed in salt, which Chenzira ordered whisked off. Though the dehydration process had not proceeded far enough to eliminate the effects of rot, it had already caused considerable shriveling, so that Neferenphet's head, plucked of all hair, resembled a skull given just enough flesh to scream out the soul's agony through the drawn-back lips and the strained, sewn eyelids. The blunted nostrils were badly twisted from the brains having been drawn out with a hook and discarded, that organ having no value.

The late Second Prophet had a hole in his throat as big around as a man's thumb.

The body bore other wounds, as well. One more to the neck, entering from the side. One just below the sternum. One directly over the heart. One to each kidney. Or where the kidneys would have been, had they not been removed. And several to the legs.

Upon discovering these, Chenzira called for the brain hook, and plunging the instrument into the wounds and measuring the depth against his hand, found they covered a span of close to eight fingers. Considerably longer than the distance the horns projected beyond the *ureas.*

Over the heart, which as the organ of both intelligence and emotion had been wrapped in salt and bandages then restored to its place, lay a sacred scarab to signify that the dead man's *ka* would rise like the sun at the completion of mummification. Chenzira plucked it from the strips of linen impregnated with resins.

"A fine piece," he commented. The giant beetle had been carved from green jade, and set in a thick base of gold.

Though officially Second Prophet, Chenzira was dressed more as a scribe, with a simple white kilt, leather sandals, and the tools of his trade draped over his bare left shoulder in the traditional manner; a leather strap with pouches for two blocks of red and black ink and another holding several reed pens. Now he took the lump of red ochre from its pouch and setting it on the embalmers' table, placed the jeweled scarab in its place.

For a moment Neferenphet's priest huffed up. Then, perhaps recalling that not only was his master dead but as a representative of Aten his corpse should not be bearing symbols of other gods, he subsided. General Kamose examined the far corner of the room with great interest. Penmaat smiled, very slightly. The Anubis priest made a disgusted chuffing sound that boomed hollowly beneath his wooden mask.

In fact a number of other amulets had fallen from the bandages, including a golden *ankh*, the symbol of life, and a jade *djed* pillar representing the backbone of Osiris. Off on a table to the side stood the four alabaster canopic jars holding the dead man's organs; a jackal-headed one for the stomach, falcon for the intestines, human for the liver, and the baboon Hapi for the lungs.

"Who decreed the Second Prophet be made ready for the Western World thus?" Chenzira asked in a voice heavy with disapproval.

The dead man's priest lowered his eyes. "Such was my master's wish, oh Prophet. This I swear. We could do no other but his bidding."

"As Akhenaten's Prophet," pronounced Chenzira, "your master has committed treason. However, the mortal man is beyond my power, and I would not punish a servant for fulfilling his master's wishes. I have seen nothing of what passes here. You would all do well to remember that."

* * *

As they climbed the stairs from the Clean Place back to the blessed light of day, the High Priest came bristling and bustling up, trailing his extensive retinue.

"What do you mean, raiding our stores?" he demanded.

They stood on the edge of the main courtyard, where span after span of heavy wagons pulled by two oxen apiece were being loaded with woven baskets of bread and cakes and clay jars full of beer by the soldiers. From the roofs of the surrounding sheds smoke poured, and Chenzira, Penmaat, and General Kamose all breathed deeply, trying to replace the scent of the mummification chamber with that of baking bread and even fermenting barley beer.

"What is your complaint?" Chenzira returned. "The Festival goes forth with the usual offerings, under the auspices of the usual gods."

"Never has the thing been done with such reckless extravagance!" roared the High Priest. "You drain our storerooms. And now I find you have ordered the slaughter of our geese and cattle to make gifts of meat and fat-sweetened cakes to the mob! Do you seek to bribe your way from this city? Have care, Blasphemer. At a word from me the people will swarm over these walls like angry bees. A word, I say."

"Then give it," Chenzira replied curtly, "if a few geese and cattle are so dear to your heart. I begin to think Amun-Re's servants live too well, Priest, that they begrudge even the god the honor of his celebration."

"Re himself has pronounced judgment on you and your false god!" the High Priest shouted. "Do obeisance to him, Blasphemer, before Hathor strikes again!"

But Chenzira had already turned away, heading toward the line of wagons to ensure that General Nizam understood how he was to distribute the offerings to Amun-Re throughout the town.

* * *

"I do not understand, Prophet," said General Kamose a little later, as they stood on Karnak's eastern wall. "Your actions make enemies of the priests and the Pharaoh both."

"I do not entirely understand either, General," Chenzira replied. He cradled Panya, a comforting though hardly inconsiderable weight, once more in his arms, having chosen to spare her the Clean Place. "But as always I seek guidance most humbly from Thoth, god of knowing."

Below them, outside the walls, lay the half-completed temple of Aten. Headless columns rose toward the sky. The marble floor between them had been thickly strewn with refuse, including apparently every animal that had died in Thebes within the last few weeks. Around the temple and stretching far back along the streets, their hostility outweighing their sense of smell, a sullen mob chanted: "*Hathor, Hathor, Hathor.*"

Chenzira set Panya down. The baboon resumed its perpetual search for insects along the worn and sand-strewn blocks of the wall.

"See how calm she is?" Chenzira said admiringly.

"Indeed, Prophet, I have remarked on that before."

"And yet we had our times, didn't we, Panya? Oh yes. See here." He held forth his hands and arms, where a number of round white scars could be seen.

"You can't beat an ape into submission, Kamose," advised Chenzira. "All you get is…well, something not unlike Queen Nefertiti, blessed be the wife and sister of Aten. It takes patience, kindness, and above all"—he tapped his heart, seat of all thought—"understanding. One must also maintain a calm demeanor. Panya serves as a most useful reminder to moderate my emotions."

"Remarkable, Prophet."

"But notice these scars. See how they always occur in pairs, matching her fangs? Why didn't the horns of Hathor leave similar marks? Why were the wounds all single?"

Kamose made a sour face as Chenzira led him into dangerous territory. "If Hathor truly is a goddess—allowing only the argument, without regard to my faith in divine Aten—then she is not bound by the rules of mortal men. Much less baboons."

"Also, the wounds in Neferenphet's legs were deeper than the length the horns extend beyond the *ureas*."

"Perhaps Hathor only left the head as a sign, not needing it to kill the Second Prophet."

"Then why did she leave blood on the horns?"

"But Prophet," said a bewildered Kamose, "if the killer was not Hathor, then who? The dancing girl? The Hour Priests? How could they have accomplished it?"

"I don't know. And I cannot press too hard against either without very good evidence. The crowd believes Hathor has exacted Re's vengeance. If I blame anyone else, the people will see it as sacrilege. It all makes you most uneasy, Kamose, doesn't it? You are afraid of Hathor, and you are almost as afraid of being afraid of Hathor, since such fear amounts to heresy before the Pharaoh. So you try to avoid thinking too deeply about the matter altogether. Useful, that, to whoever did kill Neferenphet. Unless of course it truly was this Hathor we cannot on the one hand deny and on the other not acknowledge."

Chenzira laughed at the absurdity of it all. "Sometimes I wonder if the only true divinity is Seth, god of chaos."

"Prophet!" cried Kamose, profoundly shocked, "you must not speak of—"

"I asked you once before, General, and I now ask again, in full expectation that this time you will tell me the truth. When you searched Neferenphet's room following his death, what did you find?"

Kamose looked first doubtful, then, very briefly, defiant…and finally crestfallen. "What you saw in the Clean Place, Prophet. Amulets to the gods. All heavily jeweled and set in gold."

"As they were during your first search, which you also failed to tell me."

"Most abject apologies, Prophet."

"So the Second Prophet was in fact a thief."

Having seen the second Second Prophet—or was Chenzira the third?—make off with the jeweled scarab, Kamose looked at him curiously. Then nodded. "So it would seem, Prophet."

"And you, like his priest, did not want to imperil his *ka* by denying his corpse the ceremony to gods none of us, being loyal followers of the Pharaoh, believe in. And you couldn't tell me because you feared I would report your apostasy."

Kamose hung his head. "Yes, Prophet."

"Good," said Chenzira. "Very good."

* * *

"May I have a word, Prophet?" asked Penmaat, as they walked between some of the myriad underground storerooms Chenzira had ordered emptied to feast the mob.

Chenzira dismissed the pair of lesser scribes who followed him with a wave of his hand.

Penmaat looked up and down the dark hallway, its rough unfinished stone lit only by scattered candles. "You are wondering how your predecessor came to be in possession of so many amulets."

"In fact I am not," Chenzira replied. "He got them from you. As bribes. And now you are going to bribe me."

Penmaat raised one eyebrow, less in surprise than appreciation.

"Normally such things would be done openly," Chenzira said. "It is expected. But the only riches Karnak can offer are all in the form of now forbidden gods. So the two of you had to exercise secrecy. As will you and I. But what do you expect in turn?"

"You and I are not so very dissimilar, Prophet," said Penmaat. "We deal first and foremost in practicalities. The affairs of the Temple, especially its landholdings and its relations with the wealthy of Thebes, not always recorded or even openly spoken, are complex. I do not expect to be Second Prophet under Akhenaten. But I could be of considerable value to whoever is."

"Agreed," said Chenzira. "But the Pharaoh will have many beseeching him for such office. For me to advance your cause risks creating enemies. Yet I am willing to do so, should our interests appear to lie together."

"I can ask no more. May we walk?"

Taking a torch from a wall sconce, Penmaat led him to a passage concealed by thick weavings, and down a steep, tight set of stairs. Chenzira, who bore no arms, was grateful for the presence of Panya, though the baboon did tug at the leash in a very naughty manner as she made sudden dodges at gaps in the unfinished stone that might contain nice juicy scorpions or mice.

At the bottom of the stairs Penmaat walked around a small chamber lighting candles. Gold and jeweled statues, amulets, pectorals, bracelets and earrings emerged from the dark, lying about on shelves and pillars.

"Take your pick, Prophet," said Penmaat. "Here, I have something better than a scribe's kit." Rummaging in a corner, he handed over a fist-sized leather pouch with straps to go over the shoulder. "And here is a light robe of the sort our priests wear to conceal it under."

"You prepared for this," Chenzira observed, taking up a particularly colorful Eye of Horus fashioned of electrum, obsidian, jade, and amber. Not the most valuable object in the room, but beautifully harmonious.

"As I said, Prophet, we are not so very different."

* * *

After Chenzira returned to his room to deposit several valuable tributes to the proscribed gods in his travelling chest, he ordered that the dancer and her four accompanists be released, and being given time to recover and refresh themselves, that they perform for him during dinner that night.

The dining hall stretched along the first floor of the same building. He and Penmaat, having been trained from childhood as scribes, crossed their ankles and sank easily into the traditional cross-legged position on reed-stuffed mats. Generals Kamose and Nazim sat carefully upright on glazed stone benches. The four girls of the orchestra, all in modest white linen robes, also sat on mats, playing two double flutes and a lyre, while the fourth kept time by alternately shaking a sistrum and clapping her hands.

Imiu, the dancer, was remarkable.

She wore a short linen kilt, and as she danced, her exquisitely shaped and amazingly firm breasts quivered in time to the gold and jade scales of her belt, bracelets and earrings like fig leaves in a fitful wind. Chenzira had never seen such tightly etched muscles in a woman, as they successively tautened and loosened along her shoulders, arms and legs in such a way as to put him in mind of one of the Pharaoh's pet leopards. The dancer had that same primitive force, grace…and intensity.

As her first dance ended to enthusiastic applause from the men, Imiu announced that she had composed a special dance in honor of the Pharaoh and the god Aten. For this she retrieved an *ankh* glittering in blue faience from among the orchestra. Then as the music began she bent her body back in a half-wheel and lifted the life symbol, long as two hands together, toward the sky with one hand.

The two Second Prophets and two Generals clapped loyally, no matter what they thought of Aten in their hearts. The divinity's symbol was a large sun disk shooting off rays that ended in hands, each of which held the *ankh*. No face; unlike other gods Aten was never portrayed with a face, for he existed only as a divine force, and his physical embodiment lay entirely in the Pharaoh Akhenaten.

Somehow Imiu switched the ankh from hand to hand, then foot to foot, without ever losing the wheel. Then turning, repeated the process while facing downward. If it appeared to Chenzira that her postures bore suspiciously close resemblance to the goddess Nut, along whose bent form were arrayed the stars of the night sky, what of it? Since only the Pharaoh truly understood the nature of Aten, and explained it differently as he pondered day by day, why question fine points of theocracy?

Following this strikingly acrobatic performance, Imiu returned to more conventional, and highly seductive, maneuvers across the floor. Panya wandered among the orchestra, and after plucking at them here and there only to be disappointed that they yielded up no vermin to eat, settled in happily. In turn the players, after a few uneasy looks, took a great liking to her, breaking off from time to time to pet the animal.

Dancer and orchestra alike wore white perfume cones upon their heads, as was common in these withering southern climes. As the heat rising from their bodies melted the hippo fat serving as a base, thin streams of perfume ran down their faces, or in Imiu's case her entire magnificent torso, filling the room with the scent of crushed herbs and flowers.

As the performance concluded, Chenzira asked to be handed one of the flutes. Setting the instrument to his lips he pressed out a stream of air as he ran over the finger holes in each of the twin shafts. As a young man he had gained some proficiency in the instrument, but his duties for Grand Vizier Ramose allowed him scant time for such activity now, and after starting a ballad creditably enough, his lips got tangled on the double reeds of the mouthpiece and produced a sound most like a warbling duck fart. Unable to contain their laughter, the girls nonetheless clapped appreciatively.

"Alas for my youth," said Chenzira, handing back the instrument.

Shortly after the dancers departed Chenzira excused himself to visit the toilet, where a row of low wooden stools stood over sandboxes that would be emptied by the servants come morning. Penmaat soon joined him. No one else would dare disturb the Second Prophet.

"Is the entertainment to your taste, Prophet?" Penmaat asked, handing over a fistful of jewelry.

"Wonderfully so." Chenzira held up a necklace of cowrie shells alternating with ram's horns, both finely executed in pure gold. "Beautiful workmanship."

He stuffed it into the leather pouch below his light robe, then tried to follow it with a falcon head of Horus below a projection of gold lacework representing twin ostrich plumes.

"A bit of a problem," he said, struggling with the god's head. "Can you manage?"

"Ah…yes, there, I think that's got it. Does it show?"

"I should keep my left arm down. I'll bring you a larger pouch next time."

"That would be wise. I am not a greedy man, Prophet. Not considering what you ask of me."

"Far from it, Prophet." Penmaat hesitated, avoiding his eyes. "Would the Prophet perhaps enjoy further entertainment from the troupe in his chamber tonight?"

"He would enjoy it," Chenzira confirmed, "most enthusiastically. But you and I shall both be too busy. I have detailed some of the soldiers to help in baking the bread and preparing the barley beer, while your priests concentrate on the meats and fat-sweetened cakes. Of course facilities are crowded, and cooperation not always forthcoming between your people and mine. It falls to us to make the preparations run smoothly."

Penmaat gave a brief frown before regaining his customary composure. "Of course, Prophet. But the High Priest will not approve. You are draining our stores most alarmingly."

"And tomorrow you and I will visit the wealthy of Thebes, and seek additional contributions to the Festival."

Now Penmaat could not hide his alarm. "This is most unusual, Prophet."

"The people must be put in a less dangerous mood. Right now the slightest incident could set them off."

"And the Pharaoh? What will you tell him of the Festival?"

"Why Penmaat," said Chenzira, beaming fondly. "You worry for my future. As is only natural, seeing how your own depends upon it. But the mob is here, and the Pharaoh far away. First I plan to survive the week. Then I shall craft my despatches to Akhenaten with very great care indeed, and sweeten them with tribute from Karnak. So if it lessens your burden, know that few of these little trinkets would stay in the Temple anyway. The question is simply whether they are to advance your own future, or the construction of further temples to Aten."

Penmaat bowed his head. "As you say, Prophet."

* * *

Later that night, Chenzira examined the head of Hathor.

Taking a bronze razor from his toilet kit he scraped at the horns. Beneath the gold leaf lay a surface of tin, which by tapping he determined was not solid, but likely stuffed with linen and reeds.

The horns joined and met the head in a solid lump of yellow that, scraping with his razor, Chenzira determined to be some form of resin, hard enough to resist his fingernails. The same material glued the *ureas* disc between the horns.

The horns themselves did not curve perfectly around the *ureas* to join at the base. Some small areas were flattened, some ridged. They had been bent, not cast into shape.

Chenzira sat mulling over the head, periodically invoking Thoth to lend him the wisdom to see a way past his troubles.

And when that proved less than reassuring, he pondered the possibilities offered by Seth, god of chaos.

* * *

For the next two days, Chenzira the Scribe was everywhere, always bolstered and comforted, when other comforts seemed scarce, by the company of Panya.

He kept Second Prophet Penmaat close to his side during his constant visits to the kitchens and breweries of Karnak, as well as the wealthy of Thebes, who naturally protested when he raided their stores shamelessly, but not yet sure how the wind blew with the Pharaoh, did not threaten or actively resist.

Over and over those soldiers not engaged in baking, brewing, or collecting "contributions" for the Festival led trains of ox-hauled carts laden with offerings of beer, cakes, and even meat through the streets to the lesser temples. As seat for the Pharaohs right up until the then-Amenhotep IV decided to build a whole new city for himself and his new god two hundred and fifty miles up the Nile, Thebes boasted a temple on almost every corner.

The Generals had been nervous about sending their soldiers out into the streets. They worried almost as much about the effect the unending stream of beer would have upon the mob. But led before and aft by ranks of priests, and bearing numerous statues of Amun-Re and other familiar gods, the caravans made their rounds without any major incident.

And why not? After the soldiers unloaded the jars of beer and baskets of bread and cakes around the courtyard, the crowds just had to wait respectfully while a priest made an invocation to whatever god the temple served. The divinity having absorbed all that he could hold, the mob poured in to devour the rest. It was the same way the priests ate in their own temples, which naturally encouraged very devout, plentiful, and palatable offerings to the gods.

But never before had such bounty been lavished upon the common folk, even during a Festival famous for its largesse. The food and drink just kept coming, while gradually the threatening chants of "*Hathor, Hathor,*" turned into good-natured raillery, and finally even cheers.

Yes, nearly everyone in Thebes was drunk, but what of it? The city was made entirely of mud bricks or stone; not even the most inebriated could burn it down. And the mob came to believe that having been chastened by Hathor's vengeance against the Pharaoh's first expedition, the second had duly accepted the glory of Amun-Re and poured forth such wondrous quantities of beer and cakes and, blessed be, meat—*meat!*—by way of making amends.

Of course the Head Priest failed to be mollified by the widespread religious fervor sweeping Thebes. He dogged Chenzira all around Karnak, railing until the breath ran thin in his aged lungs about how the blasphemous Scribe was no better than a thief, and that Re would infallibly render judgment once again through his chosen instrument, Hathor.

Once after the old man had to be led away choking by his acolytes after a particularly vituperative outburst, Chenzira chanced upon an object he didn't think he'd seen before, mounted on a pedestal outside one of the deeper storerooms.

"Penmaat, my friend," he said, taking up the object, "was this here yesterday?"

"I'm not sure, Prophet. But no, I don't think so. These things are rotated frequently, based on the Hour Priests' calculations of what gods' favor is most propitious. I have been too busy of late to concern myself."

"This is Sekhmet, is it not?" He admired the stylized, flattened solid-gold head of a lioness snarling fiercely below jade eyes. Baring her fangs Panya uttered a rare hiss; she held no fondness for large cats, though she loved to eat the smaller, were they careless enough to fall into her grasp.

"Indeed, Prophet."

"Oh, I must have it. You shall bring it to me tonight. As well as a larger pouch to hold it."

Penmaat raised an eyebrow. "Is this wise, Prophet? I fear the object might have been deliberately left in your path to bring you misfortune. After all, Sekhmet is the avenging aspect of Hathor, and—"

"Which is precisely why I want it," Chenzira interrupted. "I arrived with the whole city prophesying my doom. Yet here I stand, and my soldiers are cheered in the streets. My enemies are reduced to putting trinkets in my path. This shall be a trophy to raise a fond smile in later years."

"Very well, Prophet. I shall see to it."

"And I believe we shall stage the full Festival tomorrow. It is time enough, and the stores run thin."

"But Prophet," said Penmaat, alarmed, "the Hour Priests have made no such augury. And to organize the full procession upon such short notice—"

"You have been doing this for years, Penmaat," Chenzira pointed out. "And Karnak itself for at least a thousand years more. After lauding your own value, do you now disappoint me?"

Penmaat bowed. "The Festival shall take place as you direct."

"Excellent. And tonight, you may send the dancers to my chamber following dinner. I know that you shall be rushing about all night making preparations, but I think I can afford some rest after my labors."

Penmaat bowed a second time. "As you say, Prophet."

* * *

Imiu and her orchestra laughed heartily in appreciation of the cleverness of Chenzira the Scribe, as he boasted of his acquisition of the golden head of Sekhmet the lion goddess.

"Fortune favors me," he told them, eyeing their lithe figures, clad only in waist belts, appreciatively. "Not even Hathor flies in the face of fate. In fact, that puts me in mind of a story. It is said that once Re became gloomy and inconsolable. Hathor, seeking to lift him from his mood, came and danced naked before him until a smile came to his lips." He smirked at Imiu. "I am sad. Know you of a dance to cheer me, perhaps?"

"Indeed, my lord, it is my specialty," replied the dancer, letting her jeweled and gold-spangled waistbelt fall to the floor, not that it concealed anything anyway, to stand naked except for the white perfume cone upon her head.

Giggling, the four girls of the orchestra took up their instruments.

"My lord," said the dancer, "I fear my friends distract you." She dragged the ebony stool forward so that Chenzira sat with his back to the orchestra. "Now see if I do not bring a smile to your lips as wide and beaming as the sun god Re himself."

And so she did.

Following which, she said she knew of a dance sweeter still, one which might last far into the night, especially if aided by the magic of fine wine.

Dismissing the others, Chenzira called for the officer of the watch, and the wine having been delivered, ordered that the soldiers not only leave the chamber undisturbed for the rest of the night, but that they remove themselves to the far end of the hall, nor go prying about the doorway grinning at any stray sounds, upon pain of his extreme displeasure.

"Here, my lord," said the dancer, when the chamber door had closed behind them. "Lie on the bed, on your back. Try to stay very, very still." She giggled sweetly. "Just try. This is a trick I learned from a Nubian consort."

Chenzira did as he was bid. Humming softly, swaying with impossible grace, Imiu picked one of the reed mats up from the floor and came to stand over him. "Remember, stay still as you can."

And with a smile at once sweet and lascivious, she lay the mat gently across his eyes.

At once Chenzira swept the mat from his face and tried to roll up, only to find a long golden spike already flashing down toward his throat.

He threw out his left hand, and being of athletic nature, caught the girl's wrist. So strong was she, however, that her arm broke right through his grip. Fortunately he'd diverted the spike just enough that it struck his shoulder rather than his throat.

Again he tried to grab her wrist, but seizing his left arm with her own left hand the dancer forced it across his body and held him pinned while she raised the spike for another stroke.

"*Panya!*"

A bone-quivering *screech* filled the chamber.

* * *

As the climax of the Festival of Opet, the priests of Karnak bore a wooden barque holding a statue of Amun-Re all the way along the Avenue of Sphinxes to the Temple of Luxor, on the far side of Thebes. Crowds thronged thickly about, not only calling out the name of Amun-Re, but pleading for drink as well, which caused the Head Priest's face to turn scarlet.

As the procession passed through the gate into the outer courtyard of Luxor they found a veritable caravan of wagons being unloaded by soldiers, who spread about large jars not only of beer but also wine, scarcely more familiar to the mob than meat.

Declaiming loudly against Chenzira the Defiler, the Head Priest led his priests and the barque containing Amun-Re into the temple of Amun-Min, god of male sexuality, to complete the ceremony that would ensure a bountiful harvest. By custom the Theban mob was supposed to drink itself into a state where they could communicate with their dead ancestors. Never before had enough beer been provided to bring the majority to such reverent union with the deceased. But right now such communication was taking place all across the city.

As the priests entered the temple's high-columned hall, at the far end where Amun-Min normally resided they found instead…

A large golden sun disc whose rays ended in hands bearing the *ankh*.

"Does the scribe's sacrilege know no boundaries?" cried the Head Priest. "Hathor shall flay him alive for his presumption."

At that moment Chenzira stepped out from behind Aten's disc, trailed by an agitated Panya, flashing her eyes and displaying her fangs. He stood bare-chested, a white, blood-soaked bandage wrapped around one shoulder.

"Hathor?" he retorted. "Or her most human assassin, abetted by the priests of Karnak?"

A party of soldiers emerged from the temple wings pushing a bound Imiu ahead of them. The dancer was for once modestly clothed, which hid the bandages covering numerous puncture wounds inflicted by the baboon's teeth. The guards thrust her to her knees before Chenzira.

One of the soldiers handed him the head of Hathor. Chenzira swung it hard against Aten's disc. On the first blow the horns held; but at the second the cow head bounced across the marble floor. Holding a horn in each hand, Chenzira yanked them apart, the gold *ureas* between them falling with a sharp crack in the stone hall.

"Resin," he declared, "held the head of Hathor together. From this." He pulled the perfume cone from Imiu's head and ripping a piece of bark from the bottom, held it base forward to show the priests the yellow paste inside.

"The heat from her head kept it soft enough to work. After she killed Neferenphet with one of the spikes, she molded resin, head, horns and *ureas* together. By the time General Kamose searched next morning, the resin had hardened so that everything seemed of a piece."

He gestured, and another soldier held out one of the double flutes and a golden spike. "The horns were concealed in the flutes, each in one shaft so that the instruments could still play—well enough for a man with other entertainments on his mind, though I heard the difference clearly enough. This horn, which you see still in unbent form, was meant for me."

Gripping it with both hands, he strained and finally managed to bend the lower section into a rough curve.

"I am not weak, but this girl is far stronger. Strong as a quarry-man. She and her companions are not only musicians, but priest-esses from the temple of Hathor at Serabit el-Khadim. Priestesses, and assassins."

He tapped the horn against the golden disc, the clear, quiver-ing tone ringing through the temple.

"The *ureas* came from inside the lyre. The orchestra removed the objects and placed them under mats while Neferenphet, and later myself, sat entranced by the dance. After the wine had been brought, the killing was done with a single thrust to the throat. Only Panya saved me, even though I believed myself ready for the attack. Neferenphet had no chance at all. Then the dancer stabbed him additional times where the blood flow would be heaviest and the chance of deforming the horns least. She then put the head together. Any bloodstains on her limbs or streaks of resin on her fingers she washed off with wine in the cups. She then splashed it over the bloodied sheets."

The Head Priest's jaw fell open. "But..." he began, and "but..." again, but could get no further.

Chenzira held up the head of Sekhmet.

"This was to be my Hathor. Too big for the girls to bring, as you see. Fully as big, in fact, as the golden cow head. I brought it into the chamber myself. Just as Neferenphet brought the cow. Concealed under his robe with this."

Taking up the strap and pouch of leather, he gave the ends a yank. With a faint ripping of thin thread the pouch separated into one long leather strand.

"This strap," Chenzira told his audience, "was then doubled up under Imiu's waist belt. For what soldier would look very close, when such other charms beckoned so near? And where did all these things come from? I think some, indeed quite a few of you, already know."

He clapped his hands. Groups of soldiers armed with spears and shields stepped out from the colonnades.

"Seize him," directed Chenzira.

General Kamose marched forward with several soldiers and pulled Penmaat from his position at the High Priest's side.

"Impossible," gasped the High Priest.

Penmaat wore a look of resignation. Even, to the credit of his courage, a shade of amusement. "I serve Amun-Re."

"But you hid your own deeds behind the face of the gods!" cried the High Priest. "That is sacrilege of the most heinous order! You, of all—"

He staggered, so that those nearest had to grab him and lower him gently to the floor.

"Here is how matters stand," Chenzira told the assembled priests. "The crowds have been drinking for three days, and grow thirstier by the hour. Even now rumors are spreading that no more beer or wine will be forthcoming because you priests are hoarding it all inside Karnak. Any of you who wish to tell the people otherwise may return to the Temple.

"Or," he added, "we can open the gates to Luxor, that the people may see you worshipping Aten. You will of course tell the crowd otherwise. Likely the people's rage will fall equally on you and us. But we shall be withdrawing behind a wall of spears. Few men, no matter how zealous, prefer a spear in the guts to the pleasures of drinking themselves cross-eyed, slaughtering unarmed priests, and grabbing the treasures we have taken from Karnak and shall scatter behind us as need arises.

"Or finally," he told the priests, who for once hung silent upon his every word, "you can withdraw from Thebes with us, leaving the crowd to their drink and their riot. At the Pharaoh's court you will present him with the treasures we have kindly loaded on the wagons to spare you the labor, and swear fealty to Aten. As for Penmaat and Imiu, they shall be granted a merciful release right here in the courtyard, and be spared telling Queen Nefertiti every name they can think of when she asks of their confederates.

"However, if you would thus choose devotion to the divinely appointed Pharaoh, Amun-Re must first make obeisance to Aten. Decide as you will. But decide now. General Nazim! Begin the withdrawal!"

For once the priests, normally a contentious lot, were of one mind. Those nearest the barque of Amun-Re hoisted it up and in the traditional manner dipped the bow three times before the figure of Aten. Then the barque was dropped with a loud thud and the white-clad priests rushed to join the column of soldiers and wagons starting for the rear gate of Luxor as the front gates were opened for the crowd to rush in and fall upon more drink than anyone in the whole land had ever seen.

* * *

Even after numerous interviews with soldiers, priests, and after the excitement died down the people of Thebes itself, no one was ever quite sure exactly *what* had happened during the Festival of Opet.

For want of a clearer explanation most accepted the summation of Grand Vizier Ramose: that under the urgings of the Pharaoh's Second Prophet the priests of Karnak chose to turn the Festival into a ceremony to honor Aten and the Pharaoh Akhenaten, and this change coming so suddenly upon the people, the mob had rioted, looted the temples that were to be shut down in any case, then returned to their homes to nurse monumental hangovers.

In other words, the Pharaoh's directive had been fulfilled.

Even Queen Nefertiti, who declared herself certain that Chenzira should have his ears and nose cut off for *something*, agreed that as she could not quite put her finger on it, she would abide by the Vizier's judgment.

By that time Chenzira himself was far north in the Nile Delta in the guise of a merchant. For Egypt was a very large land, and the Grand Vizier had much work for Chenzira the Scribe.

And of course his loyal Panya the Mouse.

Even though we think we know something about a time period, certain stories make us realize that we have absolutely no idea what living in the past was like. That was the feeling I got as I started this fantastic story from Lisa Silverthorne, set in 18th century England.

"Impressions" marks Lisa's fifth appearance in Fiction River. *She previously appeared in our second, fourth, fifth, and sixth issues. Her short fiction has appeared in sixty other venues in genres from romance to science fiction.*

I thought I knew a lot about British traditions, but Lisa found one I'd never heard of—or at least, never thought about before. She writes,

"I was as fascinated by 1780s London and Boston as I was about their traditions. Especially death masks and their strange, dark beauty. Many times, these masks were a family's last memory of their loved ones. Or an early forensic effort used by constables to identify London's dead. One final way for the dead to speak."

Impressions

Lisa Silverthorne

I'd always tried to please my father, but when I chose to become an East End constable, he nearly disowned me. I excelled at ledgers and figures, but my passion lay far from shipping manifests and bills of lading. London's new Watch fascinated me and I was drawn to the opportunity to protect the weak against the horrors that lurked in the catacomb of East End streets. Eastcheap, where I grew up.

The Great Fire had scorched away London's diseased crust, but King George rebuilt it, haphazardly covering over its charred remains with poorly erected replacements conjoined to perverse, narrow corridors and odd-angled constructions wedged into any accommodating space. These new monstrosities made crimes easier to commit and did little to halt the streams of filth and corruption that festered along the Thames and collected in the maze of East End streets where murders were commonplace and bodies sometimes lay in the street for days before being tossed into churchyard poor holes. The stench of decay was as pervasive as the stink of raw sewage that ran in the gutters along the streets. Even in daylight, the chances of disappearing forever at the end of some cutthroat's knife blade were high.

I despised Eastcheap.

Mum cried when she saw me in my blue jacket and trousers, lantern hanging from my belt. In her hooded grey eyes, I could see her imagining all the ways she'd find her wee lad murdered in the streets like my brother, Gavin. I thought I was invincible after surviving a childhood in those streets. And I was obsessed with cleaning them up. Every journey down those streets was another step closer to meeting the Devil himself. At twenty-two, I was tired of running.

I'd been five when I saw my first dead body. And my first death mask. Of Mrs. Compton's daughter, Myrna.

She and her five children lived in the flat next door along the long, narrow alleyway near the docks. And Mr. Compton, before they hung him as a highwayman.

Myrna had been a lovely red-headed girl of nine. Gently freckled face and big, mossy green eyes, her agate-orange hair was a bright flame against the haze of acrid coal-smoke that belched out of chimneys lining the crooked streets. She sang songs and twirled around in a worn, green dress patched with blue and yellow scraps while her older brother, Robert (who hated to be called Robert), chased rats off the stoop, poking them with sticks. They always leaped away, balancing on eggshells and broken bottles in the gutters that stank of urine and horse dung. Whenever Robert found a dead one, he'd poke it until its bloated belly split, spilling entrails and maggots into the street.

His fascination with dead things always upset Mum. And shiny things. Jewelry that came up missing always found its way into Robert's hands. He'd bury them under the stoop beside his rat skeletons and other putrid things. Two years before we left Eastcheap, I'd dug up Mum's prized brooch under there one night after he'd gone to bed. My brother, Merrill, insisted he'd seen a finger bone under there.

"Andrew, look what that monster's done now," Mum whispered, peering out the oily front window through the seam in the white lace curtains, always afraid Robert would see her. She feared him almost as much as Eastcheap after dark.

"Lad's always been a bit off," Father remarked and walked away, muttering, "Vermin. Just like his father."

Whenever my brothers and I tried to look, Mum shooed us from the window, but after she'd gone to sleep, I'd sneak a look at Robert's mess outside, disgusted but at the same time, fascinated. The blood so vivid red against slippery smooth organs left tangled and drying on the bricks. What struck me most was the rat's stillness. How such a limber, energetic creature could be so quickly reduced to such terrifying motionlessness. What inside us animated our faces, moved our bodies, fueled our minds? And why was it so fragile?

Myrna never seemed to notice the rats, Robert's dissections, or the sewage. She just twirled and sang. She was the brightest light in Eastcheap.

I was the one who found her. Just after her ninth birthday. The rime reflected like glass when the sliver of moon caught it, the night achingly cold, coal-smoke rolling against the sky like thunderclouds.

I'd been running from the Devil down the dark Eastcheap streets, head down, heart slamming against my chest. I found her on the street just a block from home, her hair draped across the bricks like fabric in the market stalls, arms and legs splayed. The index finger on her right hand was missing and a bright red stain covered the front of her green dress, belly torn open, entrails peeking through the fabric, glistening and slippery like one of Robert's rats.

Her mossy green eyes stared up at the sky, vacant, empty. Disturbingly still. As if someone had blown out the candles illuminating her eyes, like they'd reached inside for that fragile, little pearl of life that had gleamed so brightly and torn it out.

No one ever found Myrna Compton's killer. A kind-hearted constable gave Mrs. Compton a wax casting of Myrna's face. Even in death, her face was quiet beauty. Like someone had captured her light in wax. Any moment, I expected her to open her eyes and smile. But the wax had seeped into every curve and line of her nine-year-old face, freezing every line of her full lips, the shape and direction of every hair in her eyebrows, and the upturn of her nose.

Like Robert, I couldn't stop staring at it through their front window. At the time, I'd been convinced that if I stared at it long enough, she would open her eyes. And tell me who'd done this to her.

The mask haunted my dreams. Always, the same dream. Myrna dancing among the rats, singing a cool, lilting melody. Until night fell. Then the world exploded into a maze of violence, the Devil at our heels as Myrna and I ran. As the beat of cloven hooves ticked closer, Myrna turned to me, her face like wax, telling me the Devil would come for me next. And I would wake up in a cold sweat, screaming and vowing to find whoever did this to her.

"Fletcher!" Constable McFarland shouted, poking my shoulder. "Pay attention, lad."

I glanced up from the death mask just brought from the morgue and stared back at the older Irishman and Lord Milford, royal patron of the Magistrate's office. Here on business today.

Tall and stocky, Mac's wild, thinning black hair, bulbous nose, bushy moustache, and ruddy cheeks made him look rough and unkempt. He only handled cases from noblemen—or when the coin interested him. And this case had both. He was intensely protective of me, insisting I was young and foolish. Fearless. With no sense of the Devil that roamed London's streets. Among the constables in the Magistrate's office, McFarland only allowed me to call him Mac.

"Forgive me," I muttered, looking away from the death mask lying on the table.

"Is this your wife, Milord?" Mac asked as I sat back in the wooden chair.

Tucked into a forgotten corner of the Magistrate's office, the small office was stuffy and cramped, creosote from the stove flume burning my eyes. We were grateful for the office space. Its walls had been white-washed and the floors had a bit of polish along with the old oak table and chairs. Constable McFarland slouched forward in the chair beside me, blue, boiled wool jacket a little faded and smelling of pipe smoke, top button missing. He glanced at Lord Milford who sat in the chair across the table.

"Of course it's my bloody wife, Constable! I demand some answers!"

In his early fifties, the short, portly aristocrat wore a velvet coat in sage, pristine white-powdered wig, and crisp, black silk breeches. He obviously spent the cold winters huddled in the warmth of a carriage or by his hearth. His small, dark eyes were pinpoints as he leaned forward in his chair, cane gripped in his hand. His cheeks were smudged with rouge, skin powdered white, a paunch stretching his ivory silk shirt to its limits. Milford was the second or third son of the Duke of Chamberton, but acted like King George II's firstborn.

The wax mask mesmerized me. They all did. This one was a pleasant oval with strong, tapering chin and gentle jaw line. Small forehead with the barest hint of creases between the dead woman's eyebrows and across her forehead. Cheekbones high and delicate. Large, wide-set eyes cloaked by unwrinkled eyelids, a delicate aristocratic nose gently sloped with small nostrils, and full, upturned lips hinting almost at a smile.

A story to tell. And I ached to hear it.

"My wife was quite beautiful, wasn't she?" said Lord Milford, his voice softening.

She looked peaceful, her face almost doll-like in its symmetrical perfection. I doubted the sun had ever touched this woman's face, leaving it like dewy porcelain.

"I would guess her about twenty-two," I said, running my index finger along the cheekbone down to the chin. "Born an aristocrat. Fair-haired, light eyes. Fair-skinned. Intelligent. Engaging. Devoted."

"Yes, lad, all very astute," said Lord Milford, steepling his fingers. "Aptly describes my apparently late wife, Sarah."

Mac preened like a proud parent and patted me on the back. "Ansel's young, but he's smart as a whip!"

"Apparently, Milord?" I asked.

Milford nodded, tapping his fingers against his hawk-like nose as he looked away toward the frosted window, making a snuffling sound as he closed his eyes. It wasn't grief because that emotion was absent from Milford's face. I saw no tears. No slumping of his shoulders, no sadness in his eyes. I knew grief; I'd seen a lifetime of it.

Grief was a carver's knife scraping away light and hope one shaving at a time. I'd watched it etch itself into Mrs. Compton's face like a blade to wax. I watched it cripple my Mum who'd grieved herself into a bitter, frail, shadow-of-a-woman after my oldest brother, Gavin, met the Devil somewhere along Eastcheap. They brought him home empty-eyed and bloodied in a dirty sheet. We buried him in the churchyard, but all that remained was his wax visage that hung on the wall from a black ribbon. I'd stare at it for hours, convinced that if I watched it long enough, Gavin would tell me who'd killed him.

After Gavin's death, we moved west across the new Westminster Bridge. Gavin's death mask hung on the wall of Father's office at the Port of London where it continued to blind him with grief. He'd curled up inside himself, unable to understand that he'd only lost one son, not a wife and three sons. I spent the rest of my childhood trying to get him to see beyond that mask, but the only emotion left in him was rage.

Squinting, I noticed something at the edge of the mask. Slight impressions. On the right-hand side.

I ran my index finger across them. They were partial imprints of fingers: ring and pinky. And some lettering. I slid the mask closer, staring until I made out the letters. They spelled Beloved. That word looked distantly familiar.

"Milord, what is this indentation?" I asked, pointing at the lettering.

The nobleman shook his head. "I have no idea."

Grimacing, Mac leaned down and ran his fingers along the mask's right edge.

"It says Beloved," I said finally, watching Milford's expression for a reaction, an emotion—the slightest twitch.

"Beloved?" Milford muttered in a gruff voice, shaking his head as he picked up the mask and pressed a monocle to his left eye, studying it. "That's rather odd, wouldn't you say?"

He set down the mask.

"With your permission, Milord, I'll inquire," I said, picking up the mask. I wrapped it back in muslin and placed it in the wooden box.

"Of course, of course," he said with a dismissive sweep of his hand. "It might be important."

Mac set out a piece of paper and inkwell, nubby quill in hand. He wet it in his mouth then dipped the quill into the ink and scritched some notes.

"Can ye both read and write then?" Milford asked.

"Aye, Milord." Mac motioned at me with the quill. "This one writes and figures like a cleric. Smart as a whip, I tell ya. Now, Milord, you claim your wife, Lady Sarah Milford, was alive when they pulled her out of the Thames. When was that, Milord?"

"She was quite alive!" Milford shouted, rapping the end of his cane against the floor. "We argued not four hours ago! I shook her. She lost her balance and fell into the Thames. A man pulled her out. Quite alive, I might add. When I came round to fetch her, a constable tells me she's passed and hands me this bloody box! I demand to see her and I demand answers!" He pounded the floor with his cane. "I'm prepared to pay a handsome sum for them, too."

Mac's eyes glimmered. "Well, Milord, we'll certainly get to the bottom of this."

Lord Milford thunked a leather pouch onto the table and grunted to his feet. "They'll be more if you succeed."

Breathing heavily, he leaned on his cane and flung open the office door. His manservant met him at the main door of the Magistrate's office, tossing a fur throw around the man's shoulders as he sauntered out into January's bitter cold.

Mac pocketed the leather pouch and rose from his chair. "We'll divvy this up later. Off ya go, lad."

I gave him a look as I stood up, crossing my arms.

"What?" He held his arms wide, an indignant look on his face. "Not trustin' the old man ta share the coin with ya? Now, go, lad. Off with ya to the morgue. Pick up the other masks and inquire about Lady Milford."

I trusted Mac with my life. He might filch a few shillings for a pint, but he'd always watched my back.

"It's not that, Mac," I replied and picked up the wooden box. "I've seen this mark before."

"At Mrs. Salmon's exhibition, I'll bet," Mac said with a snort.

I winced at that chamber of wax horrors on Fleet Street. People paid good money to glorify the Devil in London's streets. A jaunt through Eastcheap was free and promised to display at least one body among the rats.

I remember when Myrna turned nine. Her Mum made wiggs with a bit of butter icing. Myrna twirled and sang, crumbs clinging to her dress as she held out a little cake in her right hand and turned gently on the stoop, displaying a thick silver band with a small red seal on her index finger (it was too big for her ring finger). Passed down to her, not Robert, by her Mum's grandfather. She showed us the band engraved on the outside with her name's meaning. The word *Beloved* was carved deep into the metal in crisp, flowing script. She'd been so proud of that ring.

For a long time, I hadn't understood why someone killed her, but looking back, I knew it was for that ring. Cut off her finger to get it.

"For a shilling, I'll show ya around Eastcheap." Mac gave me a sympathetic smile.

Where had I seen that mark? "I think I saw that mark on another mask," I added.

As constables, we saw wax masks every day. Made from bodies that washed up at Limeswatch, bodies found along Eastcheap's catacombs, and those found along the docks. It was all we had after a body was buried. We numbered them and posted a list outside the morgue for those missing loved ones. There was never a shortage of bodies. From the Thames or the streets. In the last week, we'd had four young East End women found dead. The bodies, throats cut and bellies opened, had already been buried in secret to ward off body snatchers, but we preserved their faces in wax, hoping to avenge them, to tell the stories they couldn't.

As a lad, I'd been fascinated by the masks, as if they could speak, but now, they troubled me, haunted me when I closed my eyes at night.

"Harold Darling has a key to the storage bin where the masks are kept, lad. But don't forget to inquire after the mask makers. Harold will know who made it. He knows everything that goes on in the morgue." Mac patted my shoulder. "Off with ya, now!"

* * *

Every time I went to the morgue, wrapped in the honeycomb of streets and shadowed by tall buildings and coal soot, I felt the Devil at my heels. Today was no different.

The cold bit through my boiled wool coat and burrowed its way through my gloves, but I felt the Devil's hot breath at my neck, around every angled corner and through every stark January shadow. Felt his distant steps closer as I hurried through the stench of death and throngs of people crammed into London's dreary, grey corners until I reached the morgue's dark brick façade.

Cavernous, the silence deafening, I entered the gated door. Bodies were stacked along the walls, draped in muslin shrouds and ready for burial. The low-barreled ceiling made me claustrophobic, the smell of decay thick as I pressed a handkerchief daubed with linseed oil to my nose, wooden box under my arm. I peered around corners and down dark walkways until I found Harold Darling, keeper of the dead.

A sagging, crusty, white-haired man with bristly white whiskers and scraggly hair tied away from his face, Harold lit a lantern in the main room. I handed him the mask. He was missing most of his teeth and lisped when he spoke, but the warmth of his brown eyes and gentle manner set me at ease. With gnarled, rheumy hands, he turned the mask over, fingertips grubby and clubbed.

"We got four of 'em makin' masks in a room off the back of the morgue," Harold said, pointing down a long, dark hallway to a green door lit with a lantern. He pointed to a larger wooden crate on the floor. "New masks are all there, numbered like you asked, lad."

Harold tapped the crate with his foot. "All there. I wrapped them meself for ya."

"Do you remember the woman in this mask, Harold?" I asked, returning the mask to its muslin sleeve and the safety of the wooden box.

He nodded, brown eyes sad. "Was a young thing," he said. "Royal's wife. Not a mark on 'er. Like she was sleepin' a sweet, sweet dream."

"Lord Milford claims she was alive when she was pulled from the water," I said. "He seemed surprised by her passing."

Harold's bushy white eyebrows pressed up, deep creases carved into his brow. He shook his head. "She was cold as marble when they took her into the back," he said with a nod and picked up a ragged broom, scraping it across the grimy brick floor. "Not an hour later, a man and woman came round and fetched her corpse. The woman had similar eyes. A sister maybe? Cousin? She was so young and beautiful. Like the others."

I raised an eyebrow. "The others?"

Harold nodded, his broom moving dirt from one side of the bricks to the other. "Lord Milford's fourth wife, they tell me. Has a penchant for young ones. Gets tired of 'em quick."

A chill fluttered across my spine. "What happened to the others?"

Harold's voice got low and he stepped close to me. "I seen all of 'em, Fletcher." He touched his temple with a thick index finger.

"All beauties. But over twenty, all of 'em. First one fell from a horse, but those marks on her neck weren't from no horse. Next one died in her sleep. Next one died of a stomach ailment. Both of 'em were poisoned, Fletcher. I'd stake me life on it."

"How can you be sure?" I asked.

His eyes lit with determination. "I'll show you."

He grabbed a lantern off the wall and motioned me toward a nearby door. After fumbling a key ring off his belt, he unlocked it into a small, narrow room. He set his lantern on a table in the center of the room. Shelves and chests of drawers lined three of the walls. Where they stored the masks.

From the drawers, he removed two, wax castings, both of women's hands: one delicate with long, willowy fingers and the other squared with shorter, rounder fingers. The nails of each hand had a series of horizontal lines across each fingernail.

"See the lines, Fletcher?"

He went to another drawer and pulled out a casting of a man's hand, setting it beside the women's hands.

"Remember the nobleman that confessed to poisoning his brother?"

I nodded, remembering the Magistrate's grand case about how the Earl of Pembroke's fourth son had poisoned the third. The story had been big news throughout London.

"This is a cast of the poisoned man's hand," said Harold. "See the fingernails?"

The ridges on the man's fingernails were identical to those of the two women. I nodded.

"I been here a long time, Fletcher," he said. "I seen lots of bodies come through. The dead do speak, but you gotta know how to listen."

I opened the crate Harold had given me and studied the four other masks. All women. Each one had various impressions of letters at the edge of the mask. The facial features looked almost …shaky. On all four. The mask of Lord Milford's wife was clear and crisp, but all of them had the same impression. Despite the shaking, I was certain they'd all been made by the same person.

"Harold, why are these masks so fuzzy?"

"Maybe 'e had to 'old 'em down?" Harold cackled at his joke, but it made me squirm.

The old codger examined all four masks and his expression softened. "Shakiness is a bit odd, ain't it? If I'd seen these, I'd haf ordered 'em redone. Got some new blokes back there. One of 'em shakes I've heard. Palsy maybe?"

Had someone made them fuzzy on purpose? To hide distinguishing facial features? Had criminals paid them to foil the only identification tool the constables had? Harold's terrible joke rushed back to me. Or worse? Had the women been alive when those masks were cast?

Harold examined the masks. "Brought this lass in from Philpot. Murdered." He pointed to the second mask. "Young woman murdered on Tinney." Harold's face contorted as he picked up the last two masks. "Like children they was, no more than fourteen. Both girls kilt near Pudding Lane."

Flashes of Myrna twirling and singing rushed back to me. I winced. Swath of brilliant red hair draped across frosted pavement, green dressed stained with blood. Index finger missing. Big, mossy-green eyes as empty and dark as that Eastcheap alleyway.

I felt the Devil blow on the back of my neck.

The same mask maker had done all these masks. Except for Lady Milford's, they were all out of focus. Intentionally ruined? Or someone new? Maybe I was over-thinking things? Or overlooking something vital?

* * *

I couldn't get Harold's voice out of my head or the faces of those dead women. Not on the walk back to the Magistrate's office and not back to the morgue again. To see the mask makers. Mac thought I was obsessing again, but I had to prove him wrong.

I walked down a cramped hallway and pushed open the green door into a drafty, cramped space scattered with tables and shelving.

A young woman stood by the nearest table, looking startled as I approached. She had wide-set blue eyes and alabaster skin. Her wheaten hair was pulled off her face with yellow ribbons. Her once-blue dress was dusty with clay and stained with paint. She looked out of place.

A man with hunched shoulders stood beside her, another man and two other women working at a table behind them. On the far wall, a brick oven crouched beside a roaring hearth where large, blackened iron pots hung over the fire.

In the corner, they stared with closed eyes out of the darkness. I shivered, feeling the weight prickling across my skin.

A wall of death masks, drying yellow in the dim light like fat on a bone.

Beside the masks was a table long enough to lay a body. And two chairs with some sort of scaffolding around them. Perhaps for setting up a body to cast a mask? Strips of muslin and some sort of trowel lay on the table.

"I'm Constable Fletcher," I said. "From the Magistrate's office."

The woman with yellow ribbons stiffened, eyes filling with fear. She glanced at the man beside her.

"What do you want?" the man snapped, stepping toward me. Constables weren't well liked, mistrusted, and sometimes feared, but I had to quell their fears. I rubbed my hands together, blowing on them as I opened the wooden box under my arm.

"Forgive my intrusion, but I need to inquire about this mask."

She stared at it from a distance as if it was a poisonous snake about to strike.

"I r-remember it," said the man, his voice hard, a bit of a shake to his words.

The woman avoided my gaze.

"Did you make this mask? Miss?"

The man stepped between us. He was taller and broader of shoulder than I, his hair warm brown to my sandy blond locks. His hair was tied back at the nape, a day's beard darkening his jaw and strong chin, unlike the fuzz along my jaw line. He wore gloves with the fingers cut out, his left hand pressed against his chest. Anger burned in his grey-green eyes and something about them aroused my curiosity.

Did I see a trace of Gavin in his eyes? Or someone else from my childhood?

He stood straighter and laid his gloved hands on the younger woman's shoulders.

"She don't work here, Constable," he said in a sharp voice, glaring. Out of fear? Protection? Or both? "The rest of us make the masks and do what we're told. Is there somefin' wrong wif it?"

"Lord Milford insists that his wife was alive when pulled from the river," I explained. "He was nonplussed when given the mask. And asked us to investigate."

"Take it up wif Harold then," the man said, turning away.

The woman beside him had such light in her eyes. Like nine-year-old Myrna Compton, my light of Eastcheap. But this woman had a familiar expression that puzzled me.

Then I realized what it was. It was an uncanny likeness to Lady Milford's death mask.

"Tell me then," I began, turning the edge of the mask toward her. "Can you identify what this mark is, please?"

"I said she don't work here!" The man snapped. With a shaky arm, the man grabbed a lantern off a nearby table and held it up to the mask. He looked at me, shaking his head. "What mark?"

"It's a faint impression," I said, laying my finger above it. "It says Beloved."

The man glanced at the woman, frowning. He exchanged a hurried look with her that unsettled me.

"I'll come back later, David," she said, stepping toward the door.

The man called David handed the mask back with a shrug and returned to his work, but he kept glancing at me, hands shaking. I was clearly making him nervous.

I removed one of the other masks, setting it beside him.

"And this one," I said.

He stared at it a moment then his gaze slowly trailed up to my face.

"A poor job," he muttered, left hand against his chest. "I'll remind the staff about accuracy. Good day, Constable."

Outside, in winter's frail light, a shadow fell over me as I started back to the Magistrate's office.

I looked up. The woman from the morgue. In the clear light of day, her beauty blossomed.

"Constable, who hired your services?"

"Lord Milford." I had nothing to hide.

Fear rose in her eyes. "Why?"

"A constable told him his wife had drowned, but he insists she was pulled out of the river alive."

The woman folded her arms against her chest and began to pace. "But didn't he see the mask?"

"This one?" I asked, sliding it from its box, and held it to her face. "Lady Milford?"

Her pupils eclipsed the light blue of her irises, mouth falling open as she stared at me, hand over her mouth.

"No," she said in a tiny voice, grabbing my arms. "Please, you can't tell him I'm alive! You can't! He'll kill me like the others!"

"Who made the mask?" I asked. Obviously, she'd been alive when it was done. I shuddered. *Had the others been alive too?*

Tears welled in her eyes, her face a mask of fear.

"I can help you," I said. "I know about Lord Milford's other wives."

"You do?" she cried.

I nodded. "I have proof that they died under mysterious circumstances. But I want something in return."

Her eyes turned hard, her body stiffening. She let go of my arms.

"I have no money, Mr. Fletcher. I left Richard with but the clothes on my back."

"All I ask is an answer to my question. Who made the mask?"

"David made the mask in exchange for my emerald necklace," she said finally.

* * *

I presented my evidence to Mac about Milford's previous wives. The Magistrate consulted with two clerics, confirming that the casts of their fingernails indicated that they had been poisoned.

As it turned out, Lady Milford hadn't told me everything. She'd been planning her escape after learning about the fates of her husband's previous wives and hadn't exactly fallen into the Thames with only the clothes on her back. She'd fallen in with half the Milford family jewels. Lord Milford only wanted her body to retrieve the jewels. Which were on their way to Scotland with the *late* Lady Milford. I'd probably never discover the identity of the body left in her place.

After Mac confronted Lord Milford, the nobleman paid Mac handsomely for his silence. When I refused the sum, his lordship left London for a sudden crisis in the countryside.

I returned to the morgue to see David. About the masks. All of them—including Myrna's. The Devil followed at a distance when I met David at the door as he was locking up.

"What are you doin'?" he demanded as I shoved him inside and locked the door behind me.

"I'm here for answers," I said.

"To what?" the man asked, backing away toward the tables.

I moved toward him. Cloven hooves tapped at my back.

"You're from Eastcheap, are you not?" I demanded.

"What of it," David snarled, leaning against a table.

I had to ask the right questions. To be absolutely sure. I had to know the truth.

"You've made quite a few death masks, have you not, sir?"

He stood up straighter, smiling, chin thrust out. "Many masks. I pride myself on bein' accurate."

He pulled off his gloves, tossing them on the table. Exposing a thick silver band with a red seal that ringed his left pinky. I gasped.

Myrna's ring!

He gripped his left hand with his right, left hand shaking as he stared at me

The Devil whispered to me, hooves clacking just steps behind me. Oil lamps guttered, dimmed by coal-smoke and the twisting catacombs of Eastcheap, Myrna's song in my ears as I stepped toward the man.

"I went through all of the masks, David. Dozens. All women. All the masks looked shaken, disturbed somehow." I was an arm's length from his disgusting, smug face. I glared at him, wanting to smash in his face with my fists "Even Lady Milford. Because they weren't dead yet, were they?"

"What? No! What are you talkin' about?"

"You hunted each one down, didn't you? Smothering them with wax and disemboweling them. Returning them to the street for someone else to find."

"That's crazy!"

His nostrils flared, eyes widening as I closed the distance between us, traversing the decade or so that had passed since I last saw Myrna's face. And Robert Compton.

"Myrna was your first, wasn't she?" I grabbed him by the shirt and dragged him across the room. "Your own sister—you monster!"

"My sister? What are you talking about? Hey! What are you doing?"

I slammed him into the scaffolding chair, locking his wrists in place.

With muslin strips, I tied his hands and feet to the chair and pulled the ring off his pinky. I turned it toward the light, Myrna's eyes gleaming back at me.

"Rats weren't enough for you, were they? Changed your name, didn't you? Always hated your name, didn't you? Robert. Robert Compton!"

"You're crazy! Stop!" He was shaking violently now. "My name's not Robert!"

The Devil was at my back as I grabbed the ladle out of the pot of hot wax.

He reached for my shoulder, whispering in my ear as I dumped hot wax over the man's face. The man's screams filled the room.

I wound his face in muslin, over and over, wrapping the strips around and around his head, covering his nose and mouth until finally, the screams fell silent.

Turning the ring around in my palm, I heard Myrna's voice in my head. *The Devil's coming for you next.*

I twisted the ring around my little finger, staring at the word, *Beloved,* carved into the band. Myrna loved this ring. I would return it to her Mum in Eastcheap.

The Devil smiled upon me, his hands, at last, on my shoulders as I stared at the ring. My hands shook uncontrollably. There was a second word engraved in the band. Trembling, I fell to my knees, the word choking in my throat.

David.

The Raiders

Cat Rambo

When I turned thirteen, my father took me to New York City. He said a gentleman knew how to comport himself, no matter where he was.

The year was 1858. The city was so much larger than my native Providence that I gawped and gaped. I didn't mind my father poking gentle fun at me as we walked along. There was such a press of people on the streets, so many faces that were so different from the faces at home.

We'd just come out of a fancy new dry goods store on Sixth Avenue. I was lucky that I felt the hand sliding into my pocket. I grabbed at it and my father turned, sensing the movement. His own hand shot out past me to seize a boy by the shoulder.

He was dirty and ragged and not that much younger than me. He spat and kicked at my father, whose grasp fell away, and with that the boy darted down an alley.

I remembered his face, the freckles and dirt across his nose and cheeks, his blue eyes seemingly guileless, the ragged strands of dark hair falling across his forehead.

I didn't think I'd ever see that boy again. But I did, a few years later.

In Andersonville.

* * *

I signed up in my sixteenth year, when the War Between the States broke out, ready to go and trounce those dirty Johnnies down south. It was cold and dangerous, but I was still boy enough to love the gallantry of being a cavalryman, and to feel my blood stir when the bugle rang out over the fields. I was invulnerable as only a boy can be, even when there was shot whistling like wasps past my ears.

I didn't even mind the fellows who caught us. It was still a game then, as though I'd been caught while playing tag. They let us gather up our gear, and none went looting, as far as I could see.

But then Jeff Johnson went running towards the woods, damn fool. I don't know what he was thinking, but first thing I heard was the crack of a Sharp's carbine one of them had taken off us. Jeff went flying face forward into the dust, and lay still.

That was the moment when it all hit me, really. It wasn't a schoolboy's exercise in legions and companies anymore. Jeff's figure, lying in the grass with the red serpent slowly crawling from the body, that was real in the way historical military accounts, your Polybius and Caesar, never were. There was no dust and paper about Jeff's death, only that red snake of blood and the smell of gunpowder and copper that the breeze served up.

* * *

It wasn't being captured that dispirited me. The Rebs had us to rights and we'd been fighting through that valley for nigh on two weeks. And they didn't treat us too bad. No, what bothered me was the fellow who'd taken my horse, my good Bucaphelus and kept quizzing me about how the horse would do against a fence, or on a flat road, till finally one of his compatriots, seeing my lowered gaze and clenched jaw, touched his arm and drew him away.

I thought then I'd gone as low in spirits as any man might go. Now that makes me laugh.

They loaded us in railroad cars, as many of us as they could jam in each, and I found myself among strangers.

There was no oil for the axles and they screamed and whined in protest all the way. We'd run out of fuel every so often and the men sitting in the tender would hop out and chop wood till we had enough to go on.

By the time we got to Andersonville, all of us were dog-weary and, more than that, bored. We'd heard each other's stories and songs. Everyone had spilled their juice, story-wise. We had a fellow who liked to sing and every night we kept him at it till his voice was hoarse. We paid him with our own food and never grudged it, least I never did.

I could tell stories of the trip, of being packed in so tight that we lay on the floor, spooning. When someone wanted to turn over, he must whisper his demand to the sergeant, who'd sing out, "Roll yourselves gentlemen, and keep your hands to yourself!" so the whole mass of us would shift. Of being given meal more weevil than grain, and feeling the little crunch of the beetles between your teeth, like small wriggling seeds. Taste? By then, I didn't mind how anything tasted, as long as it filled my belly.

When we arrived they pulled us in companies off the train. We stood in dusk and the smell of pines, towering pines that stretched up all around us as though starved for sunlight, their lower limbs draped with death moss. Whippoorwills called far away in the woods. The guards pushed us down along a road lined with sooty bonfires of burning pitch pine, the fresh wood snapping and popping, and in the darkness it was nightmarish. I wondered what circle of hell this was, whether we would find ourselves in fire or ice.

A hell of filth and disease, it would turn out.

* * *

The walls of the prison were pine logs, the bark still clinging to the boles, set on end, extending a good five feet underground and fifteen or twenty above, depending on which side. Not quite square but almost, with the longer sides stretching a thousand feet. Inside, a creek narrow enough to jump across divided the northern end from the south. I didn't see that at first in all the confusion of tiny wretched buildings and tents, narrow paths winding through them, and the almost palpable stench of shit and blood and despair.

Later, I would think to myself I'd been lucky to arrive in the darkness. If I'd been able to see everything, I might've dropped on the spot.

There was plenty of jostling, but there seemed to be a welcoming committee of sorts. Someone plucked at my sleeve and said, "Awright, this way, we'll set ya up, find ya a place to sleep."

The flickering light of the torches set beside the gate lit his face and I recognized him. The boy from New York, from what seemed a lifetime ago. I hesitated. He was a fellow soldier, surely, but I couldn't help but remember his old profession.

That hesitation was what saved me, because in that breath, I looked past him and saw another from my company, Bill Stratton. I shook my head at the boy and went to my friend.

He said, "They tell me an old pal of mine is here, has been almost since the prison opened. We'll talk to him first, get the lay of the land." Bill was older than me by two years and prone to lord it over me accordingly, but just then I was so grateful for a friendly face that I would have taken anything.

We shuffled our way through the nightmarish landscape toward the southwest corner. Some had tiny fires outside their hovels, but they pressed so close, so desperate for all the heat, that you could barely see the blaze. Men lay on the ground, but I could not tell if they were dead or sick or simply sleeping.

* * *

Bill's friend was a man they called Illinois. He and his friend Henderson had been there for months, they said, and they had plenty of questions as to how the war was going and particularly if we had heard any plans for prisoner exchange. We told them what we could, and in turn they told us something of life at Andersonville.

"You're lucky," Illinois said. "The New Yorkers lurk by the gates waiting for new fish. Sometimes they just rob them, other times they do worse."

The face of the pickpocket boy flashed in my memory. "Worse?" I said.

"We call them the Raiders. Keep your belongings close to you, and stick close to people who know you. They come in little groups, swoop down, snatch everything you have, hurt you if you resist. They're scum. Bounty leapers and deserters, most of them." He eyed the brass buttons on my jacket. "I'd cut those off and hide them, if I were you. The Rebs love them and you'll be able to use them to bribe the guards into letting you out to collect firewood."

Pride and indignation puffed me up a little. "I'd like to see them try."

Illinois eyed me. His face was haggard but cheerful. "It's nice to see some fight still in you, son, but save your strength. You'll need it."

* * *

In the next few days, I found out how right Illinois was. On the second day, the Raiders hit me, led by the boy, and they didn't settle for the buttons but took the jacket as well. The boy laughed at me as I staggered to my feet and tried to swing at him.

"Take 'im out, 'enry," he cheered, and one of his fellows stepped forward. His fist came swinging at my face and then there was blackness.

When I came to, I was stripped clean as a whistle. I knew better than to try and beg off someone else. No one had anything. Finally a day later I was lucky enough to trip over a dead man who no one had stumbled over yet and I took his clothes from him. He must've been a long-time resident, for they were much mended, so much that it was almost as though the pants were a mosaic of fabric, tiny bits spliced together, and his shirt was so threaded with holes that it looked like lace.

"Why doesn't anyone fight back?" I demanded from Illinois.

He shook his head. "We tried, early on, and they fought us off. Now they're damn cocky, with that big tent down at the southern end they use as headquarters. They're better off than any of us, and they feather their nest even further by informing whenever they catch wind of someone's tunnel."

"I know one of them," I said.

He cocked his head. "How so?"

I related the incident with the pickpocket boy and described him.

"That's little Jimmy Sunshine, or so they call him. He'll steal the words from your mouth if he can."

"How can they do this?" My voice cracked at the end, and it seemed appropriate, for I realized what a boy's question it was as soon as it left my lips. Still, my indignation forced the other words out. "They're Union soldiers, just like us."

Illinois shook his head. "No," he said. "They're not."

* * *

Sometimes I dreamed of Bucephalus, not of riding him to war, but days at home, a slow canter with fresh air rushing past my face, his black mane flying. I did not dream of his new master. Why should I waste time on resenting him? In his place, I would have done the same.

I always awoke from those dreams beset by unmanly tears.

* * *

I watched the boy when I saw him, but the camp was so crowded that you could go a month without seeing someone that you were looking for. And even if you saw them, you might not recognize them, for everyone was so blackened from leaning over the pine fires, coated with a mixture like lampblack and turpentine that clung to the skin.

There was no soap. There was no clean water. Prisoners tried to take their creek water from the spot where it entered the prison, but if you stretched too far, a guard was likely to think you were trying to escape and shoot you. Around the creek the ground was filthy with excrement and the clay and sand bore a pale brown froth that smelled worse than anything I had ever experienced.

But worse than that, worse than anything, was the hunger. When he'd first arrived, Illinois said, the rations had included an occasional sweet potato or piece of salt beef, but now all they gave us was cornmeal, and moreover, meal that had not been sieved after the grinding, so sharp bits of the outer shells were still mixed in it, making any meal painful.

In the late spring, the word went round, the commander of the prison, John H. Winder, would be inspecting us. We were assembled in front of the north gate and already the guards had told us that one man breaking rank would deprive us all of rations that night.

So we waited. And waited. While the Georgia sun hung overhead, corpulent and self-satisfied as it stroked the sand into shimmering heat.

Finally he came. Two adjuncts walked with him, and the little group was trailed by a colored boy dressed in livery and rolling his eyes as though in terror at the dangerous Yankees he found himself among. None of them spoke a word as Winder strolled through the gate.

There is evil born of ignorance or want, and then there is another kind, spawned from the meanest emotions within the human soul. An evil of intent, rather than neglect.

That is what I saw in Winder's grey eyes.

He said to the man he was with, turning to face him and gesturing at the ranks drawn up. "A sorry lot!"

"Indeed." The other man examined us with interest. "They seem far past half starved."

A chuckle crawled out of Winder. "You boys do your part out there, and I here." His lips turned in a smile, and he said, "Whose part is the larger, I wonder? I have done more here to diminish the Northern ranks than twenty of Lee's companies could manage."

At that, anger crawled in me, setting me to shaking, and only Illinois' touch on my hand kept me still.

"They'll shoot you if you rush him. Don't give him cause to add another death to his tally now. His time will come," he whispered.

So I kept still, despite the anger coursing through me. But I must confess, seeing the confidence in Winder's stride, the well-fed jowls such a contrast to my companion's sunken face, that I found myself doubting for the first time. This was hell. Would our side come for us, so far here in the South?

Winder kept our rations from us that night, although no man had broken rank.

* * *

The Raiders grew bolder and bolder. Every day, they preyed on the weak. Some poor souls had cracked, and they wandered like shaggy ghosts through the camp, stumbling, sometimes babbling or singing to themselves. The Raiders amused themselves by edging the men towards the "dead line" that circled us, marked with a flimsy bit of wood, some ten feet away from the stockade wall. Step over that and the guards would shoot you. The Raiders would come up and ring some fellow, shove him from one to another, laughing uproariously, and when the game was over, they'd push him towards the line and laugh even harder when a shot rang out and he fell.

"Can't anyone do anything?" I said to Illinois. "Winder won't."

Illinois looked me over before nodding at another man sitting near us. "Sergeant Leroy has been talking to me about that. Go fetch me Limber Jim and Ned Carrigan. And keep your mouth shut. If they find out we're planning something, we're sunk."

That was the day the plan was born.

* * *

Sergeant Leroy Key was a tall man, but sparse-fleshed. He was a Westerner, also from the state of Illinois, and with my exception, kept his plan confined to other Westerners. He told the guards of his plan and somehow got it approved.

Why did the guards agree? To them it was an amusement to see us trying to regulate ourselves. I do not think that most of them considered us human. To see one of them leaning from his tower, eyeing a man staggering too close to the deadline, raising his rifle to shoot and then boasting to his fellows that he killed a Yank was not uncommon.

Key kept it as secret as he could but we knew the Raiders had learned of it when they tried to drag him out of what he called his tent, but was really a blanket-covered hole dug into a sandy slope, in order to kill him. He fought them off; told the rest of us that we'd move the next day.

That was when I finally encountered Jimmy Sunshine again. We were both up at the creek mouth, filling buckets. He gave me an unfriendly look from his eyes, still blue but no longer so innocent.

"You an yer friends think you can come up against us?"

"I know you," I said.

"Sure you do. I was there that first night you came in, I remember."

I shook my head. "No," I said. "We met in New York."

For the first time a look of interest came into his face. It transformed it, made it something human other than the devilish sneer that rode it. "Yeah? When?"

"You tried to pick my pocket."

His face closed to me.

But I hadn't meant it as an accusation. I wanted to ask him how he had come to this pass, how the war had treated him, how he had come to Andersonville.

But he turned away with his bucket. As he went, he tossed over his shoulder, "You'll see. Ya think ya are all so high and mighty but we run this place."

"For now," I said, but so softly he could not hear me.

* * *

You would have thought the Raiders learning of our plans a setback, but it proved the opposite. For word got to others. All of those who had suffered under their depredations now thought that perhaps our movement might succeed. They gave off discussing escape or how best to cook the daily meal ration (dumplings, gruel, or cakes) and all the talk was about us, and whether or not we would succeed.

That night, the Raiders sang in their tent, howling out the words in triumph. They thought there was no way we might prevail, and they celebrated their victory in advance, buying sorghum whiskey from the guards.

And so in the morning, we marched on them.

We had armed ourselves with clubs. All the camp had gathered to watch us, 15,000 men or so, standing on the hillside, a solid mass of faces.

We marched on them as orderly as any soldiers' company. And then the fight began and all became chaos.

I have had enough of war; I will not speak of my actions on that day.

* * *

When all of it was over, we had captured the Raiders and confined them to the small stockade the guards had agreed to let us use.

Key made sure that all of the formalities were observed. He organized a court-martial, finding thirteen sergeants, and making sure that all of them were as new to the prison as could be, in order that they would hold no prejudices. The accused were confronted by witnesses, they were allowed a defense, and in the end six of them were sent to hang.

Jimmy Sunshine was not among the six. He was not important, not a leader. He was among the hundred or so that were left.

"What will happen now?" I asked Illinois.

He said, "We'll have to let them out of the stockade."

I was outraged and said so. "So they'll all just get off scot-free?"

"Oh no," said Illinois. His voice was sad and tired. "They won't." He pointed near the stockade and I saw the crowd gathering at the gate.

They formed two parallel lines, lines made of hundreds of men, most still carrying those clubs.

The sight filled me with satisfaction. I pushed my way into one of the lines. We waited.

When the first raider stepped through the gate, his face pale with apprehension, a great sigh of satisfaction went up from the crowd. He took to his heels immediately, realizing the situation, but the crowd would not let him break out of the lines. Instead he ran between them and the blows fell on him as he ran.

When I saw Jimmy Sunshine prodded through the gate, I raised my club and waited.

He ran quickly, his arms raised to protect his face, wavering from side to side as blows landed. Just as he came to me, he staggered in the sand, going to his knees, his sweat-sodden black hair clinging to his scalp, bruises already blooming all along his forearms and face.

Until that moment I had been filled with rage. So many moments fueled it: my comrades dying of gangrene or dysentery, the careless laughs of the guards after shooting a man, the black mane of my horse fluttering as he cantered away from me with a Rebel soldier on his back. That soldier had not meant to hurt me so, he had only been doing what he was meant to do, but the Raiders had betrayed their own. Had committed evil intentionally, and this boy was among them. My jaw clenched; my fingers tightened.

He lifted his blue eyes, wide and desperate, to mine, and saw my anger. He tried to pull away, even as my hand lifted.

I thought of all that had been taken from me.

If I struck him, though, I would lose even more.

I dropped the club on the sand and he staggered back to his feet and kept running. He ran like a black horse, and at least one of us was, for a moment, free.

Technically, "The Monster in Our Midst" marks Kris Nelscott's first appearance in Fiction River. *But honestly, Kris Nelscott is one of my mystery pen names, and I've had a story in every issue.*

To date, all of my Kris Nelscott stories have been set in the 1960s and 1970s. The bulk of them feature an African American private detective named Smokey Dalton. The latest book in the Smokey Dalton series, Street Justice, *appeared in March. That series has been nominated for the Edgar and the Shamus, and it won the Herodotus Award for the Best Historical Mystery Novel.*

A new series featuring a female detective will appear in the next two years. The first short story in that series, "Sob Sisters," was chosen as one of the top ten short stories in Ellery Queen Mystery Magazine *in 2013.*

But "The Monster in Our Midst" is set in 1918, in a time that I also find fascinating. I've been planning to write a lot about Red Summer, so named by James Weldon Johnson because of all the riots and murders that happened as whites tried to defend the Jim Crow laws. African Americans were fighting back. The NAACP grew by 45,000 members that summer alone.

As I researched Red Summer, I learned the risk that so many African Americans put themselves in as they tried to get justice. One of those African Americans was named Walter White, a name that has since been co-opted by the television series Breaking Bad. *The historical Walter White was a true hero, and even though he's a peripheral character in my story, he was the story's inspiration and, in some ways, its heart.*

The Monster in Our Midst

Kris Nelscott

I ask not only black Americans but white Americans,
are you not ashamed of lynching? …The nation today
is striving to lead the moral forces of the world in sup-
port of the weak against the strong. Well, I'll tell you it

can't do it until it conquers and crushes this monster in its own midst.

—James Weldon Johnson
NAACP Field Secretary
The National Conference on Lynching
May 10, 1919

She found the postcard next to the cash register at a general store in a small town in Arkansas. The hand-tinted photograph caught her attention. She picked it up and nearly dropped it in surprise, then glanced at the stout man who owned the place.

He had been measuring a pound of dried beans for her onto a white scale mounted on a solid oak counter. The entire store smelled of spices and coffee, with an undercurrent Virginia pipe tobacco.

The stout man had dark mistrustful eyes and a fat, petulant mouth. He wore a heavy apron over his white shirt, and his black pants had worn gray at the knees.

He was measuring her as surely as he was measuring those beans.

"My," she said. "Is this what I think it is?"

"I dunno, miss," the stout man said. "What do you think it is?"

"Is this that nigra what gave you all the trouble last fall?" she asked. "I heard about these dealings the first time I came through here—what was it, September? Everyone was talking about how safe they was feeling, now that it'd all ended."

Apparently, she sounded sympathetic enough. The stout man smiled at her, although the smile didn't reach his eyes.

"That'd be the one," he said.

He scraped some of the beans off the top of the pile, then tied the white bag he'd put them in.

He paused, then asked pointedly, "Who're your people?"

She'd run into that question before, and knew how to reply, no matter what name she was answering to.

"My people are in Atlanta now," she said, "but I was raised due south of here. I'm Lureen Taylor."

"Thomas Mosby," he said, almost begrudgingly.

"My husband's passed," she said as if she were a lonely woman, unable to stop sharing, "and I don't like Atlanta. So I'm looking for a good community with solid values where I can live out my days in relative quiet."

She wasn't that old, but old enough to make the story believable. It usually softened men like Thomas Mosby, although it didn't seem to soften this one, maybe because he had seen her surprise when she picked up the postcard.

She still held it between her thumb and forefinger. If she wanted to stay in this little community for even a few days, she needed to alleviate his suspicions.

"I heard about such cards," she said, waving it slightly. "I have never seen one made from a real event. Usually I seen the photographs of buildings or the paintings from history, never one from a real moment."

She still couldn't bring herself to look at it closely.

"We been recording important doings here since before the war," he said. "We commemorate the things we're proud of."

The test comment. She smiled. She was committed now.

"Like you should," she said, and ran her gloved hand over the postcard's surface as if it pleased her. "Add this to my purchases, please."

"I can post it for you," he said.

"Can you?" She looked pleasantly surprised, even as she felt dismayed. She didn't have people in Atlanta. She only knew one person there, and only because she'd been told to watch for him. Their paths had crossed on a dark and rainy afternoon three months ago in West Texas. He hadn't seen her, hadn't realized who she was, and probably wouldn't recognize her now.

But she kept track of him there, knowing the danger he'd been in perhaps better than he had.

The kind of danger she was in now.

Thomas Mosby stared at her.

"Do you have a pen?" she asked. "I'll just put a little note on it, and we can send it. That way, my people will know I'll be all right here."

"I most surely do, Mrs. Taylor," he said, wiping his hands on a towel. He came over to her, handed her a pen and inkwell, and watched as she wrote:

Since you worried I would end up in a community of strangers, I thought I should let you know how safe this little town makes me feel.

She signed it *Love, Lureen*, and then addressed the card, hoping against hope that nothing else would rouse Thomas Mosby's suspicions.

As soon as the ink was dry, he took the postcard from her and put it in a mailbag, but not before looking at the photograph. He nodded at it, as if he approved.

She forced herself to look down at the rest of the pile, since she couldn't buy another. Mosby would ask why she wasn't mailing that one, and they both knew a genteel woman wouldn't keep the postcard as a souvenir.

The body hanging from the streetlamp was mercifully blurry. But the body was clearly male with skin darker than the skin of every person in the crowd. Some were looking up happily, others holding pistols. One young man near the post held a Bowie knife as if he planned to use it.

She wasn't going to ask if they'd cut and dried some actual souvenirs. She didn't want to hear the answer, suspecting it would be in the affirmative.

"It was not two blocks from here," Mosby said. "Right outside the courthouse. The new sheriff, he thought that he could send that boy to Little Rock. And, truthfully, that boy might be in Little Rock, if Little Rock is your version of hellfire."

Then Mosby laughed, a loud braying sound that hurt almost as much as his words.

The hair rose on the back of her head, but she smiled anyway, as if she thought him the most amusing creature she'd ever seen.

She took her coin purse out of her bag. She couldn't stay in the store much longer before she started shivering.

"How much do I owe you, Mr. Mosby?" she asked.

He told her. After she handed him the money, he held the small cloth sack he'd prepared for her.

"Welcome to Abbotts Creek, Mrs. Taylor," he said.

"Thank you, Mr. Mosby," she said. "Words fail when I try to tell you how happy I am to be here."

* * *

The postcard arrived on Emerson West's desk on a bright May morning, in a stack of mail bundled and tied with a harsh brown string. The warm yellow sunlight streamed across his oak desk, which he'd had made special back when he opened his detecting agency a decade ago.

He liked the early mornings; the office was brighter than it would be for the rest of the day, giving him a sense of possibility. He hadn't lost his optimism in the face of everything he'd investigated, or the frustrations he encountered. But sometimes he needed something as simple as sunlight to remind him of the good in the world.

Fortunately, most of the jobs he had done since he returned to Atlanta had been small ones such as accompanying clients who couldn't read or write to the courthouse to fill out paperwork, thereby ensuring that the white government clerk didn't misspell or simply fail to file the pertinent form. Some jobs were a little larger, mostly occasioned by America's entrance into the war a year ago April. So many young men had joined up without telling their families, and finding the documentation or getting someone to reveal the military records was harder than it should have been.

Now, with 1918 not quite half done, rumors had started that the war would end within six months, but Emerson had no idea how. The newspapers proudly proclaimed that thousands of men per day were sailing overseas to get involved in Europe's conflict, which meant that thousands of men would die there.

Emerson was privately glad that he was too old to consider going to war. Twenty years ago, he would have proudly joined up, although back then, he would have had to make a choice between enrolling under a lie to become a respected soldier or telling the truth and serving in a segregated unit.

His light brown hair, pale skin, and blue eyes made it easy for him to pass for white. He had studiously avoided passing because it meant disavowing his family. His mother had skin the color of coffee with cream. His father was darker, but was at least one-quarter white. Emerson's paternal grandfather had been the man who owned his grandmother. Emerson's mother never said where her white blood had originated.

Emerson had never pressed her, and now the time had passed. His parents both died ten years on now, just after he married. His wife was gone too—childbirth had taken her and the baby—and Emerson saw no point in making new ties.

These days, he passed more often than he had in all of his youth. However, he only did so when he needed information for his detecting business.

The detecting agency had started as a lark, but it had become his life. And because he was now free of family and obligation, he could go places, and do things he would never have considered as a much younger man.

The postcard slid out before he even had a chance to untie the string. He saw the back first, his name written above the words "Atlanta, Georgia," which were the only things that served as any kind of address.

The postmark had been made four days before in Abbotts Creek, Arkansas. He did not know anyone there. He had never heard of Abbotts Creek before this moment.

The same confident hand that had addressed the card to him had also written:

Since you worried I would end up in a community of strangers, I thought I should let you know how safe this little town makes me feel.

Love, Lureen

He didn't know anyone named Lureen. But he had seen this handwriting three times before. Before he looked through his files to make certain his memory was accurate, he turned the postcard over—and dropped it, wiping his hand on his black pants almost without thinking.

He let out a breath, reminded himself that he had seen worse, and picked up the postcard. It was a photograph showing a man hanging from a street lamp, with dozens of whites around him, most of them looking like they had achieved something great.

The dead man was blurry, probably in his death throes, and if he had been touched up, he had only had his skin darkened. But other spots of color were added throughout the post-card—red neckties and handkerchiefs, some light pink added to women's cheeks and lips, and a bit of silvery paint along parts of the lamppost.

In thick white ink along the bottom, someone had written *September 19, 1917.*

Emerson turned the postcard back over. He couldn't look at the dead man any longer, nor could he stomach those jubilant white faces.

He had spent nearly two years investigating lynchings for the National Association For The Advancement of Colored People. Walter White, who had started the Atlanta branch, had hired Emerson to accompany him on several trips into rural Georgia to investigate reports of lynchings.

White, like Emerson, could—and often did—pass.

Once Emerson was trained, White engaged his services using NAACP money to send him all over the South to gather information. Emerson had gone to Louisiana, Alabama, and Mississippi, and things had mostly gone smoothly. The only time he felt truly unmasked was in West Texas, not because he got caught or even challenged, but because he couldn't pass for a Texan. His accent was wrong, and the attitudes he'd learned to mimic, so common in the rest of the rural South, seemed dangerously liberal in the tiny Texas towns to which he'd been assigned.

Emerson sat in his office chair and looked at that postcard. He had heard from Walter White just last week, and White had said nothing about a new case. The NAACP was turning its findings into a report they would publish to help support Congressman Leonidas Dyer's anti-lynching bill.

With the war, the excellent performance of the colored troops on the field of battle, and the horrible race riots last year in Dyer's home state of Missouri, the NAACP felt the time was right.

With all that Emerson had seen, he had no idea if there was a good time for that sort of bill, even with strong white Republican support. But his was not to question. His was to gather facts, so that the report to the NAACP was accurate, not filled with hate-talk and rumor.

He'd been paid well to venture into communities his father could never have walked through. And Emerson tried, always, to keep in mind the victims, especially the ones who were murdered and buried without so much as a by-your-leave. He suspected that some of the young men he'd searched for these past two months had not joined up to fight in Over There, as the song said, but instead, had died horribly in some dark Georgia backwater, where no one would talk to outsiders, not even outsiders with the right accent and skin color.

But his beliefs didn't matter. He kept doing the work, knowing someone had to report the truth. He knew that very few people could even attempt it.

Generally, the request for information came from the Atlanta or New York NAACP offices, not directly like this. But if the handwriting here was from the person who had sent the previous postcards, then perhaps he owed her enough to figure out why she had sent the card directly to him.

He stood and went to the matching wooden filing cabinet and unlocked the bottom drawer. That was where he kept his lynching files. He was afraid—even now—that he could get in trouble for the work he had done, so he kept them hidden. If someone wanted the files badly enough, they could break in, but he knew the lock would discourage the most casual searcher.

Emerson pulled out three, all of which had come from Walter White. Two had been handed to Emerson in the Atlanta offices; the most recent one had been mailed from the New York office. He opened the files, one on top of the other, and pulled out tri-folded envelopes that White had included in the larger envelopes he sent.

The Atlanta trifolded envelopes had been addressed to Walter White at his former home address in the city. The New York trifold was addressed to Walter White care of the National Association For The Advancement of Colored People, New York, NY, the same sort of vague address that had shown up on this postcard.

Inside those envelopes were postcards decorated with equally grim photographs, and a single page from what clearly had been a much longer letter, detailing what little the correspondent knew about the depicted scenes.

One postcard was an actual illustration, with a hand-drawn caricature of a young colored man dancing across flames as he tried to flee white hooded members of the Ku Klux Klan. The illustration looked like something from a minstrel show, and disturbed Emerson almost as much as did the two photographic postcards.

Their subject matter was the same as the one on Emerson's desk. He did not look at the photographs again; he did not need to. They were indelibly embedded in his mind, graphic depictions of murder, something the photographer (and those who sent the postcard) believed to be a celebration.

None of those postcards had any writing on them. The letter writer had found them and sent them, along with whatever the correspondent had discovered, to Walter White for investigation.

But the one Emerson had just received was different. It had writing on it. It was addressed to Emerson directly.

And it was signed *Lureen*.

He had always suspected the handwriting belonged to a woman, although he could not say why. Now, he had confirmation of it.

Emerson ran his fingers along the postcard.

He needed to speak to White before he went to Arkansas all alone. And Emerson needed to discover if White knew more about this mysterious Lureen than he had told Emerson in the past.

* * *

The Atlanta Branch could not afford the expense of a telephone, not even one with a party line. But the office did have use of a telephone at the Atlanta University, and that telephone was expensive and private.

Emerson had graduated from Atlanta University eighteen years ago now with a teaching degree he had used for only a decade. Still, he was proud to say he was part of the oldest Negro university in the United States—not that anyone asked any longer.

The telephone was located in the office of the president, and could only be used with advance permission or on NAACP business. Emerson had placed the postcard in an envelope, planning to use it with the secretary if she refused to let him call the New York office.

She did not refuse. Apparently, she understood the look on his face.

The president's office was book lined and smelled of cigars. Papers strewn about the desk did not concern Emerson, but the secretary covered them with a blotter, apparently worried that he would snoop.

He stood at the front of the desk, and picked up the black candlestick telephone. He placed the cone-shaped receiver against his right ear and spoke into the mouthpiece, asking the operator to call the New York office of the NAACP. He hoped she would not remain on the line after the call connected, but he couldn't guarantee it.

He also couldn't ask her to sign off, because that would alert her to the private nature of the call, and would probably make her more likely to listen in.

A young man answered, and Emerson asked for Walter White. The young man set the receiver down and went in search. Feeling nervous, Emerson glanced at the clock on a nearby bookshelf. The local branch would be angry if this call went on too long. He hadn't approved it through them, and telephone calls were expensive.

White answered within a few minutes.

Emerson quickly told him about the postcard, and concluded with, "I want you to decide what I should do with this. I can forward it to you. However, if you would like me to investigate, all I need is the promise of an authorization and payment. I still have half your fee from the last job in my bank accounts and can fund this trip myself."

White did not answer immediately, which made Emerson's heart pound. He knew that the connection had not been severed because he could hear the hum of the wires.

Finally, White said, "I am disturbed by the method in which the postcard reached you. It is not our agreed-upon method."

Emerson knew that, which was why he was calling. He was about to say so, when White continued.

"The woman who calls herself Lureen here is to contact me with evidence she finds of lynchings that she believes I am unaware of. I am then to dispatch an investigator, or to go myself in some cases."

Emerson closed his mouth, and silently cursed the infernal machine he was using. He couldn't see White, which interfered with the communication. He knew that White spoke deliberately, a habit that had served him well, and often his voice remained calm while his blue eyes blazed with fury.

Emerson wondered if that were true now.

"You can reach Arkansas faster than I can," White said. "I would like you to investigate. Your normal fee will be awaiting you when you return."

"Let me clarify," Emerson said. "You want me to do what I usually do. You want me to gather facts on the lynching from last September."

"Yes," White said.

"I am not going to search for Lureen," Emerson said, deliberately not making that a question.

"Good heavens, no," White said. "I would hope that she has left the vicinity already."

"Hope is one thing," Emerson said, thinking of the missing young men he had been unable to track down. "But it is not certainty."

"Indeed," White said. "However, my agreement with this woman we are calling Lureen does not include running to her rescue. She does know that we have a legal budget should she get in trouble with the law."

Emerson's heart was pounding hard. "Does a legal budget matter? Isn't she in danger of dying the same way the man in the postcard did?"

"Generally, no," White said, his tone so curt that Emerson knew he wasn't to ask more about the woman.

Still, he couldn't resist one last question. "What is your agreement with her?"

"She found us," White said. "She does this of her own accord, for reasons she has not explained. Every time I have offered to pay her or asked her to have an assistant, she has not only refused, but she has gone silent. However, I did ask her one favor three months ago. I asked her to keep an eye on you, and if you got into trouble to contact one of our branches—and me—immediately."

"West Texas," Emerson murmured.

"Yes," White said. "We lost our normal investigator there. We have not found him to this day. I was afraid the same might happen to you. I wanted her to let me know the moment trouble began."

"And that's how she knew my name," Emerson said.

"Yes," White said. "It was quite a risk, since, to my knowledge she and I have never met. But I believed she would give you no trouble in Atlanta."

"She hasn't," Emerson said, although he wondered what the post office thought of his receipt of such a postcard.

"I could send a different investigator if you are worried," White said.

"Are you?" Emerson asked.

"It is unusual," White said, "and she knows what you look like. There is more risk than you would normally face."

Emerson clutched the center of the candlestick phone. He already knew these jobs were dangerous ones. And as White said, Emerson was closer than someone from New York or Boston. Emerson was a trusted investigator. So many others lacked the finesse to work in the rural areas where the bulk of these murders occurred.

"I understand the risk," Emerson said. "I accept it. You will get the usual report from me in a week or two."

After he hung up the receiver, he sat for a moment in the unfamiliar office, breathing in the lingering cigar smoke.

He had just volunteered to go back into the fight, one that had already exhausted him and taken most of his sleep, as surely as it had stolen a lot of his good nature.

But the images he had seen, the stories he had been told, would not leave his mind. He would get little rest here or in Abbotts Creek.

He set the telephone down and stood up.

He was going to go, even if it was the last thing he ever did.

* * *

Abbotts Creek was in Phillips County, slap dab in the middle of the Arkansas Delta. For such a small place, the town itself seemed prosperous enough. Emerson's train had veered past what was clearly the main street that had several red brick buildings that seemed new—no more than fifteen years old.

The train station itself looked to support a much larger town. It had two levels and a large arrivals area, with solid wood benches and marble floors. The entire interior smelled new.

As Emerson and four others emerged from the train, the ticket agent behind the big arrivals and departures window, looked up, smiled and nodded, then returned to whatever it was he'd been doing.

Emerson let out a small breath. He would most likely be fine. He had a card identifying him as a reporter with the *Atlanta Journal*, only the name on it was Earl S. West, since he'd learned that the name Emerson wasn't sufficiently Southern for some whites. In fact, it suggested a Northern man of liberal education, something his father aspired to, but which had become a handicap for Emerson in communities where he was unknown.

Usually, there were signs posted about the nearest boarding house. He couldn't see any, so he walked over to the ticket agent. The ticket agent was a small man, with freshly cut red hair, and thin mustache. He looked to be about Emerson's age, and just as tired.

The ticket agent had changed the sign behind him mentioning the next day's train, and seemed about to close up.

"Beg pardon," Emerson said. "I'd be much obliged if you could point me to a boarding house."

The ticket agent looked up, frowned at him, that friendly smile gone as if it never had been. Had the ticket agent been looking at someone else when he smiled a few moments ago?

"Miss Dottie usually takes new arrivals," the ticket agent said. "But they usually write ahead. Who did you say you were?"

"I didn't say." Emerson smiled as he spoke. "My name is Earl West, and I'm afraid I'm horribly unfamiliar with the local customs. I ask your forgiveness for that."

"You should ask for Miss Dottie's. It's her you'll be inconveniencing." The ticket agent made a show of stamping some documents. The slap of the stamp echoed in the large space. "What business brings you here?"

Emerson reached into the pocket of his waistcoat, and pulled out his credentials. "I'm a reporter with the *Atlanta Journal*. We're doing a series of articles on the recent sharecropping troubles, and we'd heard that most communities in the Delta had had some difficulties."

The ticket agent's face shuttered even more. "You a union man?"

The question surprised Emerson, and he decided to let the emotion show. "No," he said with emphasis. "Who'd be wanting to unionize?"

"Some carpetbaggers been talking to the nigras around here, stirring them up, saying payments is off. Trouble started last fall, been spreading all over the Delta. Surprised you hadn't heard."

Especially given the story that Emerson was telling.

"I'd heard about the troubles and the discrepancies. There's talk like that from here to Mississippi," Emerson said. "I didn't realize there was actual union men stirring up the nigras. That's unusual, don't you think?"

"I do," said the ticket agent. "I always think there's something wrong when one of our own decides that he don't like us much no more, and decides to spend his time agitating the darkies."

Emerson suspected that some of the ticket agent's word choices were designed to irritate any white outsider who was visiting these parts.

"I just came to report on the trouble," Emerson said. "We haven't seen much of it yet in Georgia, but my editor doesn't want anyone to be getting ideas."

"Those what had ideas are gone now, praise the Lord," The ticket agent said, and pounded that stamp one more time.

Emerson nodded, knowing better than to push harder. "If I could trouble you for directions…?"

The ticket agent looked up. "Miss Dottie's is two blocks south on Elm. Go outside, turn left and walk straight. Can't miss it."

"I thank you," Emerson said, and then walked out of the train station, the heels of his shoes clicking on the marble floor. He felt alone and uncomfortable, just like he had every other time he had done these investigations.

He stepped out of the cool station in the warm sunlight, blinking at its brightness. Wood sidewalks and a well flattened dirt road ran through the center of town. He saw no automobiles, but several fancy horse-drawn carriages. Lots of men and women on foot, almost all unconcerned with the handful of new arrivals at the train station.

Except for a group of white men across the street. They sat outside a building with a fancy restaurant inside, chawin' and spitting into the nearby spittoons, and watching him like they'd been told to.

The train station was on Cherry Street. Second Street took him past the men and onto what was most likely Elm.

Emerson walked with purpose, as if he had come to Abbotts Creek dozens of times.

The men, all wearing white shirts tucked into black pants held up with suspenders, watched him. He watched them out of the corner of his eye, careful not to appear as if he were actually staring at them.

He crossed into the street, felt the softness of the dirt, which suggested there'd been rains here recently, and then stepped onto the wooden sidewalk.

As far as he could tell, none of the men followed him. He took that as a good sign. He'd been followed too many times in too many other towns just as small as this one in the past.

The next street up was Elm and sure enough, the boarding house was in the middle of the next block—a white clapboard house with gingerbread trim and a well-kept fence. A sign outside said:

Boarding House
Inquire Inside

He squared his shoulders and walked the half block, feeling as if every eye in the town was on him. He opened the gate, and walked across a beautiful path ringed with red and pink flowering plants that he couldn't name.

The porch had wear on its main steps, and a large brass knocker covered the main part of the solid wood door.

He knocked twice, then waited.

The door eased open part way.

"I'm enquiring about a room," he said to the dark crack between the door's edge and its jamb.

"Two dollars per day, ten dollars per week," said a strong female voice. "Includes breakfast and supper, both at seven sharp. If you don't arrive for the meal, you don't get fed."

A strict boarding house then. He'd stayed in some that were lax. "I presume payment is up front?"

"Yes, sir, and I do not refund." The door still hadn't opened all the way.

"If you have room," he said, "I would like to pay for two nights."

He hoped that would be all he needed. He always felt as if he was on some kind of good-luck clock when he did this work.

The door opened the rest of the way. Emerson stepped inside. The interior smelled of roasting beef mixed with heavy perfume. The door closed behind him before his eyes adjusted enough to see the heavy-set woman in front of him. She wore her steel-gray hair in a bun. An apron covered a long blue dress that had seen better days.

"I have a register," she said. "Come with me."

She led him into the front parlor. There, someone had set up a counter with some fresh flowers in a vase on one side, and an open register on the other.

She handed him a pen and an inkwell, along with a printed card that he had to fill out with his name, his home address, and the length of his stay.

He did all of that, using the address for Atlanta University as his own, and marked down two nights.

He took four dollars from his wallet, and handed them to her along with the card. She took the money and set it with the card, but did not put either away. Apparently she did not want him to know where the money was kept.

Then she shoved the register at him. He paused before signing his name.

The register went back two weeks. On the page across from the empty line where his name would go was the name Lureen Taylor with the city and state left off.

He paused for a moment too long.

"I require my guests to fill out the register," the woman said.

He did, not apologizing for the extra time it took him to do so. He signed his alias, and added that he was from Atlanta. He decided not to ask about Lureen Taylor. He would find out soon enough if she remained at the boarding house.

The woman nodded, then said, "I'm Dottie and this here's my house. You will treat it like a home and not some way station, are we clear?"

"Yes, ma'am," he said.

"Your room is six stairs up. It is the only room on the landing. It's a mite small but you're not staying long. If you decide to stay for a week or more, we'll find you something more comfortable."

"Thank you, ma'am," he said.

She almost smiled. It looked like that was as friendly as she got. "Stairs are back in the entry."

Apparently, she wasn't going to take him up there.

"Much obliged." He turned around, taking in the horsehair furniture that looked like no one had sat in it in this century, the occasional tables covered with expensive glassware and shelves with all sorts of little figurines. He did not pause to examine them.

Instead he returned to the entry, and saw the stairs off to his right. He took them, saw the landing, and a door to his left.

The room was more of a walk-in closet than an actual room. He had to duck once inside, because the bulk of the room was under the stairs. A narrow bed with a handmade quilt pushed against the only long wall. A chamber pot peeked out from under the bed. A short table stood beside the bed, with a wash basin and matching pitcher on top. A kerosene lamp had left black stains on the underside of one of the stairs.

A tiny round window, the size of a portal, had been drilled into the wall behind the bed. The window opened, but just barely.

There was no closet, no bureau, and no place to store his things. No wonder she had said that if he decided to stay longer he would get a nicer room. No one could live comfortably in this one for a week.

He set his satchel underneath the table, as far from the chamber pot as he could. He would have thought that a nice house like this would have indoor plumbing. Perhaps it did on the main floor, but he had not been informed of it. He would have to ask somehow, without offending anyone's sensibilities.

He pulled out his pocket watch. He had two hours until dinner, which meant many of the businesses were closing. He sometimes had to think what an average traveling man would do, and he supposed someone like him would not wander the streets, looking for someone to speak with.

So he removed his shoes and spread out on top of the covers, hoping to get some rest.

The next thing he knew, a gong had sounded below.

He assumed that sound invited all of the boarders to supper.

* * *

The large oak table in the dining room was set for eight. When he arrived, two men were standing near the sideboard, looking at a decanter and glasses. Emerson could only assume they had hoped for some kind of alcohol, but he doubted they would find any. Arkansas, like Georgia, prohibited the sale and manufacture of liquor, and genteel homes like this one did not serve any of it, even if the owner indulged.

The entire first floor smelled heavily of that roast beef, and his stomach growled. Emerson introduced himself to the men as Earl, but he did not mention his profession or give any reason for being in Abbotts Creek.

"You're in luck," one of the men said. "Dottie makes the best roast beef in the entire Delta."

The other man nodded in agreement, then added, "Pay attention to her hints. If she mentions that she's low on potatoes or needs coffee, then volunteer to pick some up from Abbotts Mercantile. We've learned that if we buy some of the supplies, she rewards us with good down-home cooking."

Emerson smiled and said he would remember that. They exchanged small talk for a while—both men lived in the house and had since their wives died, claiming living here gave them the opportunity to talk with people they wouldn't normally encounter.

They were inviting him to tell them about himself. Instead, he said, "I see that Miss Dottie also takes female boarders."

"Yes," said the first man. "When there are women in the house, we men are confined to the outhouse out back. Fortunately, the last woman left here near to a week ago."

So much for Lureen. He tried not to look disappointed. As the other boarders showed up, Miss Dottie banged the gong a second time.

This close, it sounded as if the entire house would shake.

The men sat down in what seemed like their usual places, and then Miss Dottie entered, without any food at all, which surprised Emerson. His surprise only lasted a moment though, because a young colored girl, wearing a maid's uniform, staggered in under the weight of an uncarved roast.

Emerson had to catch himself from helping her. In this town, among the white folk, this girl was an invisible servant, not a lady deserving of assistance. He studiously avoided looking at her, so that he wouldn't acknowledge her, even as she brought out the rest of the meal.

One of the men carved the roast, then Miss Dottie said grace. She sat at the head of the table, and presided over the conversation like a queen instructing her court.

Emerson didn't dare bring up any troubles or the sharecropping information he had received. He definitely couldn't discuss lynching in mixed company, nor could he comfortably mention race issues.

Finally, he managed to turn the conversation to other guests, asking Miss Dottie who the most interesting boarders she had ever had were. She demurred, saying it wasn't her place to discuss her "people."

"Miss Dottie always has a fascinating mix," one of the men said. "Every time I stay here, I meet someone new."

"I was saying earlier that I was surprised to see a female name on the register," Emerson said, hoping he sounded prim.

Miss Dottie's gaze met his, and he felt her measure him. She finally understood why he paused.

"I've been to very few boarding houses that mixed male and female," he added, disapprovingly.

"We have no women here now," said one of the other men.

"I like them," said the first man who'd come into the room. "They always liven up the conversation."

"Except that last woman, what was her name?" asked a different man. "Mrs.—?"

"Taylor," Miss Dottie said. "She left."

"Left town?" Emerson asked.

"She didn't say." The man who spoke sounded disappointed.

"We suspect that Dan here scared her off," said one of the other men. "He was too interested and she wasn't comfortable."

Emerson looked at the man they had called Dan. He was one of the men who lived here. He was short and balding, with a round belly. Certainly not the most appealing fellow in the room.

Then Emerson caught Miss Dottie's eye. She was still staring at him. Something had set her off. Maybe she hadn't liked Lureen Taylor.

He would have to tread carefully. He wanted to ask more questions, but didn't dare.

"I saw no reason for her to leave," said one of the other regulars, maybe in defense of the man named Dan.

"She didn't belong here," Miss Dottie said tightly, and the conversation died as if it hadn't existed at all. Everyone turned their attention to the meal before them.

Emerson looked up after a few minutes to find Miss Dottie still watching him, her gaze flat and cold.

He made himself smile, and vowed to keep quiet for the rest of his stay in this place.

• • •

His vow lasted for less than an hour.

He needed to stretch his legs, and he didn't feel safe enough to walk in downtown Abbotts Creek. So he took the pipe he rarely smoked and stepped onto the porch.

One thing he did like about nights in faraway places—the soft perfume of spring flowers, the rich sweet cut of pipe smoke, and the comfort of a good wrap-around porch. Miss Dottie's had a swing and well cushioned wicker chairs.

But he didn't sit. Instead, he stood near the railing and looked out over the quiet street.

After a moment, the man named Dan joined him. Emerson waited, not certain if the man wanted to defend his actions with Lureen Taylor or if he was just here for a companionable evening.

The man reintroduced himself.

"Dan McCall," he said, extending his hand.

"Earl West," Emerson said, and took a puff off his pipe.

"You didn't say what brings you to these parts," McCall said.

"It's not for discussing around ladies," Emerson said.

McCall looked at him sideways.

"I'm a reporter with the *Atlanta Journal.* We're doing a series of investigative reports about the agitators who are stirring up the sharecroppers in the Delta and beyond. My editor's worried our own boys might get Ideas, and he wants to use other places as a cautionary tale."

Emerson hoped he hadn't over-explained. He had done that before, and it had been something which made people suspicious.

"Don't believe what they tell you," McCall said. "It ain't northern agitators coming down here. There's some white lawyers from Little Rock who seem to believe that how we do business here ain't proper."

"Don't you do business how you've always done business?" Emerson asked. He wished he'd had time to study up on this. Ironically, he was going with what he had learned from the papers.

McCall shook his head sadly. "There's money now. The war, and all. Cotton prices are good, and them nigras, they see a dime and want a dollar. The white lawyers say we gotta write out receipts and payments, pay everyone equal for the same labor. They're even researching cotton prices, see what white landowners are really getting paid, and making sure they give the right amount to the sharecroppers."

Emerson took another puff of his pipe to hide his feelings. He hated the sharecropping system. It was little better than slavery—with all the rents and food taken out of the payments, and often nothing left for the sharecroppers to save or use to move elsewhere.

He hadn't realized that cotton prices were up because of the war, but it made sense as did McCall's interpretation. Money did bring in agitators, and for good reason. When money flowed, people thought about cheating.

"I'm surprised that you're talking white Southern agitators," Emerson said. "I'd thought Northern boys'd come down and stirred up things. I'd heard about how you'd dealt with that boy last September. I'd been hoping to use that as the focus of my article, how Abbotts Creek dealt with those who believed the bunkum those bolsheviks peddled."

McCall scratched a match on the wooden post beside him. The match flared with a stink of sulfur. He used it to light his pipe.

"That boy? Moses Ross." McCall stretched out the name, making fun of it with his tone. "He wasn't sharecropping. He just got too big for himself. Heading off to some school in the North or maybe Atlanta."

Then he glanced sideways at Emerson, trying to gage a reaction. Emerson kept his expression neutral, that of a man hearing a tale which did not concern him, instead of the story about the horrifying end to someone else's life.

"One dark night just before Moses left, someone knifed Willis Bowden to death, left his wife bloody and terrified, and we all know who done it."

"That boy," Emerson said softly. He'd heard these stories before. "The wife said so."

"Oh, no," McCall said. "She was so out of her head, she said she done it. We told her to hush up, and she did. She ain't never said it again. Not that she has need to. Willis didn't treat her the way a Southern lady should be treated, but he did leave her money."

And gave the town an excuse to make an example of an uppity Negro, Emerson thought, but didn't say.

"The sheriff arrested Moses Ross. We all knowd he liked Mrs. Bowden. But that boy, he kept saying he didn't do nothing. His family was gonna use his school money to fight what everyone knew to be true. Took about ten days before everyone was ready, but the sheriff—who had all those misguided reform thoughts—finally saw things our way."

So, the sheriff wanted actual law and order. Emerson nodded, but not in agreement with McCall. Just in understanding.

Which chilled him.

He had to change the subject. He didn't want to seem too concerned with Moses Ross's death. Nor did Emerson want to hear any more details. Not at the moment.

"What about those white lawyers?" he asked. "How're you going to stop them from agitating?"

"We catch them," McCall said. He spoke with such calm deliberation, it sounded as if he were talking about a picnic. "We don't touch them, though. We just make them watch what happens to them they're trying to convince."

Emerson had seen something similar in Alabama. Northern labor unionists got hauled to a lynching, and were expected to cheer. If they didn't, they were afraid they'd die. They didn't die. They left and reported the incident to the *New York Times.*

"Does it work?" Emerson asked, keeping his tone calm and barely interested.

"Don't know for sure," McCall said. "But we ain't seen none of them Little Rock folks for months now. And they better hope we never see them again."

He said that last with great force, as if he were trying to convince Emerson, as if he thought Emerson was one of the lawyers.

Emerson wasn't quite sure how to convince McCall that he wasn't.

"Anyone else I should talk to about the ways Abbotts Creek is protecting its own?" he asked.

McCall puffed on his pipe for a moment. The smoke had a touch of vanilla, making it even sweeter than the usual blends.

"We got a meeting coming up five days from now," he said after a moment. "But we usually don't take outsiders to it. Maybe a few of us'll talk to you. Don't mind hoods, do you?"

The Klan.

Emerson's heart beat harder. He wasn't sure if he had just been threatened or if he'd just been approved for membership. He wasn't sure he would know unless he let the men talk to him.

"No," he said, "I don't mind hoods. But I'd best extend my stay. I'd only planned to be here two days."

"Do that," McCall said, and something in his tone made the shivers run down Emerson's spine again.

He had no idea if he was hearing things that weren't there. His fears and imagination often put him in as great a risk as his actual identity did.

But he thanked McCall, and then stood in what he hoped was companionable silence until the house lights went out.

* * *

Emerson slept with his satchel open and his pistol near to hand. "Slept" was too powerful a word for the half-awake state he kept himself in all night. Clearly he didn't feel safe, even here.

He kept playing McCall's words over and over in his head. Emerson slowly realized that he had what he needed. What the NAACP wanted for its reports weren't so much the gory details as why a lynching had been committed. Not the official story, the one told to outsiders, but the real story, the one the community knew.

Such as protecting a woman whose husband beat her so severely that she took a knife to him in the middle of the night. Clearly, the locals hadn't wanted to prosecute her, but felt someone had to pay. And reminding the colored community that rising above their station was a bad idea was simply an added bonus.

Emerson knew he couldn't stay here until the meeting. He wasn't sure he should stay any much longer. He took his satchel down to breakfast, figuring if anyone asked, he could say he had his papers in it.

He wasn't sure how much more information he would gather, but he did want to answer one more question for himself. He wanted to know what happened to Lureen Taylor.

Breakfast provided no answers at all. It was served at the long table in the kitchen. Miss Dottie was there, and she wasn't willing to talk to him. Instead, over the fine biscuits and gravy, she said, "Mr. McCall says you'll be needing a room for three additional nights."

Then she looked pointedly at the satchel, and added, "But I see that he's mistaken."

Emerson shook his head. "He's correct. I simply carry my satchel with me because it has my research."

Her lips thinned, as if she didn't believe him.

"Well," she said. "I'm not sure if I'll have a room. I will know this afternoon. I will tell you when you return."

Then she stepped over to the counter and opened one of the bins.

"Lord a'mercy," she said. "We're in need of flour. I have no idea how I could have let us get so short of something so important."

Then she closed the bin, crossed her arms, and looked at him. He would have understood even without the stare. If he brought the flour, he could stay.

He smiled, and nodded, not quite willing to verbally commit to her blackmail. After finishing his meal, he set his plate near the others by the sink, then thanked Miss Dottie for her hospitality.

He had put her in an awkward situation. Either she had to ask him if he planned to return with the flour or she had to trust him.

He rather liked her look of dismay.

He went out the back way, using the porch to reach the front. The town seemed quiet, even for a weekday morning. Although it was coming on nine, most folks had probably been working since sun-up.

He walked to Abbotts Creek Mercantile. He'd best take care of his purchase first. Besides, a general store in the morning was always a great place to get information.

The mercantile was only a few blocks from Miss Dottie's. Two wagons were tied up outside. As Emerson approached, two women came out of the mercantile. One had her hair covered with a scarf, the other wore hers in a knot on top of her head. The shorter war fashions hadn't really hit this community; both women wore dresses that brushed the wooden sidewalk.

Both nodded at him in greeting. He nodded back. Then he held the door for an elderly woman, who wore a black dress with a bustle and a hat that partly obscured her face. The dress shushed at him; expensive silk, mostly likely widow's weeds, probably passed down from an even earlier generation. Mourning was nothing if not ubiquitous.

He followed her inside. Every general store between here and West Texas smelled the same—a hint of coffee, the faint scent of tobacco, and a dry edge from all the goods in barrels on the floor.

The elderly woman picked up a basket and wandered toward the sewing goods. The owner stood by a counter, his meaty arms crossed, his fleshy face florid.

He stared at Emerson, much the way that Miss Dottie had the night before.

"Help you?" the man asked.

"I hope so," Emerson said. "I'm here for some flour for Miss Dottie."

The man smiled. "Be needin' a few more nights at the boarding house, eh?"

"I'd ask how you knew, but apparently she does this often." Emerson did his best to sound amused at her petty blackmail.

"Keeps one of our best boarding houses in business," the man said as he headed to one of the barrels.

He took a white sack and a scoop. He opened the barrel and started carefully scooping flour into the sack.

"What brings you to Abbotts Creek?" he asked.

"I'm with the *Atlanta Journal*," Emerson said. "We're doing a story on sharecropping—"

"What'd you say your name was?" the man asked.

"I hadn't," Emerson said. "My name is Earl West."

The man tied the bag, then weighed it on the large scale behind him. One pound exactly.

"You from Atlanta?" he asked.

The question seemed to have more import than a casual enquiry.

"I am," Emerson said, refraining from saying that all the reporters from the newspaper lived in Atlanta. Instead, he added, "We're starting to have similar troubles in Georgia—"

"Do you know a gentleman named Emerson West?" The man set the pound of flour next to the cash register.

Emerson was so surprised to hear his own name that he wasn't quite sure what to say. He approached the counter, and saw the pile of postcards beneath it. Then he saw the sign propped against the cash register listing this building as a post office.

He felt cold.

"There are a lot of Wests in Atlanta," he said, hoping that would stop the man's questions.

"There are Mosbys in Phillips County," the man said, "and we're mostly kin."

Even the colored Mosbys? Emerson wanted to ask, but didn't.

"Atlanta's a big city," he said, hoping he didn't sound too argumentative.

"I been," Mosby said. "It's not that big."

Emerson frowned. He could let it pass, or he could say something. He opted for bluntness. "Are you implying something, Mr. Mosby?"

"Lady come in here not one week ago, bought one of them postcards you're near, and sent it to an Emerson West in Atlanta. Now you're here. And I've been hearing of government men, investigating our justice here, trying to change our laws because they saw things they like better in France. Just making sure you're not one of them."

Emerson pulled out his credentials, happy that his hands didn't shake. "I'm not with the government."

"You wouldn't be from one of them new-fangled nigger associations, would you?"

"Do I look like I am?" Emerson asked, hoping he sounded offended instead of frightened.

Mosby let out a small unamused laugh. "For all I know, you're high yella."

Emerson's breath caught in his throat.

Mosby's beady eyes bored right into him. "I been hearing tell of high yella niggers from some advancement association mixing with good folks, trying to stop some of our organizations from doing right. I even heard one of them high yella niggers is named White. Might think another would be named North, but West'll do."

Emerson's mouth had gone dry. His cheeks were warm. He had actually flushed. He obviously couldn't hide his reaction, so he had to give it lie.

"I have covered stories all over Dixie," he said with as much indignation as he could muster. "And never once have I been called a nigger before."

Mosby reached over the counter and grabbed a handful of postcards. He spread them next to the flour. The first postcard was the same as the one Emerson had received. The next two pictured men hanging from trees, one surrounded by a crowd, the other by four men in white shirts and hats. One of the men looked like Mosby.

The last postcard showed a body being burned—or worse, a man being burned alive.

Emerson made himself look at them. Then he thought about his pistol in the satchel. He'd always feared he would come across a moment like this, when he was directly confronted, and he often wondered what he'd do.

If he shot this man, Emerson would guarantee his own ugly death.

He worked alone.

What he had to do was survive to the next day.

"You trying to scare me?" Emerson asked, voice flat. "Because I came to Abbotts Creek to understand your justice, and perhaps bring a taste of it to Georgia, not to have it threatened against me."

"I heard that this nigger association collects information on nigger killings," Mosby said. "I got me a cousin in L'siana who met this White feller, didn't stop him before he left. Heard tell this White was drummed out of the South, had to go to New York City to escape."

Emerson had no idea how to deal with this kind of bluntness. He'd heard of it, but never encountered it. And didn't know how a true white man would respond.

He decided to stick with indignation. "How much do I owe you for the flour?"

Mosby stared at him. Emerson stared back.

Finally, Mosby looked down. "This ain't a town for niggers."

"That's fairly obvious," Emerson said. "Do you think if I was one I'd be here?"

"I don't think nothing," Mosby said. "We've had lots of agitators."

"I'm not one of them," Emerson said. "But I assume you don't want to sell me the flour."

"I don't need your money," Mosby said. "And you don't need to talk to Miss Dottie no more."

Emerson didn't know how to argue with that. He needed to leave Abbotts Creek before he really did meet with the Klan. But now, he had to find out what happened to Lureen. He had a hunch he knew, and he didn't like what he was thinking.

"You said a lady sent one of these postcards to a man named West," Emerson said, "and somehow that made you think I was colored. I do not understand how a lady's postcard would make you think that."

"Miss Dottie didn't like her," Mosby said.

Emerson's stomach twisted. "I gathered that. I also had the sense Miss Dottie doesn't like everyone."

"Miss Dottie knows people." Mosby looked down at the postcards, almost wistfully.

Emerson felt cold. His heart was pounding so hard it was probably audible.

"So," he said, "will I be seeing a postcard of this lady next time I'm here?"

"No." Mosby's tone was flat. "But not for lack of trying."

Emerson's gaze met Mosby's again.

"Because you couldn't get a good photograph?" Emerson asked, afraid of the answer.

"Because there was nothing to photograph." Mosby gathered up the four postcards and put them back on the pile. "Now you get. I'll tell Miss Dottie you have no need of her hospitality any longer."

"Then she has no need of that flour," Emerson said, hoping the emotion in his voice sounded like rage. "Of course, she already has my money, so she can afford her own. Do tell her that her boarding house will not get a good review in the *Atlanta Journal.*"

"We'll be watching for it," Mosby said.

Emerson glared at him a final time, then gripped the handle of the satchel and left the store. He paused, his back to the wall, looking to see if anyone was waiting for him.

Cherry Street was empty.

The door banged behind him and he jumped.

The elderly woman peered at him from beneath her hat. She carried a sack in one hand. The other was hidden in the pocket of her silk dress.

He hoped to God she wasn't carrying a lady's pistol.

He looked at her, trying not to seem afraid.

She stopped beside him, and also looked at the street, not at him.

"Miss Taylor took the train to Little Rock seven days ago," the woman said softly. "Before she did, she asked me to give you these."

She pulled the four postcards out of her pocket, and slid them to his nearby hand.

Then she backed away from him and spit on the wooden sidewalk. "Now, you git!" she said. "We don't need no agitators here."

She crossed the street, shaking her head as if his very presence offended her.

He was trembling. He watched her go. He hoped no one had heard any of that. She would get in trouble for helping him, and she could get him in trouble for threatening her.

In the distance, a train whistle sounded. It was later than he thought.

It was always later than he thought.

He stuffed the postcards in his satchel, next to the pistol. Then he walked the block to the station, just in time to board the train.

M. Elizabeth Castle contributed two stories to our Crime *special edition. One of those stories, a cozy mystery written in haiku form, has received a favorable mention in every single review we've received for the volume.*

Her stories are always fascinating and always powerful. "Blood and Lightning on the Newport Highway" is no exception.

About the story, she writes, "I have roots in southern Appalachia, and find the people and history fascinating—especially the era just after the turn of the last century, when coal wars and Prohibition brought change and opportunity. When I lived in Knoxville in the early '90s, rumor had it that neighboring Cocke County's major cash crop was marijuana. I expect this was true, given the area's colorful history regarding the production and transport of illegal substances. And I bet that a certain bar tucked well off the highway out there still serves white lightning in Mason jars during their Saturday night bluegrass jams."

Blood and Lightning
on the Newport Highway

M. Elizabeth Castle

Jacksie Douglas ate more leftover fried chicken and collards than me and Uncle Hep and J.D. put together, though I don't suppose J.D. counts, seeing that Mamaw's constantly on him about growing boys needing to eat like growing boys and not like birds.

I sat on the wood bench between him and Jacksie, protecting my brother from Jacksie's flying elbows.

Jacksie'd scared the tar out of me earlier—"Davie! Hey, Davie!"—when he stepped from between the oaks behind the shed where I was chopping wood before supper, sweating through my undershirt in the cool spring evening. Then again, I probably wouldn't have noticed a black bear lumbering by the cabin—I was taking out my frustrations with Hep and Papaw on the woodpile, and having thoughts about going to Knoxville to work in the mills there despite Hep's flat refusal.

Now Papaw watched with his little half-smile as our hulking guest sopped up the last of the greens with his cornbread and popped the whole thing into his mouth. Papaw says he doesn't see much now beyond light and dark and shapes, what with the cataracts turning his eyes from brown to milky-blue over the last couple of years.

"That sure was good, Miz Monroe!" Jacksie said, swallowing the last of it down. "Davie said you might have pie." His wide, soft face was hopeful. Jacksie lived for pie, it seemed, and Mamaw made the best in Cocke County.

"Why thank you, Jacksie," she said as she stood and took his plate. "And I believe I do have a pie in the kitchen." Across the table, Uncle Hep shot me a glare and rolled his eyes. I gave him my most innocent shrug. J.D. caught the exchange and grinned. I had no doubt he knew Hep was still angry at me from our discussion earlier. That boy don't miss much.

We took our pie to the front porch, despite the chill in the air. Papaw and Mamaw sat in their matching oak rockers, made by Papaw's papaw as a wedding present. Hep took the newer rocker like he usually did, his crutches leaning against the cabin's rough-hewn wall. Me and Jacksie took the bench, the mate to the one inside, and J.D. perched on the rail next to the cinderblock step to the packed dirt of the yard.

Between bites of pie, Jacksie told us that his pa sent him around the mountain on account of he had some news. Jacksie, for all his size, didn't have the brains God gave a chicken, but he could remember simple messages. He shoved another huge bite of warm apples and flaky lard crust into his mouth, savoring it as he hadn't bothered to savor his supper. Then he furrowed his brow and thought hard and swallowed his pie and finally said, "Pa figures ya'll oughta know before the next time Davie goes to town to fetch supplies for the stills." He put his last bite into his mouth.

"Find out what, Jacksie?" Hep's voice was soft. He wouldn't have used that tone with me. For someone as short and uncharitable as my Uncle Hep, he always showed an odd patience with our idiot neighbor.

Jacksie chewed and swallowed and said, "Oh yeah. He told me to say that Charlie Virgil been seen over in Knoxville two nights ago. They heard him saying he was headed for Newport."

Jacksie said it like he was telling us he saw a deer up on the overgrown mountain trail. But Papaw and Uncle Hep both sat up straight like they been stung. And Mamaw set her little plate on her lap and leaned back with her eyes closed.

J.D. looked between them, frowning. "Who's Charlie Virgil?" It was the first time he'd spoken since he got home from school.

I glanced at Jacksie, who was still smiling as he picked the last crumbs off his plate. Papaw answered. "He's the revenuer what run your pa and Hep off the road."

* * *

Jacksie didn't stay much longer since it was getting dark. He said his goodbyes and stomped through the yard and disappeared behind the woodshed. He didn't use a light, never seemed to need one. We heard a quiet rustle of rhododendron, then silence.

"No idea how a man that big and slow in the head can be so quiet in the woods," said Papaw, shaking his head. He brought out his hand-carved pipe, filled it and lit it, puffing deliberately. He didn't need to see for that. He passed it to Mamaw, who puffed and passed it back. The sweet smoke hung in the air.

"You think Virgil's after us?" I asked.

"Can't imagine he's not," said Hep. He'd leaned back, and now scratched the stump of his left thigh through the sewed-up denim of his overalls. "Knowing him, it's personal. That judge made a fool of him six years ago."

The sheriff told us the crash most likely killed Pa instantly, sparing him from the fire that destroyed the Model T and the load of moonshine him and Hep were running to Knoxville. Virgil took it badly when the judge threw out his case, ruling there was no evidence Hep had been in the car that night. It came down to Virgil's word against the Cocke County deputy who'd showed up and found Hep twenty feet down a ravine.

Right after that, Virgil had disappeared. We got word later he was reassigned to help the Prohibition effort up in Chicago. Everyone in these parts figured it was a demotion.

Papaw nodded. "Even if he ain't here for us, he's still gonna try to give us grief." He puffed his pipe and said to Hep, "We need some eyes and ears in town. You and Davie go over tomorrow morning. Take the Dodge."

"Me, too," said J.D.

"You got school," said Mamaw.

Hep grunted. By now it was nearly full dark and I could barely see him. The only clear feature was the jagged scar on his cheek that stood out in pale relief. "Wagon makes more sense," he said.

"Take the Dodge." And Hep nodded once, still unhappy, but Papaw had used the voice that even Hep obeyed.

＊ ＊ ＊

The next morning, I cranked up the Dodge and backed it carefully out of the barn and across the yard to the rutted track that led off the mountain.

J.D. was already off to school and Papaw had headed out at dawn on the mule to work on the set of five stills a mile or so around the slope. They weren't the closest ones to the cabin, but they were the easiest to get to. The mule knew the way and Papaw didn't need much sight to check and adjust the mash. We'd be setting them up to distill after this weekend's run.

I parked the Dodge by the porch and after a moment, Hep came out the front door. He carried a pie in his free hand.

Hep used two crutches only when the other, less-obvious injuries from the wreck were paining him. He hadn't used just one in awhile.

He slammed the car door and grunted under his breath as he turned to lay the crutch on the reinforced floorboard behind us.

"You okay, Uncle Hep?" I said. "Need me to fetch your other crutch?"

"No. Get this thing moving."

The ride to Newport takes about an hour, but once you're over Jackson's Ridge, the road flattens out and runs down the valley. It's still a rutted mess in the springtime, but at least we didn't have to listen to the Dodge's engine wind out over the hills.

If you continue on the Newport Highway toward Knoxville, another thirty miles finds you at the curve in the road that took Pa's life and crippled Hep. I was glad we didn't have to pass that today. Hep was surly as it was, and I probably wasn't going to make things any better.

"Who's the pie for?" I figured I'd start easy.

"Preacher."

That wasn't easy. Hep hadn't been to church since the wreck, and it was a point of contention between him and Mamaw. "Why didn't Mamaw come along? She could have brought it to him herself, visited with her friends in town."

"Said she needed to work in the garden." His head was turned toward the window, making it hard to hear him over the wind. Definitely surly.

I took a moment to enjoy the drive, the clean green of the valley and the crisp spring air carrying the faintest whiff of the hot summer to come.

"Uncle Hep, about last night." He turned from the window with a frown and I hurried on. "I think you and Papaw are making a mistake not letting me go find work in the mills. I know I can get a good job."

It took him a moment to reply. "You got any idea how big Knoxville is, Davie? You're barely eighteen. You know what that place will do to the likes of you?"

"It'll give me work and I can send the money home like Rafe does, and Matt and his brother too."

"We need you here."

I yanked the Dodge to the left to avoid a particularly bad rut. Hep hung onto the window with one hand and the pie with the other. When I got us straightened out, I said, "Rafe says they're begging for workers. He says I can come live with them in their apartment. And he told me what he makes, even after food and rent, I could send enough you can hire both the Ward brothers and have some left over."

"It ain't about the money."

"How's it not about the money?

"It's about family."

"Family?" Everything was always about family. I swerved to the right, maybe a little harder than I needed to. "I'm trying to help the family. Not much longer and Papaw won't be seeing a thing. And J.D.'s got years before he's big enough to help with the runs."

I was taking a chance bringing up the Knoxville runs. The fact that he couldn't take up Papaw's slack stuck in Hep's craw, and never fiercer than when the Dodge was involved. No matter how much he might want to, a one-legged man just can't drive.

But there was no way around it with Papaw going blind. I'd been driving the Knoxville runs since late fall, Hep beside me in the front seat with the shotgun, and—less often now—Papaw in the back.

I glanced over. Hep was turned toward the window but his shoulders were tight. When he didn't respond I said, "You know we could use the help. I just figured this is a good way to get it. I go work in the mills—" and get out of Cocke County to see the big city "—and you and Papaw get a couple of strong backs. It don't have to be forever. Just for awhile, then I'll come home."

Although I wondered about that last bit. What if I decided to stay in the big city? Or go further west, maybe even to Memphis. What then?

The Dodge jounced over the ruts for nearly a full minute before Hep turned to me. "It sounds real easy, don't it?" he said. "You worked it out all simple. But you got it wrong. You got a duty to your family. To your papaw and your mamaw, and to me. And especially to J.D. You got a duty to him."

"Duty?" He sounded like a Marine, but I didn't dare say that. "What duty I got to him?"

"Your pa and ma are dead. Me and your grandparents, we do everything we can, but you're his brother. You got a special duty to help him grow up. Keep him safe. You can't do that if you're off in the city. You need to be here. Your job is to protect your little brother."

I should have noticed the warning signs. I should have heard the tightness in his voice, seen the tension in his jaw, the beginnings of the flush in the scar on his face. I should have said nothing. But I was wound up by then. "Like your duty to *your* brother?" I said. "Like you protected Pa?"

I regretted the words as soon as they left my mouth. And for a second I thought he might let it pass by. But he said, "Stop the car."

"What?"

"Stop, I said!"

I slowed and stopped the Dodge in the middle of the dirt road. The engine wheezed and died. Hep slammed the door open and grabbed his crutch. "Get out."

I got out and he met me in front of the hood. I stood there before him in the packed and drying ruts of the road, and he stared at me, and some small part of me noticed the sun and the scent of the wild wisteria off in the woods somewhere, and another small part noticed that he had to look up a little to meet my eye and when had that happened. But mostly I saw that the jagged scar on the side of Hep's face had turned bright red and writhed like a angry snake as he clenched his jaw.

He looked at me like he was taking my measure. And I had come up short.

I thought he was gonna belt me one. Lay me down flat right there in the road. And I braced myself 'cause I knew I deserved it.

But after another second or two, he turned away and crutched back to the passenger side of the car and got in, slamming the door so hard the heavy car jolted on its springs. After a moment, I remembered to breathe.

Neither of us said another word until we got to Newport.

* * *

Hep stayed in the car as I offered the pie to the preacher and gave him Mamaw's regards. "And how is your grandmother?" he said. He didn't give me time to answer, but instead glanced past me at the Dodge and asked about not seeing me or J.D. in church. I just shrugged and ended the visit as fast as was polite. He hadn't asked me inside.

Hep scowled at the neat little whitewashed clapboard house with its neat little yard and fence as I got back into the Dodge and cranked the engine.

"He tell you you're going to Hell?" he asked as I pulled into the street.

"No. But he wanted to, I think. Told me you're going."

"I reckon I am. But he's not one to judge."

"What do you mean?" It was only a couple of blocks from the preacher's house to downtown, and I was looking for a place to park the Dodge.

"I mean he's been known to imbibe. More than a little."

"Really?" I was so shocked at the notion that I nearly plowed into the back of Jonathan Campbell's Ford truck.

"Careful!" said Hep. Then, as I followed the tailgate of Jonathan's truck, "I suppose God's laws about drinking don't extend to preachers." He gave me a sharp look. "Don't you dare tell your Mamaw."

"No sir."

I parked the Dodge across the street from Whitney's Store, in front of the Newport Saloon. Jacksie's ma would be somewhere in the dim insides. Some folks say Jacksie's slowness is because she was stone drunk most of her time carrying him, and the alcohol scrambled his brain. The preacher says she's being punished. I figure it's Jacksie what's being punished and wonder about the fairness of that.

"Go on in," Hep told me as I killed the engine. "Tell Nate we need six bags this time. Load 'em in the trunk. I'm gonna have a word with Mack."

Half a block up the street, Deputy John MacAllister leaned against the side of his Chrysler, thumbs hooked over his gun belt, the wide brim of his hat pulled low against the morning sun. He'd seen us and was waiting for Hep. I waved as I crossed the street and he nodded back.

It was Mack what saved Hep's life that night. When he showed up, the Model T was already on fire and Pa's body and the moonshine with it. Virgil and the other revenuers were standing back watching the flames. But Mack saw the break in the undergrowth at the side of the road, fought his way down the ravine and found Hep tangled in the bushes. He'd used his gun belt as a tourniquet for Hep's mangled left leg, hauled him up the slope just as the Sheriff arrived. Over the revenuers' objections, they'd loaded Hep into Mack's car, and Mack drove one-handed those final forty miles into Knoxville, siren wailing the whole way, Hep bleeding and unconscious next to him on the front seat. They said when he pulled in at Fort Sanders Hospital, Mack's hand was cramped so tight, the docs had to pry it off Hep's leg.

A gaggle of little kids squealed and chased each other around the side of the store. About half of them were barefoot, reveling in the springtime lack of shoes. Or maybe growed out of them over the winter.

I threaded through them and the bell on the heavy oak door dinged as I pulled it open and stepped through.

It seemed like half the old moonshiners in the county were gathered inside Whitney's place. Most of them glanced at me as I entered, some nodded, a couple smiled.

One of my earliest memories is of Pa holding me up to the long wood counter that runs the length of the store. On the far end Mr. Whitney keeps jars of candies, all different kinds, and I pointed at the one with the jawbreakers as big as my fist. I remember the sharp smell of the pine floors, and the laughter of my Ma as she said they were too big and to pick something else. But

I don't remember her face so well, and J.D. doesn't have even the sound of her voice, since she died birthing him.

Now the store smelled like old moonshiner.

I walked up to the counter and Nate Whitney grinned at me from the other side. His bald head gleamed in the electric light and his apron was spotless as always. "Gonna need six bags today, Nate," I told him.

"You know where they are," he said.

"I'll pick 'em up on the way out," I said and turned to the table of a half-dozen old men sitting on stools and chairs around Nate's checkers table. They greeted me with gap-toothed smiles and handshakes.

I glanced at the checkers board. "What, nobody playing?"

"Waitin' fer you," said Henry Davidson. He gave me a nearly toothless grin, his wiry gray-on-white beard bobbing against his chest. "Pull up a chair, boy."

"No thanks, Henry," I said. The old man might look like he didn't know his own name, but he was shrewd as a fox and would wipe the board with me. "We heard Charlie Virgil's back, poking around these parts."

"We done heard that too," said Levi McCoy. He was even older than Henry, and his snow-white beard reached to his frayed belt. "Hain't seen him, though."

Henry cocked a bushy eyebrow at Levi and moved a checkers piece onto the board.

"I seen him," said Asa Ferguson. "He done come around my place asking a bunch of questions, what I been doing since he went north, how's business."

"You done talked to him? What'd you tell him?" asked Levi. He got over his shock enough to move a checkers piece of his own.

Asa cackled. "Asked him if he seen anything around what looked like I was still shinin'. Told him I was retired. Too damn old any more."

"You lying through your teeth," said Henry. Asa's boys had taken over his stills, moving them deeper into the mountains. But like the rest of them, Asa wouldn't retire until he was planted in his grave.

"Did he buy it?" asked Levi.

"Don't know. He looked around some and left when my old lady woke up from her nap. Guess he didn't like her threatenin' to blow his head off with her shotgun." He cackled again. Henry made another move.

"What do you suppose he's up to?" I asked. A revenuer making house calls—and risking getting shot—just to ask questions wasn't right.

"Who the hell knows what goes on in that revenuer's mind," said Levi. The others nodded and murmured their agreement.

"There's talk about problems up north," Henry said. "Revenuers cain't keep up. Your turn, Levi."

"Revenuers never stood a chance from the start," said Asa. "Move that one, Levi." Levi moved a different piece.

"Heard on the radio last night there's talk of repealing the Eighteenth," said Nate from behind the counter. "End this whole mess."

Repeal the Eighteenth Amendment? "What happens to us, then?" I asked.

"Nothing happens to us, boy," said Henry. "We do like your daddy did, and your Papaw does, and his papaw before him. Even if them boys in Warshington repeal the Prohibition, half the counties in these parts'll stay dry till Revelation. There'll always be want for good moonshine."

"So what's Charlie Virgil doing, then, coming back here?" I said.

"Making trouble," said Levi.

"We run him out six years ago, we'll do it again," said Asa.

"He don't got the sense God gave a wood tick," said Henry. "Now, if we don't get a hot summer, we're gonna be in a hurt come fall, what with last year's corn bein' light."

The conversation shifted to the weather and the minor annoyances of the business they and their families had been in for generations. And back around to how they were lucky the Sheriff turned a blind eye to the runs to Knoxville and Chattanooga and elsewhere. Of course, he took his payment in kind, but that was part of the price of doing business.

I listened and watched Henry tromp Levi at checkers as they talked. Levi didn't even acknowledge his utter destruction, just collected the pieces and reset the board.

Before he moved out his first piece, the bell on the door dinged. The old men stopped their conversation as Hep entered. He glanced and nodded at them, then met Nate at the counter.

"Hey, Hep," said Nate. "Hain't seen you since fall."

"Guess not." Hep reached into his pocket and pulled out a neat wad of bills, peeled off about half of them and set them on the counter. Nate glanced at them then popped the till open and put them under the change tray.

"How's your pa doin'?" he said. "How's his sight?"

"'Bout the same," said Hep.

"That's too bad," said Henry. "Give him our regards. Tell him he needs to come into town."

Hep nodded and turned to me. "Got the car loaded?"

"Not yet."

He leaned on his crutch and raised his eyebrows. "Well?"

"Don't be sore at the boy, Hep," said Levi. "We done sorta detained him."

"I ain't sore. Go load the car, Davie. I'll be out in a minute."

So I headed out the back of Nate's store to the bigger of his two sheds where he kept his stockpile of feed corn, and began humping fifty-pound burlap bags around to the Dodge.

I was dropping the last bag into the trunk when Hep stepped out onto the wide porch, the door dinging again as he pulled it closed. He turned to me and wasn't looking behind him.

"Bobby! You get yourself back over here!" The woman hollering at one of the laughing children came from the other side of the porch, also not looking, and she ran full-bore into Hep just as his head whipped around in surprised recognition. His reaction was lightning-quick—he braced his shoulder against the rough logs of the wall, caught her elbow with his free hand to steady her, saving her from a sure fall. When she'd found her balance, he inclined his head and said, "Didn't know you was back, Dottie Mae. Sorry to hear about your husband."

"Hep." The single syllable carried the bite of a mountain stream. She pulled her arm away and straightened. "You go straight to hell, Hep Monroe."

The expression on his face didn't change. He nodded at her and crutched down the steps.

"Guess she's still mad at you," I said as I slammed the trunk.

"She's got a right."

Dottie Mae and Hep had been an item before he enlisted, and when he got back from the Marines, it rekindled and they engaged to be married. It fell apart after the wreck. Not for lack of trying on her part, though. She visited him in the hospital in Knoxville every one of those long eight days while he was unconscious and fighting for his life. And when he finally came around, she stood there and cried for him as the doctors told him his brother's body had been burned to a cinder and by the way, we had to cut off your leg to save your life.

He'd already come home from service quiet and moody, and by all accounts, the wreck seemed to push him over some line. He railed at the doctors, cursed them, told them they should have let him die. He pushed everyone away from him, and especially Dottie Mae, telling her that a useless one-legged moonshiner could never be a proper husband.

She didn't believe him at first. He remained hard and silent until one night he yelled at her—a thing he'd never done before—and called her names that could be heard across the entire ward, names that shouldn't be repeated in *any* company. She'd left and didn't come back.

When the docs discharged him, he came to live with Papaw and Mamaw, who by then had taken on me and J.D.

Six months after Hep forced her away, Dottie Mae married a strapping young man from up the road in Kingsport. Couple of years back her strapping husband died in a mining accident somewhere across the Virginia border, leaving her with three little kids to raise.

"How long she been back?" Hep asked as I turned onto the Newport Highway and headed toward home.

"Three months."

"And you didn't think to mention that to me?"

"Mamaw said not to." I'd take his wrath over her quiet disappointment any day. "Reckon she wanted to spare you."

He snorted and shook his head in irritation.

"You hear anything from Mack?"

"Yep."

After a moment, I said, "You gonna tell me? Or do I need to find it out from J.D. when he listens on you talking to Papaw?"

Hep almost—*almost*—smiled. "Looks like Virgil was asking around in Knoxville who the major suppliers are from Cocke County. He's gone out and talked to a couple of them. Told them things were gonna change. The supply lines were gonna get consolidated and they best be ready."

"Consolidate the supply lines? What's that mean?"

"I'd guess he thinks he's gonna come in here and try to take a piece of the business in these parts." He scratched the stump of his leg. "Or all of it. Run some extortion on us hicks."

"But he's a revenuer."

He turned to me. "What difference that ever make?"

Neither of us said anything for awhile, then Hep said, "Gotta wonder, though, why he didn't stay in Chicago. Mack says Sheriff's looking into it."

* * *

Six miles before our turnoff from the Newport Highway, we came around the curve to find a roadblock. Two cars, one a big black Ford with "Tennessee State Patrol" painted on the side, and the other a big black Dodge with no markings. The Dodge looked a lot like ours except newer and shinier.

A Fed, then.

I hit the brakes and the Dodge slowed, the back end wanting to slew under its load of three hundred pounds of corn. Hep cussed under his breath and said, "Virgil." He looked over and said, "Do what they want unless I say otherwise."

I was already breathing fast. "Okay." I brought the car to a stop twenty feet away from the roadblock. My hands were shaking on the steering wheel.

Two troopers in identical black trooper uniforms and hats approached us. One had a revolver and the other carried a Tommy gun. Both were aimed at us.

We occasionally got stopped by the Sheriff or one of his deputies, but they never searched the car and they never drew their guns. "Oh crap," I whispered.

"Davie. Look at me." I did, and Hep said, "Keep your head about you. Don't do anything stupid."

I glanced at him, and wondered how he could look so calm. But he was, and it helped. "Okay, Hep. I hear you."

He nodded. By then the two troopers had reached the car. Both of them were big, but the man that sauntered behind them was even bigger. No uniform, no hat.

He stopped just off the front fender on Hep's side of the car, and the troopers walked up to the windows.

"Get out of the car," said the one on Hep's side. A toothpick stuck out of the corner of his mouth. They opened the doors.

"Do what they say," Hep said to me. To the trooper, he said, "I got a crutch in the back. Need it to stand up." The trooper scowled, opened the back door, retrieved the crutch and shoved it at Hep.

"Hands up, assholes." They prodded us toward the waiting man. He smiled as we stopped before him.

This, then, was Charlie Virgil. A bear of a man, his shoulders straining the seams of his dusty suitcoat. "Hold the boy," he said. The trooper with the revolver moved behind me and pulled my arms behind my back, trapping my wrists in a painful grip. The other trooper took a couple steps in front of us and pointed the Tommy gun at Hep. Virgil held his own pistol loosely. With the firepower standing next to him, he hadn't bothered to aim or even cock it.

"Well, I declare," drawled the Fed. "Boys, this here's Hep Monroe." He had an odd accent. One of the Carolinas, maybe.

"Virgil." Hep's earlier calm had been for my benefit—he leaned easily on the crutch, but I could see now he was anything but calm. His scar had turned red and seemed to pulse with the flexing of his jaw. And his stare would have melted iron.

Virgil holstered his pistol and sauntered up to Hep. "How you been, Hep? Haven't seen you since your little accident. Hear you and your pa been busy these last six years."

Hep said nothing, but his eyes blazed fire.

Virgil turned to glance at me. "This one can't be yours, he's too damn good-looking. Must be Ephraim's boy."

"Leave him out of it, Virgil," said Hep. His voice was a low growl, barely contained.

"Now, how can I possibly leave him out of it. Especially since you brought him into it. Haven't you figured out that any time you're in the passenger seat, bad things happen?"

The trooper holding me chuckled and I caught a whiff of stale garlic from his breath. The other trooper hadn't moved, except to switch the toothpick to the other side of his mouth. He still had that Tommy gun pointed right at Hep.

Then in a lightning-fast move, Virgil kicked Hep's crutch out from under him. Hep fell to the packed gravel with a grunt and Virgil dropped onto him, his weight knocking the air out of Hep's lungs. Hep twisted and lunged and I suppose if he'd had two legs instead of one, he'd have thrown Virgil off him for all that the Fed outweighed him by eighty pounds. And he almost did it. But almost doesn't count.

At the same time I lunged forward, but the trooper holding me hauled me back by the wrists. The pain of it made me yelp. I felt cold metal against my jaw.

Virgil had Hep pinned underneath him now, his arm twisted up against his back, cheek grinding into the gravel. "I know what you are, Hep," Virgil said. "Or should I say, what you were. You so much as twitch, and Trooper Mays will blow that boy's head clean off."

Garlic-breath—Mays—chuckled, and the one with the Tommy gun and the toothpick stepped forward with a grin.

Hep flicked a glance up toward me, his breaths short and hard. But he didn't move. The Fed shifted so his mouth was closer to Hep's head, and in the process kneed Hep in the ribs.

Virgil seemed to savor the moment before speaking. "He begged for his life, your brother, did you know that?" he said. "He was trapped in the car." Hep tensed, and Virgil punched him hard in the kidney. Hep grunted. "All that heat coming off the engine, all that fuel and white lightning everywhere, and Ephraim trapped and bleeding." He leaned closer. "Good chance the whole thing would blow. Just needed a single spark."

Hep's breaths wheezed through his nose.

"He cussed me at first," said Virgil. "Then when he realized he was trapped and I wasn't gonna help, he begged me. Your brother begged me for his life, Hep. It should have been you driving, it was always you that drove. But you didn't that night, did you?"

Hep closed his eyes. He relaxed under the Fed's weight. I couldn't move, and even the two troopers seemed frozen.

"How come you didn't drive that night, Hep? It should have been you that died screaming in that car, not your brother. Why didn't you drive?"

Hep opened his eyes and they blazed with hatred. "Fuck you, Virgil."

"One spark, Hep," Virgil said. He held his hand out in front of Hep's face, thumb and forefinger pointed at him like a gun. His finger curled. "One spark. That's all it took."

With a wordless snarl, Hep lunged uselessly against the Fed's weight.

Virgil laughed and pushed himself up and off Hep. He brushed the dirt off his jacket as Hep rolled onto his back and got his arms under him. Virgil kicked him in the ribs. I lunged again and Garlic-breath tightened his grip.

Virgil stood over Hep and said, "Times are changing, and you hillbillies need to figure that out. There's gonna be a consolidation in these parts, with me at the top. And you and your pa best play nice."

He leaned forward and waited for Hep to look up at him before he said, "Or what happened that night will look like a birthday party." He turned to the troopers. "Let's go, boys."

The instant Garlic-breath let me go, I ran to Hep and hauled him upright. He gripped my shoulder for balance and support and we both glared as the lawmen returned to their cars and roared off past us back toward Newport.

* * *

I knew better than to say anything. Hep sat stiff and silent for nearly five miles, breathing shallow, not bothering to wipe the blood off his face where the sharp gravel had cut his cheek. I turned up the road toward the ridge and let my hands and eyes do the job of keeping the Dodge in the ruts on the switchbacks. I tried to calm the shaking in my hands.

When Hep finally spoke, it was so soft I almost didn't hear him.

"What?" I said.

"I was drunk."

"Drunk? When?" I hadn't seen Hep take a drink since I was a little kid. Not since before the—oh.

"That night. That's why your pa was driving. 'Cause I was too drunk."

"Hep—"

"Virgil was right—it should have been me that died that night. I failed your pa and he died, because I was fucking *drunk.*"

I opened my mouth, but no words came out. We crested the ridge and I kept the Dodge in low gear as we descended the switchbacks. The road turned along the valley and flattened out and I mashed the gas pedal.

And then Hep surprised me. He shifted to stare straight out the windshield. And when he spoke, I could barely hear him over the rattle of tires against the road.

"I'd only been home couple of months," he said. He frowned as he spoke, as if the words came hard. "I was finding it tough to…to adjust." Hep had been nearly ten years in the Marines, lying about his age to go fight at the end of the Great War, then being sent all over the world afterward. He'd come home when my Uncle Elias got killed in an accident at the sawmill.

"It was different when I came back," he said. "The people, the mountains, they didn't change, but everything was different. Elias dead, and you'd got all big and there was J.D. running around looking just like your mama. It was hard coming back and trying to live a normal life. Hard after what I saw over there…what I did." He stared out the windshield, not seeing the road or the woods that pressed in around us as we passed. "I found out right quick, you go away and you can't come back. But there I was."

Hep had never talked about his time in the Marines. This time I had sense to keep my mouth shut as I kept the wheels of the Dodge in the ruts of the road.

"It ain't no excuse. I was weak and I was stupid, thinking I could find help at the bottom of a Mason jar. Every day I think about what happened. Every single day I think about your Pa and how I failed him. How I failed everyone."

I glanced over and saw—truly saw—my uncle for the first time. Not the grim and bitter man I'd thought I knew, but a man struggling under a tremendous weight of guilt. And in that light, I began to understand his reaction to me wanting to leave to work in the mills.

"I'm sorry about what I said back there. I was mad and it just came out." There was nothing else I could say.

"You had the right of it. And Virgil did too."

"I'm not so sure. Either way, it don't mean I need to be saying it. And Virgil's an ass."

He just grunted and looked out the window.

* * *

Hep had a bruised kidney, and a cracked rib or two from where Virgil had kicked him. It made it all that much harder for him to get around. He slept that night in Papaw's big rocker on the porch. I suspect it was as much him guarding the place as an inability to sleep lying down.

The next morning, Mamaw made a half-hearted effort to force Hep to take it easy for the day. But we had our Saturday run to make that night and work to do.

Since Hep couldn't do it, Papaw sent J.D. around the mountain to the North Fork to check on the two sets of stills—seven in all—hidden away in a holler toward the Douglas farm.

"Take your pa's shotgun," Hep told him. "If someone you don't know sees you out there, shoot 'em in the leg."

J.D. nodded and scampered off to fetch Pa's double-aught Remington.

Mamaw had already set to rough-grinding the corn we brought back. "You keep your eyes open, boy!" she called after him from the porch, not altering her rhythm on the foot-pedal that powered the stone grinder. "And no lollygagging in the woods! Be home by dinner!"

"He'll like as not stay out till supper," said Papaw with a chuckle.

"Like as not," she said with a sigh.

Papaw and me took the mule the half-mile the other direction. We had three stills hidden down there. We'd load up the last of the moonshine, and if we had time, break down and clean the stills to get ready for the next batch.

Before we left, Hep had me pull the Dodge into the yard. He was going to check the engine and tires, get the guns and ammunition we might need for tonight. "Virgil caught me by surprise," he said. "He won't do it again."

* * *

At the site, Papaw's hands were sure as he filled the jugs with 'shine. "This is a good batch," he said.

The site was hidden in a small clearing by the river, which still ran loud with spring runoff. In another month it would be a mere trickle over the rocks. Papaw's old Winchester leaned against a nearby tree and the mule browsed nearby.

"I ain't seen you make a bad one." I worked on the Mason jars, filling them up and screwing the rings tight onto the metal lids. We didn't worry too much about sterilizing them first. Any germ that got in would drown right quick and right happy.

Presently Papaw said, "You still wantin' to go to the mills in Knoxville?"

"I dunno." I'd been thinking about what happened yesterday. What Hep had said.

"Well, you decide to go, I reckon there's not much I'm gonna do to stop you."

I paused with a Mason jar in one hand and the lid in the other. "But…you still don't want me to."

"We need you here, no doubt about that. But I understand a young man's need to see a bit of the world. Can't keep him cooped up on the mountain. I went off, came back. So'd your pa for a little while, went to Kingsport. And Hep, well."

Hep most likely would still be gone if Uncle Elias hadn't died in the sawmill.

"He says I got a duty to J.D."

"You do. Just like Hep had a duty to your pa and Elias. And what happened to them was no more his—" the old man cocked his head, his rheumy eyes focused on nothing.

"What?" I said. I didn't hear anything but birds and river.

"Cars, coming up the mountain. Couple of them."

"Expecting anyone?"

"Nope." He set the jug down and as he corked it, I heard them too. "Fetch the mule, boy." But I was already on my feet.

* * *

Papaw had kicked the mule into a trot and I struggled to keep up with it on the overgrown trails. I was out of breath by the time we got to the cabin. The car engines had shut off, so Papaw had me circle around the back while he rode into the yard from the trail—there was no hiding the mule's clop-clop approach.

As I made my way as quiet as I could around the woodshed—hard because I was still panting—I heard Virgil's voice. "Hello Matthew. It's been a long time. Don't you be touching that rifle of yours, lest I have to shoot you."

"What're you doing here?" Papaw said. I heard him slide off the mule.

"I came to talk. I got a business proposition for you."

"We ain't interested, so you can just turn around and head back down the mountain." The old man's voice was hard.

"I think you ought to listen to what I have to say," Virgil drawled. "Word is you're all but blind, so let me lay out the situation."

I eased up to the outside corner of the woodshed and squatted down to peek around. I could see Papaw standing with one hand on the mule's flank, and the same two troopers from yesterday standing next to their car. Garlic-breath held a shotgun pointed at the porch where I couldn't see. Toothpick held the Tommy gun at the ready.

"I got a pistol against Hep's head, and my boys got great big guns pointed at your wife. So what I want you to do is go join her on the porch and then we're gonna have a nice talk."

I risked poking my head out further and saw that Virgil was standing close behind Hep. He had Hep's arm twisted up behind him and his other hand held his gun against Hep's temple. The crutches lay close to the porch where they must've fallen. Hep's weight was on the ball of his foot, and his knee was slightly flexed. He didn't look so much concerned or angry as watchful and waiting.

Virgil and the troopers were looking over at Papaw, but Hep caught my movement. His eyes narrowed slightly and his gaze flicked to the far side of the cabin. I nodded and pulled back.

"He tellin' the truth, Hep?" said Papaw. "He got a gun to your head?"

"Yep."

Papaw nodded. "You alright, Evvie?"

"Just madder'n a hornet," she replied.

I had retraced my steps and crossed the gap between the woodshed and the cabin. The troopers were still looking toward Virgil and the porch.

"You got no cause with her," said Papaw. "Let her get safe inside, and I'll go set on the porch and you can point your guns at me."

I moved as quiet as I could along the back of the cabin.

"I'll be staying out here, Matthew," Mamaw said.

"You git inside, woman!" snapped Papaw. His voice cracked across the yard like a slap.

"Shit," said Virgil. It came out with three syllables. "Go on inside, then," he said. I heard the door slam and Papaw shuffle across the yard.

By then I'd made it to far side of the cabin and Hep's tiny lean-to what he and Papaw built so J.D. and I could sleep in the cabin's loft. I eased the thin door open and slid into the dim inside. Then I smacked against his chest-of-drawers and fell, landing awkwardly half onto the floor and half onto Hep's narrow cot. Heart thumping, I froze, listening for sounds like Virgil or the troopers had heard me. All I heard was Mamaw's steps across the boards inside.

I breathed again, and eased off the cot. The spread had hardly creased, still tucked tight and square at all four corners.

Under the cot was three cases. I felt past the largest, which contained Hep's long-bore military sniper rifle, and instead reached for the two smaller ones.

Light footsteps from close inside the cabin, and I looked up as I slid out the second case. Mamaw pulled back the inside window's curtain. She nodded as if she'd expected to see me and gave me a ferocious grin. "That Fed's a fool," she whispered. "Shouldn't'a never let me outta his sight." She held up Papaw's shotgun. "You be careful," she said, and disappeared, the curtain falling back into place.

I heard Virgil and Papaw's voices, but couldn't make out what they were saying. I opened the first case and smelled gun oil. This was the Luger that Hep had gotten off a German soldier in the Great War. And it occurred to me that though he'd never said, he must've killed that soldier. I wondered how many other soldiers he'd killed and if their deaths weighed as heavy on him as his brother's.

The other case held Hep's big Smith & Wesson service revolver, also smelling of gun oil and also loaded.

I shoved the Luger into the back of my pants and carried the revolver as I slid out through the door into the back clearing that led to the outhouse.

"—don't have a choice, Matthew," Virgil was saying. "You can play along and we all make money, or I can kill you and everybody here. Tragic hillbilly accident." One of the troopers laughed.

I reached the corner of the cabin and peered around the porch. The mule still stood in the yard, oblivious. Hep and Virgil hadn't moved, but Hep's scar had flushed red. Papaw must be up on the porch where I couldn't see him. Garlic-breath still had his shotgun pointed toward the porch, but he'd let it drop. And Toothpick was alert but not aiming at anything.

Virgil and Hep were closest to me. Which was a good thing, cause I only had one shot to hit Virgil in the head. Then I'd have to turn my attention to Toothpick and his Tommy gun.

"Sounds to me like you make all the money," said Papaw.

I raised the revolver and Hep shifted a tiny bit to his left, opening up Virgil a little bit more.

And then, before Virgil could answer there was a rustle from behind the woodshed.

Everybody turned, and I realized later that if I had been prepared, I could have taken the opportunity to shoot Virgil right then and probably both troopers too. But I didn't.

And, to my surprise and dismay, J.D. stepped from around the woodshed. He held Pa's shotgun braced against his bare shoulder, and it was almost as long as he was tall. He had it aimed square at Toothpick, who gave a slow, dismissive grin. But what I knew, and Virgil and those troopers didn't, was that J.D. knew how to use that gun, just like I knew how to use the revolver and the Luger. Papaw and Hep had made sure we could hit a target with every gun in the house, except for Hep's sniper rifle, which he wouldn't let us even touch.

J.D. didn't say a word, just glanced around. Toothpick raised the Tommy gun and pointed it at J.D. Garlic-Breath still had Papaw covered on the porch.

"Boy, you put that shotgun down before you hurt someone," said Virgil. J.D. didn't so much as flinch. "Do it, boy, or I'll be putting a bullet in your uncle here."

"Reckon you'll shoot him anyways," J.D. said. "Kill him like you done Pa." The shotgun didn't waver.

Virgil scowled. "Fine. Go on, then, shoot him," he said. Toothpick flicked a startled glance at Virgil, who ignored him and continued, "Then the other one shoots you. And I shoot your uncle then your grandpa." J.D. hesitated, then started to swing the gun toward Virgil and Hep. Hep shook his head and J.D. swung the gun back. At any second I expected Toothpick to open fire.

I stepped out from the side of the cabin, raising the big revolver and pointed it at Toothpick's chest. If he flinched, I'd take him down.

"Shit!" said Garlic-breath. He whipped his shotgun around to me.

"Sonofabitch!" snarled Toothpick. But he didn't move that Tommy gun off J.D.

"You twitch and I'll shoot," I told him.

Virgil laughed. "Looks like we got a standoff, then, boys." He called to the porch, "Matthew, looks like your boys are all set to die in a gun battle today."

I glanced from Toothpick to J.D. They stood less than ten feet apart. That Tommy gun would cut my brother in half. J.D.'s eyes were wide but he still held Pa's shotgun steady. Hep's revolver was heavy in my hands. I swallowed.

"J.D., Davie, put 'em down," said Hep. "Virgil, call off your dogs. Nobody's gotta die today."

J.D. frowned and shifted his weight. The shotgun lowered an inch, then another. "Davie, you too," said Hep. "Virgil. Tell your boys to—"

"Davie! Hey *Davie!*" Jacksie Douglas stepped from behind the rhododendron at the far side of the woodshed.

And a lot of things happened at once.

Toothpick whirled and opened fire on Jacksie. The roar of the Tommy gun was louder than anything I'd heard. I had a split-second to register the shock on Jacksie's face as his knees crumpled.

Then I shot Toothpick, squeezing the trigger three times without pausing. Toothpick went down, still shooting, then the sound cut off and he lay still.

I heard the blast of a shotgun, and looked down, half-expecting to be hit. Another blast and I swung the revolver toward Garlic-breath. But he had crashed backward against his car, leaving a blood smear across the lettering on the door. He still held his shotgun, so I fired at him, once, then twice more until he dropped it. The hammer clicked on an empty chamber and I dropped the revolver.

No more gunshots. Now I heard Papaw yelling, Virgil cussing. He and Hep fought for Virgil's pistol. Across the yard, J.D. had dropped Pa's shotgun and stood staring at Jacksie. "J.D.! Get down!" I sprinted across the yard and as I passed Hep and Virgil, they hit the ground and—

And I was on my back, looking at the trees and sky, the report of Virgil's gun echoing against the side of the mountain.

I rolled over and Virgil was on top of Hep. A second shot, a third, muffled, and they both lay still.

"Hep!" I tried to get up but there was a pain in my leg. I did it anyway and Virgil moved. "Hep!"

Papaw hollered, "Davie! What's happened!" and Mamaw's "Oh, Lordy!" I spared a glance toward the porch and saw the blown out screen door. Mamaw still held the smoking shotgun as she helped Papaw to his feet.

Virgil rolled off Hep and I fumbled for the Luger. But his eyes were wide and unseeing, his chest covered in blood, and Hep coughed and cussed and pushed himself to his elbows.

"Hep—" I said. His face and chest were also covered with blood.

He looked down. "His, mostly," he said. "That's twice in two days," he said to Virgil. "You're a heavy sonofabitch." He gave the dead revenuer a chilly smile. "Dead sonofabitch now."

Then we heard sirens, getting closer. Turning off the Newport Highway.

"Lordy, now what?" said Mamaw.

* * *

Deputy John MacAllister leaned on the porch rail and shook his head as he surveyed the massacre in our yard. "Lord have mercy," he said, for about the fifth time.

Hep had pulled me onto the cinderblock porch step, looked at the wound in my calf, bandaged it up, and declared the bullet had gone through and that I'd keep the leg. Then he'd handed me the Smith & Wesson and a cleaning rag. J.D. sat on the rail above me. He'd spat on Virgil as he walked by.

Mack had told us that the Sheriff telephoned Chicago to find out what Virgil was doing here. "Come to find out, he got himself fired," he'd said. "Got a warrant on him for extortion and graft and all sorts of other such activity."

The Sheriff was in Newport getting the judge to swear out a warrant on Mays and Harris. He'd heard Virgil and the troopers planned on coming our way, and sent Mack up the mountain ahead of him to avert what he figured would be a bloodbath.

Now Mack pushed his hat up. "Sheriff was right, but it looks like I got here a little late."

"A little," said Papaw. He and Mamaw sat in their rockers. Each was cleaning a shotgun.

"I suppose Virgil thought he'd try the same thing, that nobody down here would know he wasn't a Fed no more," said Mack. "He made a mistake messing with you all. Sheriff will say for sure, but I bet ya'll won't have to worry about no charges."

"What about Jacksie?" said J.D. in a small voice. Hep had covered Jacksie's body with one of Mamaw's quilts.

"Don't worry, we'll get him to his Pa," said Mack.

"He just wanted some pie," said J.D. "We got here and I saw the guns and I told him to go home and he wouldn't, so I told him to stay back and don't say nothing. And he said okay. But he didn't."

"No, he didn't listen to you," I said. "You told him right and it's not your fault what happened to him, J.D."

"He's right, J.D., it ain't your fault," said Mack.

"Yeah, I know, but, I shoulda protected him…"

Some part of me thought I should have protected Jacksie too. But I don't know how I could have. And I came damn close to losing J.D., and the thought of that made me ill inside.

I glanced behind me at Hep, who sat on the bench, the Luger broken into pieces beside him even though it hadn't been fired. Now I had some small taste of what he felt every single day.

He met my eye and I could tell he knew exactly what I was thinking. Then he surprised me and gave me a little smile, one like I hadn't seen since before the wreck, and he looked like a weight was lifted off him. And maybe with the death of Charlie Virgil, it was.

I'm staying here, I mouthed at him. He inclined his head and returned his attention to the Luger. I turned back to the revolver in my lap and the six of us waited for the Sheriff.

Michele Lang is one of my favorite writers, and I'm so happy that we can finally include one of her short stories in Fiction River. *When Michele writes historical fiction, it's usually in the form of historical fantasy like her Lady Lazarus series from Tor Books. But she also writes crime, science fiction, and romance. Her next novel, the latest in the Ms. Pendragon series, is urban fantasy.*

She sticks with straight crime here. She writes,

"I survived the 1970s in New York. The New York City I knew growing up did seem to be turning diabolical, and I wanted to tell the story of how a girl and her friends stood together at the edge of that particular abyss."

Deathmobile

Michele Lang

The first time I ever saw the business end of a switchblade, I was eleven years old and standing in the shadow of the giant rocketship-shaped monkey bars at the Woodcrest Community Park. It was smack in the middle of July, smack in the middle of a Wednesday. Jonesie, that crapulous creep, flicked the knife open, right in front of all the little kids and the grandmas heading for the big cement pool, just because I told him he was an asshole for pushing Fat Donna down the stairs.

Jonesie was crazy. The world was crazy.

The summer of 1977, the world seemed like it was going completely out of control, losing its moorings, coming unglued. In those days, I was in the habit of imagining the people in my world as cars. It helped me to see the world as a little less crazy, somehow.

Jonesie was a Ford Pinto. A shoddy piece of crap that spontaneously combusted upon the slightest contact.

Sweat slicked Jonesie's pudgy face, and he smiled behind the glinting silver of his blade.

"You like this, chickie?" he said, under his breath. "You like it, Rocky?"

I wasn't scared, not exactly. My bare toes gripped the volcanic hot sand under my feet and I took shallow little sips of air. I had no witty response to make to that knife…it reflected the baking sun and half blinded me.

I heard more than saw Tony Tiepolo come down from the spaceship and jump down to the cement base, then walk to where I stood, staring at the knife. Now Tony was a Lincoln Continental. Classy, fast, with suicide doors. I was too young to love a boy, but I loved Tony anyhow.

Tony took in the sight of the flicked open switchblade without comment. Instead, he pointed past us with his chin.

"The narc," was all Tony said, but that was enough to bring Jonesie to his senses. He snarled something under his breath and the switchblade folded back up like a silver demon and went into some pocket of Jonesie's cutoffs.

But my brain couldn't let go of the image of the knife, brandished a couple of inches from the tip of my sweaty nose. I saw it in negative, superimposed over the gleaming painted metal of the spaceship monkey bars, stretching four stories high into the jewel blue sky.

The narc was the guy in the black tracksuit that had been following us kids around all summer, until this moment at the height of the July scorch. It was the summer of 1977, and the city of New York was getting ready to explode. Gerald Ford had told NYC to drop dead a few years back, and we were doing our best to oblige.

But we weren't dead yet. We'd just survived the great blackout of 1977 and the looting. And at least Tony and I had so far survived the hunting of the crazed killer, Son of Sam, as he evaded capture and killed girls and lovers all through the five boroughs and beyond.

We lived in the suburbs, on Long Island, in meticulously manicured neighborhoods, divided and measured and carefully tended. But even then I knew the distance and safety was only an illusion.

New York paid for everything in my world, no matter that we lived about fifteen miles away. I lived in a postmodern mansion that looked like something out of a disco nightmare. All white stucco, with white staircases stretching up into nothingness. I lived in a neighborhood full of white stucco mansions, filled with families where the dad worked in "construction" or was away "on business" upstate and would be back in three to five.

The money flowed through the city until it reached the suburbs. My dad worked in the city. But my dad was no druglord or gangster like my neighbors.

My dad was a cop.

My dad was a cop, but I knew enough and had the instincts to be wary of a narc. Wary enough to think maybe he wasn't a narc, but something even worse. Somebody working on a hit, or maybe even Son of Sam himself, expanding his operations into the suburbs.

"Here he comes," Tony said under his breath.

Jonesie scuttled away, but me and Tony held our ground.

This guy, with his black tracksuit and reflecting sunglasses, looked like a Mercedes with tinted windows. What my Jewish friend Anna called a Deathmobile. This guy was a Deathmobile.

We watched him walk across the playground until he stood right in front of us.

"You Edith Malley?" he said in a low voice, a toothpick sticking out of the corner of his mouth.

Nobody called me Edith, nobody who mattered. My father called me Little Rocky, and he was Big Rocky, so for all intents and purposes I considered Rocky to be my name.

"Who wants to know?" I said, fake tough but knowing I was too little to pull off the fake.

"I want to talk to you about your dad," he said. He took another step toward me and Tony took a step toward him.

"Get outta here," Tony said, somehow sounding respectful in his tone despite his words. "She's a little girl, and you're some stranger hanging out around a playground."

The Deathmobile guy looked around, like he was seeing his surroundings for the first time. Sweat slicked down my back, and I could feel the sun blisters forming on my freckled Irish skin, on the bridge of my nose and across the tops of my shoulders.

I squinted and just looked at the guy. He looked down on me, his hands jammed into the pockets of his shiny black track pants. "I want you to tell your dad something. He's a target, okay, but I can make that go away. Tell him it's his decision. Okay?"

It was definitely not okay. *Target*…I'd heard my mother hissing the word on the phone when my dad was at work. Saw the piles of ripped open envelopes from some lawyer in the city, heaped up next to the other bills. Payment due.

For the last three months or so, before the appearance of the man in the tracksuit, Target was like some secret incantation of doom in my life. And now this stranger was saying it out loud, in front of my best friend, on a frickin' playground.

I just stared at him, stared Mr. Deathmobile down while he waited for me to say something. I didn't start shaking until after the man in the black tracksuit gave up on me, turned on his heels and walked away.

"What an asshole," Tony said.

I licked my lips and tasted salt. I was shaking too hard to reply.

* * *

Within 24 hours after that, Jonesie was dead.

It was a Thursday morning, just as blazing hot as the day before, with a humid edge to it that portended a thunderstorm later. My dad was out of Scotch.

So he gave me a twenty and instructed me to get a fifth of the good stuff from the liquor store at Four Corners.

I hopped on my bike with the banana seat and the pink and white plastic streamers coming out of the handlegrips, and I was more than happy to help out. A cold can of Tab was always my reward, and though it was before noon, it was hot enough out for me to crave some shade and that sweet saccharine chemical lemon goodness.

I zoomed along Woodcrest Road, a noble knight on her mighty steed, and reveled in the solitude. As an only child you'd think I would be looking for more human connection. But my mom spent her days chain-smoking on the sofa, looking out at nothing through the giant plate glass window of our living room, her eyes bloodshot. I sneaked around her like a mouse, but honestly I probably could have screamed and jumped on the white modular couch in the sunken section of the living room and she wouldn't have registered the fact of my existence.

And my dad was off working an awful lot, and when he had a day off for no reason in the middle of the week like he did now, he ran out of Scotch a lot.

Getting out of the house was a pure pleasure.

So I zoomed along on my bike, the hot breeze evaporating the sweat off my forehead. Woodcrest Road, once you got past the development with the space-pod white mansions, was rural-looking until you got into the town at Four Corners. So I could pretend I was a character on that TV show *The Waltons* or a friend of Laura

Ingalls and that I was more likely to meet up with an Indian or a grizzly bear than some housewife decked out in gold lamé, heading to the market for some Saucy Susan for a cookout.

As I coasted down the hill, thinking these profound thoughts, I saw a flash of orange in the ditch. And without thinking I slammed on my brakes, so hard I almost flew over the handlebars. I knew by instinct what I saw even before my mind could convert the crazy quilt of clashing colors into a coherent image.

I flipped down the kickstand, stood the bike near a spruce tree. Then I peered into the deep shadows down in the ditch, absent-mindedly worried about poison ivy.

And then I said to hell with poison ivy, and I walked down, over brambles and thorn bushes, to what waited for me at the bottom.

Yeah, Jonesie. The switchblade he'd waved in my face was now jammed in under his ribs. He was wearing a hideous canary yellow tee shirt, so the blood over his chest looked more orange in the dappled shade than red.

I heard a squawking, squeaking sound and only belatedly realized it was me. I scrambled back out of the ditch, scratching the crap out of my bare legs in the process, and sat on the hot-as-hell asphalt, trying to get my breath and not succeeding.

He was so obviously dead it didn't make any sense to try to save him down there. His eyes were open, and the blood looked old. I didn't let myself see any more, or smell anything, or deduce anything.

HE'S DEAD! HE'S DEAD! That's all I heard in my head, a klaxon horn blasting in my brain. I climbed on my bike and started pedaling like a mad thing, heading absurdly for the liquor store instead of home. I almost wiped out taking the corner into town but by then I had used the bulk of the adrenaline out on the pedals.

Ran into the liquor store, told Marty behind the counter what I saw.

He never blinked, didn't even raise his voice. Just picked up the phone. Called my dad first, and then he called the cops.

*　*　*

By the time I got home, it was almost sunset. We rode up in a wood-paneled Country Squire station wagon, the passenger window cranked all the way down. Tony was waiting for me on the front doorstep when I got there.

"Hi." I waved from the passenger seat, utterly exhausted.

My dad got out of the car, wordlessly nodded at Tony, and unlocked the door and went into the house. Who knows where my mother was…probably still chain-smoking on the couch.

"You think it was Son of Sam?" Tony asked. How he knew what had happened, I had no idea.

"Maybe," I said.

"Let's go sit by the pool," Tony said.

Too tired to protest, I followed him around the back of my house to where the pool stretched, mirror smooth, uninhabited. I collapsed on the redwood lounge chair next to the cabana. No words I had in mind to say.

"Jonesie was a jerk, but he didn't deserve to die," I blurted out, surprising myself.

Tony shrugged. "That's never the question, if somebody deserves to die or not," he said. "The question, is why?"

I stared at the water. My eyes felt puffy, too tight somehow. My nose hurt from sunburn, the scratches all over my bare legs itched like hell.

"I don't know," I said finally.

"My ma says she thinks that Son of Sam is a bunch of people, not just one guy."

I forced myself to look at Tony, even though I would rather die than cry in front of him. And I was afraid that if I looked at him, looked into his warm brown eyes, I would cry.

But I looked anyway. Because I had something extremely important I had to say to him, right now. Before he said anything else. "Forget Son of Sam, okay? Your dad has an alibi, Tony. Mine doesn't."

His face got red, like I'd slapped him hard.

"Rocky…"

"The cops thought *he* did it. Not Son of Sam."

Tony looked around, like he thought the Deathmobile guy was hiding in the bushes or something. "Forget it. Don't get involved."

I knew exactly what he was talking about. It was the code we all lived by…my mother chain-smoking by herself, Tony not even asking why his dad had been gone for over a year. Don't ask questions. Don't see the obvious.

Which is exactly what I'd done when I saw Jonesie in the ditch. I didn't want to see what I was seeing, so my brain scrambled it up for me, and I saw random patterns and not a kid stabbed to death on Crestwood Road in broad daylight.

I didn't want to fight with Tony any more than I wanted to cry in front of him. So instead I took a deep shuddering breath and inhaled the chlorine smell emanating from the water. I watched the sunset reflected in the surface of the kidney-shaped swimming pool, and I zipped it.

But even at eleven years old, I was lousy at forgetting.

* * *

I slept terrible, all churned up by terror and remorse.

The first thing I did the next morning was call Tony up on the phone.

Meet me at the cornfield at noon. I'll make it worth your while. Okay.

I'd make it up to him, my mean words. Somehow. Though I wasn't sure how.

* * *

The cornfields stretched for miles behind the development we lived in. An artifact of the Long Island of farms and wilderness that had existed before my kind invaded from the city like a cloud of locusts.

Crows and hawks hung suspended over rippling cornfields, the flat leaves shivering and trembling in the endless summer breeze. Wandering through the fields, I startled pheasants, wild turkey, foxes. The sun beat mercilessly down, and in all the times before I'd gone there to escape my daily life, I never saw another person there I hadn't brought along with me or arranged to meet there.

It was a great place for a serial killer to strike.

I got to our meeting place five minutes early. I knew Tony would be more or less on time, but I wanted a couple of minutes alone to think. It's like I had to digest the fact of Jonesie's demise before I could even pretend to forget it. And I wanted Tony to know at least I tried.

Mr. Deathmobile stood in my secret spot, and I just couldn't believe it. I rubbed my eyes as if I could knuckle the sight of him away, but no.

"I been waiting," he said, like I was late and he was pissed.

"Sorry," I said automatically, used to getting away with an apology. Not this time.

RUN AWAY RUN AWAY RUN AWAY the klaxon horn screamed in my head again. But like in a nightmare, this time my feet grew roots and I was stuck to the ground.

Cicadas droned over the field, so loud I couldn't hear myself think a sane thought. My heart pounded so hard I swayed. But I couldn't move.

The man smiled. Took off his sunglasses and perched them on his head.

"FBI," said a voice behind me.

I turned around.

It was Tony's dad, Victor Tiepolo, and in that moment he looked like a golden Rolls Royce. He'd been gone for a year or more, but I recognized him instantly.

When I turned back around, Mr. Deathmobile had a gun in his hands, pointed right at me. It was like a black hole that sucked the whole universe into a silver circle, staring at me.

"That's a .44 Bulldog. What Son of Sam uses," Tony's dad said. Now his voice sounded very far away, like he was speaking out of the spirit of 1776. The voice of authority.

"Jimmy Breslin swears up and down that he is working alone," Mr. Deathmobile said. "He doesn't know shit."

"Are you…Son of Sam?" I managed to wheeze out.

"Shh," Tony's dad said.

I couldn't take my eyes off the gun, but I kind of glanced side-wise back at him.

Wish I didn't. Tony's dad was covered in sweat, and he was green, he was so pale. So much for keeping a poker face. He was terrified. For me.

"You couldn't be Son of Sam," I went on, thinking out loud. "You woulda shot by now if you were. He's a hit-and-run kind of guy."

"You should be a cop, kid," the guy in the black tracksuit said. His mirrored sunglasses fell off the top of his bald head where he had perched them, but he never took his eyes off me, and the gun never wavered.

"My dad is a cop." I said it proudly but also as a warning.

"Your dad is a crooked cop."

For a minute I wasn't sure if Tony's dad was speaking or the Deathmobile guy. I didn't care.

"Take it back," I said to both of them.

Out of the corner of my eye, I saw Tony walk up, dead on time like always. He froze.

"Dad," he said, his voice cracking.

It was a crazy standoff like in a John Wayne movie.

"You want my dad to go down for Jonesie," I said, my brain almost bleeding trying to work some rationality out of this bizarre madness. "You knew people saw Jonesie try to scare me with the knife. In the playground."

"Shut up, Rocky," Tony's dad growled.

Deathmobile smiled harder, and he looked like a skull with dead, sunken eyes. "Go on with your theory, what you know. Or I'll shoot."

A deathly calm settled over me. I spoke to the silver circle that had swallowed up the world.

"I don't know nothing. It's just, Tony told me to ask why? You're setting my dad up to take the fall as a kid-killer. But why do you want my dad to go down? You said he's a crooked cop. Maybe he is, but he isn't a kid-killer like you."

I stared at the gun, the barrel stared back at me. My heart still galloped and boogied like a wild thing in my chest trying to leap out.

I thought hard. "You want to shut my dad up. Maybe he's a crooked cop who knows too much and is willing to talk. Or, hey, maybe he's just playing a crooked cop on TV."

"Put down the gun," Tony's dad said.

BLAM

A shot rang out and I thought I was dead dead dead.

And Mr. Deathmobile slow motion pitched forward into the dirt at my feet.

I watched the blood pooling out from under him into the rich farm earth. My ears buzzed like huge swarms of killer bees were attacking my brain.

"Whoa, easy," Tony said, and he grabbed my elbow before I blacked out altogether.

My dad stood behind the mysterious dead stranger, his own weapon smoking in his hand.

Tony's dad walked into my line of sight, and I was so amazed at the whole scenario, Tony's dad appearing out of nowhere, my own dad saving the day, that I forgot to barf on my flip flops. Forgot to look for bullet holes on my own body.

"Dad?" I said, stupid and scared and totally brain-scrambled at this point.

"You got good instincts, Rocky," my dad said.

"There's two kinds of cops," Tony's dad said. "The honest ones that stay bought, and the rats that sell anybody out to save their own skin. Thanks, Malley. You got me out early from upstate, and I know why. I got a tip from the Boss that this scumbag was coming after your little girl, and I wanted to return the favor."

"Are you in the FBI?" I asked Tony's dad. That's what he'd said to the dead guy in the black tracksuit.

"Nah, that scumbag was in the FBI," he replied. "Shooting was too good for that two-timing little fucker, pardon my French."

Tony's dad turned to face Tony. "I gotta go…west for business. Tony, you the man of the house now. If anybody comes looking for me, you didn't see nothing. I wasn't here, you got that?"

Tony didn't answer. His face was gray like a stone.

"I'll look out for your boy," my dad said. "One good turn deserves another. You get out of here. I'll deal with the cops."

And like a racehorse at Belmont Park Tony's dad shot out of the field and out of Tony's life forever. I watched him run, and before I knew it I was crying, I didn't know why.

I looked at Tony again. But he wouldn't look at me.

* * *

Less than a month later, Son of Sam was under police custody. The first victims had been stabbed with a hunting knife, right under the ribs, and a long time later, Son of Sam claimed he was part of a satanic cult that needed "blood for Papa."

But that summer, it was his four-door yellow 1970 Ford Galaxie that gave the game away. They found a rifle in the back seat, maps of the neighborhoods where he had struck before, and a threatening letter to the chief police investigator of the Omega Task Force charged with capturing him.

What the papers didn't mention was that he also had maps of Woodcrest, Long Island, in the back seat, along with another note, addressed personally to my dad, Officer Patrick Malley. My dad told me so.

To this day, I don't know the true identity of Mr. Deathmobile. My dad didn't want me to know, and right quick I'd learned Tony's wisdom was sound and led to a long life and happiness in my morally swampy part of the world.

I'll give you my best guess now, though, since my dad is no longer alive, and neither is my beloved Tony Tiepolo—he was fast and classy, but the suicide doors got my Tony in the end.

The guy in the black tracksuit *was* FBI, and my father was getting too close to him and his associates. Deathmobile's associates were enemies of my father's associates, who happened to live in the same neighborhood, who happened to need a

Rolls-Royce bagman let out early from upstate for whatever shadowy reason.

The cops fought a proxy war for their masters, and because my dad's friends controlled the tap on Tony's phone, he and Tony's dad both got the tip I was meeting Tony alone at the cornfield. They were both nervous about Jonesie getting shanked, and didn't want us to end up next.

So the hitman and the crooked cop saved my life, and Tony's life. Their children, the inheritors of this crazy, mixed-up world.

And for all I know, the end of Mr. Deathmobile saved my father's life from the murderous rampage of Son of Sam himself. The map to our house in the back seat of his yellow Galaxie surely gives me pause.

But I'm not quite sure. Like many incidents in my puzzling childhood, the pieces just didn't fit together, didn't quite make sense.

Maybe my dad just made it all up. Or maybe the cops planted the map, to send my dad some other kind of cryptic message. Maybe Son of Sam himself was yet another proxy in another twisted story of corruption and sickness, the Rotten Apple of 1977.

But I don't think so. It's like I said…the world itself was coming unglued, dismantled, some pervasive evil had overtaken my little corner of a big and deadly city. David Berkowitz was a 1970 Ford Galaxie, bright yellow and dented, driving the wrong direction near Bath Beach, ticketed and discovered on a technicality. And as he himself insisted, the world was full of Sam's sons, full of Deathmobiles. They didn't have to know each other to be related.

In such a world, a funhouse mirror world, the smartest way to live was to laugh a little too loud, ride your bike really fast to get the feel of freedom under you, and amnesia the holes in the world after you got forced to look at them. Remember, but not remember. Not an easy trick to learn.

My dad was a police cruiser, hugely powerful and painted over to look like something else. He was forever leaping away from me, into the dark.

Me, I was a little Volkswagen. Also yellow, absurd, yet I was brave and quick and on the side of the lovers and the dreamers walking the city alone at night. Outrunning the bigger, more powerful Deathmobiles of the world.

And even though the world was out of gas, I somehow kept driving anyway.

JC Andrijeski first appeared in our pages in our sixth volume, Moonscapes, *edited by Dean Wesley Smith. But then she returned two more times—in our seventh volume, as well as in the special edition,* Crime. *Each story has a different setting and a different style.*

Which seems to be an Andrijeski trademark. She's currently writing a new adult series called Allie's War *that's romantic alternative history, a dystopian series called* The Slave Girl Chronicles, *and the* Gateshifter *series about shape-shifting aliens and a tough-girl PI from Seattle. In addition, she writes nonfiction for such places as* NY Press *and holistic health magazines.*

When I envisioned Past Crime, *I hoped I'd receive a story like "The Stonewall Rat." I was so thrilled when I saw the title and the author, because I knew the story would have such power.*

JC writes, "I've always had a fascination with New York, maybe because I lived there for a number of years, and civil rights are a passion of mine. Given that I hadn't seen any crime fiction centered around the riots at the Stonewall (or even much set in the gay scene at all, truthfully), I wanted to see if I could combine the two things and capture something of that moment in history."

She has, quite effectively.

The Stonewall Rat

JC Andrijeski

I waited at Stonewall's bar for an hour before the kid showed up.

Even after he got there—walking with that teenaged swagger of his, smoking a hand-rolled cigarette probably more than half-filled with shake-weed, slim-hipped in tight jeans and a skin-tight, black t-shirt that made him look like more of a boho throwback than a full-blown hippie creature of the night—I just watched him for awhile, fascinated, in spite of myself.

No question the kid was an eye magnet.

Textbook jailbait, really…or, (possible but unlikely), well-crafted to look that way. I knew that last was just wishful thinking on my part, though.

Still, the kid wasn't a rube.

He knew the effect his presence had, no question. So as much as he did the cherry thing, even feigning the school boy, not-sure-what-I-am schtick, I knew his type well enough to see past it, even though he was good.

Really damned good…spooky good, given he didn't look older than fifteen.

Then again, he'd probably been fawned on by this scene ever since he first showed up in the Village, likely wearing clothes a lot more ratty than the ones he wore now, if he was anything like most of the street kids in this neighborhood. Maybe before that, in Hometown USA, whichever corner of nowhere he came from…wherever most of the queers and street kids in the rest of the bars in Greenwich came from…he'd had his share of chicken-hawk admirers there, too. Maybe that's how he ended up here. A few too many people I knew had been thrown out of their homes and disowned by their parents, fingered in one fashion or another by the good and plain Christian folk of…Whereversville.

None of the kids in this part of town had happy stories to tell, though.

Despite a lot of lobbying by the Mattachine Society, (and, well, those of us in the community with a damned conscience, which was the vast majority of us, thankfully), and a lot of attempts to drive the butchers out of our bars, that kind of pedophile crap still happened a lot in this part of town. Down there, there wasn't a lot that could be done, since our whole damned existence was illegal, and anyway, most of those kids had no place to go, and no money to live on beside what they earned the hard way. Most straights thought we were all like that, anyway, so who could we even call to complain?

I really hoped the kid was older than he looked.

I also hoped he wasn't seriously stupid enough to be ratting out the Mafia's blackmail scheme to the cops.

I watched him in a kind of unwilling awe as he worked the room, doing it with a skill that made me shake my head in spite of myself, smiling at just how smooth the little bastard was. The longer I watched him, the more I doubted my initial impression, too.

Maybe he was closer to eighteen. One could only hope.

He'd clearly been doing his schtick long enough that the regulars all seemed to know him. He also didn't bother to steal outright; most of his marks handed over their bread willingly, so he charmed and seduced instead, lifting bills out of wallets with a practiced ease, all the while making them laugh, making them feel like they'd gotten their money's worth.

He was a hustler, and obviously had been for awhile.

He'd obviously conned someone into letting him in here, too. I hadn't yet seen him without a drink in his hand, an eager flame to light his cigarettes, or a few suits hanging around, hoping to spend even more on him, I guessed. The latter type seemed to be his primary meal of choice…Wall Street banker types who came for the anonymity, and because they preferred trolling where the cops would turn a blind eye. Kid probably had a fake ID, too.

The Stonewall itself was a shit hole, of course.

I sat at the main bar on the furthest end from the door, where I could turn my head and see the primary dance floor crammed with sweaty, twenty-something bodies, or turn it again and see the east window by the entrance, where the kid and his admirers had more or less parked themselves at a table, at least when he didn't drag one of them out to the rickety dance floor.

If I turned around in my chair altogether, or used the worn-through mirror on the back of the bar, I could also glimpse some of the action through the doorway into the secondary dance floor, which the more flamboyant queens more or less staked out as their own, particularly in terms of the jukebox.

The Stonewall was owned by the Mob, like everything in this part of town.

Dirty, watered-down drinks, glasses that maybe got a pass through dingy, soapy water before they got reused. Roaches (both kinds) and butts scattered all over an uneven, water-warped floor already sticky from beer and vomit and whatever else. So much smoke it was hard to breathe by about midnight, between that and the smell of unwashed bodies and stale booze that permeated the cracked wood furniture and walls. The music was deafening, the speakers crap, but everyone was having a good time most nights, and most of what you heard was laughter.

I looked around the dank insides of the bar for about an hour before the kid got there, squinting through the dim light, which wasn't more than a step or two above no light at all. Only pulsing gel lights and black lights broke the darkness, and it took some getting used to, even for me, to be able to see through that seizure-inducing flashing well enough to identify faces.

Between that, and the jukebox blaring a slightly warped-sounding version of "Over the Rainbow" by dearest Judy, who'd passed just a few days before, and the laughing and the shuffling feet and the up-and-down cadence of conversation and the occasional cackle of a tranny through the doorway into the next room, where I could see the shimmer of sequins and teased hair and red-lipsticked mouths…it was hard to concentrate.

Before the kid showed up, my roaming eyes were often taken the wrong way by other patrons. I'd already shaken off more than a few offers to dance and refused a few watered-down drinks bought with soggy tickets. To discourage more of the same, I pulled out the warm soda can I'd bought with me and popped it open on the bar, using my dented church key.

I earned a frown from the bartender for that, but I pretended not to notice.

It didn't stop the offers coming, but at least it gave me an excuse. Not being a regular, I was fresh meat in here, and while a few of those offers were tempting, I couldn't go there, not while I was on the job.

I needed to find out if the kid was our rat before the next raid.

Stonewall might not be my usual hangout, but I'd been in there before, sure. Pretty hard to avoid the place entirely, if you were someone like me, so yeah, I'd been there…but no one knew me there, really, and I usually had to pay extra to get in because I look like a double-life man, too, if in a different way than these Wall Street hawks.

I've never married, though.

Truthfully, I pretty much knew what I was from day one, and the rumpled suit and clean-cut look is as much cover as I could afford back then, and as much as I needed. When you grow up with nothing, you got a lot less motive to give in to that kind of headache, anyway. That was for the bozos with something to lose, which wasn't me. In some ways…a lot of ways, maybe…I'm grateful. Even a willing beard was an extra mouth to feed, and I could barely keep my cat in milk and mice, much less a whole other person.

I'd worked jobs at the Stonewall before.

My partner, Robbie—meaning my work partner, not any kind of in the life, double-speak type of deal, and who's an uptight, crotchety bastard if there ever was one, despite being two years my junior at the ripe old age of twenty-nine—sent me on this job. Which isn't to say he was like me (he wasn't), or that we were open about that kind of thing (we weren't).

We had, what you might call, an understanding.

Robbie hardly ever spoke to me about anything personal, and he sure as hell never mentioned my "affliction," but he knew. They all fucking knew, even though I hadn't been beaten up for that fact for a goodly number of years, not in my own neighborhood, at least. The cops we sometimes paid off and sometimes shared info with knew. The neighborhood wise guys knew. My sister Mary, my little brother Frank…my father, who I rarely saw sober for more than a minute at a time anyway…they all knew.

We all pretended. It was easier that way, and really, pretending was about as tolerant as people got.

Still, when this job came up, or any job like it, Robbie sent me.

Watching the kid who'd been fingered as the possible rat, I smiled a little, shaking my head as I saw him give a shy grin to one of the older bankers he'd finally settled at a table with, in that same far corner by the window. I figured he was sizing the guy up as his next Santa Claus, and while I got it, sure, it still turned my stomach a little.

Charlie Dickens…that's what the kid called himself.

It had to be a fake name, of course.

Kind of a funny one, too, and more clever than most of those I'd heard from hustlers working the corner of Christopher and Greenwich.

He saw me staring at him that time, though, and our eyes caught.

He looked away a few seconds later, but when I watched him make excuses and wind his way through the crowd, drink ticket in hand, I knew, somehow, that he'd be coming my way.

I wasn't sure how I felt about that, either.

I wondered if I'd stupidly tipped him off as to why I was there, staring like a dumb ass, then realized that half the queens in the room were probably staring at Charlie off and on, and I'd seem no different from them.

Still, I figured I'd have to make the approach if I wanted to talk to him, and I still hadn't decided if that was a good idea or not… or if I'd be better off just watching him until I had a better idea of what he was up to.

…so when he slid up next to me, pressing the length of that young body against my side and thigh, I nearly jumped out of my skin.

I might have even made a sound.

Moving back in reflex, I managed to control my expression before I looked up, quirking an eyebrow in his direction.

To cover up my shock, I took a drink of the soda I'd brought with me, and then a drag of my cigarette, too, probably looking a bit weird in the process. I was on the high end of the age register for this club, but no Santa Claus, and I saw Charlie look me up and down to determine the same for himself. He summed me up and probably knew the balance of my bank account in less than a few heartbeats, and while I couldn't help but be appalled, I also couldn't help but see his obvious disappointment at what he saw.

"How old are you, kid?" I asked him, more to see what he'd say.

"I'm legal," he said, giving me that dazzling smile of his.

I couldn't see their color well in here, but I knew his eyes were blue, contrasting longish, almost-black hair.

"Sure you are," I said, ashing my smoke. I didn't bother to keep the skepticism out of my voice…or my disapproval.

"Not a chickenhawk then?" he smirked back.

"No. Is that what you're looking for?" I blew smoke in his direction. "Because I think you could do better, kid. Why don't you come back in here when you're really eighteen?"

He frowned a little, but gave me a closer, sharper once-over.

"You a pilgrim?" he said.

I smiled. I couldn't help it. "No," I said, shaking my head. "Just not into toddlers." I frowned. "Seriously, kid. Why don't you go home?"

He gave me a contemptuous look, such that only a teenager can give.

"Are you a quiff?" he said.

I shook my head again, grimacing a little that time. "That's not a polite word," I reminded him, ashing again.

"It's not a polite world," he shot back.

He'd obviously wanted that reaction though, and smiled.

I bet he thought his comeback was pretty clever, too.

"Too bad," he said, leaning into me again and forcing me to move the stool entirely. "…About the quiff thing, I mean."

I watched as he handed two rumpled drink tickets to the bartender. He also gifted the burly guy working that side of the counter one of those shy, schoolboy smiles, which earned him a wink, but a good-natured one.

"You should listen to the Chief, here, Charlie," the bartender advised the kid, motioning his head towards me. "He's a wise one. Maybe you should do as he says."

"The Chief, eh?" Charlie said.

He cocked an eyebrow himself, looking directly at me. I headed him off, a little disconcerted that the bartender knew who I was.

"You don't seem hard up for cash," I observed to Charlie, glancing back over at the Wall Street bozos in suits. They were staring at me with an open hostility now, waiting for him to return. "Or admirers."

"Maybe that's not what I meant," Charlie said.

"Whatever you're up to, you should stop, Charlie," I said, jumping the gun before I knew I was going to do it. "It's been noticed."

He frowned, staring at me. I saw a lot of intelligence in those eyes, too.

"What on earth are you talking about?" he said finally. He smiled again. "Did you drop some acid before you left home tonight…Chief?"

I frowned a little, but didn't try to answer. I couldn't decide what he'd figured out about why I was there, and why I'd been watching him. I'd made it pretty clear I wasn't in the market for what he was selling.

I decided to play along, anyway.

"You a big-time business boy?" I said. "You know, in case I win at the horses in a few years, and your balls actually drop?"

He rolled his eyes, giving me a hard look. "You a killer queen?"

I shook my head, answering him honestly. "Nope. Too old." I took another drag of the cigarette. "You aren't, though. Then again, the war'll probably be over by the time you're old enough… am I right?"

"How old?" he countered, ignoring my question.

"Why do you care?" I said, smiling. "I can't afford you, right?"

"Who are you, really?" he said, turning to face me directly that time. "I've never seen you in here before. Are you sure you're not a tourist?"

"Not a tourist," I said, with a single shake of my head.

"What are you?" he said.

"Haven't we covered this?"

"You know what I mean. Spic? Mulatto? What?"

"Oh." Understanding, I shook my head, a little annoyed. "Sioux." That made him frown more. "Soo?"

"You know." At his blank look, I grinned. "Big Chief. Kill white man."

He laughed, more in surprise that time, I think. It looked to me like the first genuine smile I'd seen cross his face that night, in either case. It opened up his features, making him look even younger.

"Why aren't you drinking, Chief?" he said to me then.

"I am drinking," I told him, nodding down to my soda can.

He squinted at it, then at my church key still sitting on the bar, and gave me a bewildered look. I knew it was a little weird that I'd brought my own church key in there. But I'd found church keys to be handy for a lot of things over the years, not just poking holes in cans. Even so, I swept it off the top of the scuffed bar, disappearing it into my jacket pocket.

"You going to use that on me?"

"You don't have anything I want to drink, kid. Trust me."

"You know what I mean," he said.

"I do," I said. "Maybe I already gave you some advice tonight."

He frowned again.

Then he surprised me again, digging into his pocket and handing over one of the gifted drink tickets he'd just won by working the room. Sure, he probably had about twenty of those stuffed and crumpled in his various pockets by then, sweated through from dancing and even from previous trips in here on other nights. And yeah, I don't drink alcohol, for a lot of reasons, my father being the main one, although I wasn't about to explain that to young Charlie Dickens, either. But I was surprised, yeah. Grifters weren't generally known for handing out their winnings, not even toddler grifters. Was this supposed to be a bribe? Or maybe a peace offering of some kind? Or just a show of bravado?

Either way, something about it touched me in an odd way, reminding me again just how young he was.

"Have one on me," Charlie said, placing it on the bar with a lordly kind of air. He was still watching me closely. "Maybe I'll see you around."

"Maybe," I said agreeably, leaving the ticket where it lay.

That seemed to tick him off, too.

Either way, he looked more annoyed as he dragged the two watered-down gin and tonics off the bar and hauled them back to his admiring coterie, who continued to stare suspiciously at me from their smoke-filled corner of the bar. Watching Charlie as he made a big show of handing over the two drinks he'd gotten for his new friends in their expensive suits, now crunched against the wall as the inn began to fill up and the witching hour grew closer, I frowned a little, too, catching a glance he threw my way.

The bartender must have seen me staring.

"Nothing you can do, Chief," he said kindly. "He's just another lost soul, poor kid. You can just hope he'll survive it."

I nodded, but didn't answer him.

Maybe Charlie Dickens had gotten to me, just a little.

Maybe more than I really wanted to think about right then.

* * *

In 1969, Robbie and I had been in business for almost six years.

We technically worked as private dicks, starting at the end of '63 in a crappy tenement on Forty-Third in Hell's Kitchen, after I got my license. I asked Robbie if he wanted in, given that he'd gotten kicked off the Force (he said as some kind of "example," but really, he got caught racketeering, which was no surprise, really) and he needed the bread, with a wife and two kids and a third on the way. Robbie probably took some shit for setting up shop with me, but he did it anyway, getting his own license a few weeks later and pitching in on the rent and the business cards and keeping the lights on and whatever else.

The neighborhood wise guys, the Westies, who ran the whole area by '65, just tolerated us at first. Then, after a year or so, they became our primary customers. After all, Robbie was from the neighborhood. Meaning, not only was he born there, but he was a mick, like them.

And yeah, okay, that might have been part of why I asked him.

We were friends, though, too, mostly because our mothers knew each other, back before mine died in '58. Everyone still called me "Chief," of course…Robbie, too. Some of the baby Westies, new recruits out of Brooklyn and Queens, mistook me for a Puerto Rican and had to be set straight by the neighborhood guys, but mostly I got left alone. Like most New Yorkers, the neighborhood wise guys were happy enough to kick their own, but that didn't mean they wanted anyone else to do it…so I had protection, just like anyone else. After Robbie and me opened up shop and started doing odd jobs for the Family, then no one bothered me at all, even in spite of what I am.

It probably helped that I'm a big guy.

Six-foot-two, in my socks.

The Stonewall job came to us like a lot of jobs did. Someone who worked for someone from the neighborhood walked up the four flights to our office, dumped a wad of cash on Robbie's desk, told him what they wanted, and walked out.

No unnecessary explanations…nothing but the bare bones.

There's a rat in the Stonewall.

We think we know who he is, but find out for sure…and then explain things to him.

I didn't want to kill no kid, I'll tell you that, but I couldn't screw around, either. This was a Family job. Not even Westie family, but Family-Family. Some Mob-boss senior thought something was going in Mob-boss junior's "screw you, Pop" side project, the fairy bar on Christopher Street.

He wanted that shit to stop, now.

That's where some of the details got fuzzy, but I got the gist. Some wrestling match was going on with the Mob and the cops, either Vice or Alcohol and Tobacco, and someone was playing both sides of the fence.

Everyone joked about "gayola," the pay-off that gay bars had to pay the cops just to stay in business, but I'd heard whispers of more than that going on, in the form of blackmail and whatever else—meaning street kids on the Mob payroll blackmailing some of the richer clientele who had more to lose by being outed as queer. Maybe the cops heard those same rumors and were pissed off from not getting their cut. Maybe they found a kid and turned him, found the right things to say, maybe threatened him with jail or an orphanage or just offered a better deal than what he'd been getting, and he was too dumb to turn it down.

That's what made sense to me, anyway.

After all, Stonewall was hardly a secret to the cops, and everyone knew all the homosexual bars in New York belonged to the Mob.

They could sell people like me and those Wall Street bozos watered down drinks stolen from the backs of trucks without a liquor license, not bother to wash the glasses, let the place smell like vomit and piss…and we'd still come, if it meant we could hang out in the dark with a minimal chance of being beaten up or arrested. If it meant we could dance and laugh and pretend we were human, if only for a few hours some night. Even with the gayola, the Mob still made a killing on those places, just like they had with speakeasies under Prohibition…all because it was illegal to sell a queer a bottle of beer in the fine city of New York.

After watching Charlie in action that first night, I couldn't help but believe he might be their guy. He really might be running a scam like that, despite his age. He was smart enough, cocky enough, and he definitely would have been marked by the Mob as good hawk-bait in a blackmail scheme, given the types of admirers he attracted. Of course, I still didn't have any proof. I wasn't making any kind of move at all until I knew for sure, and even then, I still had no idea what I intended to do with him, if he ended up being our rat.

I knew I wouldn't get that proof at the Stonewall, though.

I'd need to know more about where he went when he wasn't hustling, which meant I needed to follow him.

Which is exactly what I did, the very next night.

* * *

Like most of those hustler kids, Charlie had a routine.

To his credit, he didn't do a lot of selling on the corner. But then, he was fishing with higher-end bait than most of those kids, and he'd probably earned his stripes out there already, living on the street in ways I didn't want to know about.

Nowadays, he crashed in an apartment on Bleeker Street.

He spent a lot of time there, too, from what I could gather, when he wasn't at Mama's Chick'N'Rib or Washington Square Park, or one of the head shops, record stores or crash pads in the Village haunted by other street kids who called this mess of maze-like streets their home. He seemed to do at least one circuit a day of the above, but didn't spend a lot of time anywhere but one of the tea rooms where a fair few of his favorite prey tended to hang out to give him presents. Even then, I didn't see a lot happening other than the requisite fawning and cash dispersals before Charlie went on his merry way.

In fact, the more I watched Charlie, the more I couldn't help thinking he had to be a gold mine for the Mob boys running the blackmail scam. Why hadn't the Mob tried to reason with him?

Why had they just painted a target on the kid's chest?

I knew the answer to that, too, though.

The kid was disposable to them. They didn't see what I saw— the talent, the beauty, that sharp intelligence, any of it. They just saw another cleaned-up street kid, with a line of thousands just like him, waiting to take his place.

They saw a queer punk who'd dared to screw with their livelihood.

I'd talked to a few other street kids, anyway, looking for more dirt.

I got told Charlie was a black widow and a vampire, which didn't exactly surprise me, but I wondered how much of that was jealousy, too. Most of those kids were hustlers, too, and probably wanted the kind of scores Charlie had carved out for himself, between the Mob and those rich hawks.

I paid off his building's supe to find out more about his habits…and also who paid his rent, knowing somehow, it wouldn't be Charlie Dickens himself. Turned out the apartment was owned by some big time brokerage house, one of the ones gobbling up the mom-and-pop variety over the past six months, or so the supe told me, and I later read about in the news. Some kind of "crisis on Wall Street" thing having to do with a lot of crap about trade volume and adding machines that I didn't bother to try and wrap my head around, other than to note it had thrown a lot of those suit-wearing cats out of work.

More than I'd realized, according to the supe.

I heard the usual complaints from the superintendent, too, who thought he had me figured from my clothes to be like him, so ranted up and down about queers and communists and hippies and all the usual crap you hear from old timers who hate what the Village turned into. Somewhere in that, though, he seemed to give me a second look through those coke-bottle glasses of his and remember that I'd shown up there, asking about Charlie Dickens.

Not long after that, he clammed up on me, too, and wouldn't say another word, so I wondered if he figured I was just another fruit looking for Charlie, or maybe wondered why else I might be looking for the kid.

In a weird sort of way, I found that touching, too.

Even though the guy hated queers, and wanted to boot Charlie out, he didn't seem to want to see Charlie Dickens get hurt, either.

All in all, I spent two days following Charlie, knowing at the end of the second that I had a few more before I had to make up my mind for real, before the next weekly raid happened some-time early the following week. It was only Friday, after all, and the place had just been raided on Tuesday, so the cops would leave it along until after the weekend.

I decided I would go home. Take the night off. Think on things.

Pet the damned cat.

But I didn't end up doing that, either.

Because when I was halfway back to Hell's Kitchen, walk-ing on foot up the sidewalks that would eventually lead me back to my apartment building, I ended up turning back around and walking all the way back to Christopher Street instead. I'd barely admitted to myself the reason why before I'd already crossed half the distance between me and Stonewall…or even a few minutes later, when I plopped myself back at that bar, another warm soda and my church key in hand.

Only then did I admit to myself that I'd already made up my mind, that I already knew what I wanted to do.

By the time I'd finished that first soda, I even had a plan.

I already knew Charlie was the rat.

I figured I would confront him. I'd tell him who I was, then talk the kid into skipping town…maybe even escort him to a bus headed somewhere that night, without him going back to his banker-owned apartment, and without Robbie knowing what I'd done until after the fact. I'd use my half of the deposit on the job as the bribe. It wasn't much, given what he probably got off his hawks, but I figured between that and the threat on his life, I could make Charlie see reason.

The kid wasn't stupid. He would go.

And I could do my little bit of good in the world this one time, however small.

* * *

The kid got to the Stonewall late.

It was nearly midnight when he finally showed, and by then I'd paid some other kid to bring me a few sodas, and I was kind of jerked up on sugar and caffeine. I'd forgotten they'd buried Judy Garland that day until they kept playing her songs over and over and I noticed a bit of a pall over some of the older set. The younger kids didn't give a hoot about Judy, of course…the music changed in the front room once enough of the under-thirty crowd showed, but in the back room I'm pretty sure it was all Judy all night for that other set.

But hell, it was Friday night, so who was I to judge?

By the time Charlie got there, it was a full house. He was avoiding me, too, and I was wishing I'd gone home like I'd planned, or at least tried to corner him outside, before he'd hunkered down with all of his admirers.

It wasn't until after one a.m., after I'd given up on talking to him inside and figured I'd try to find him again tomorrow instead, that someone pressed up against me on my right side, for the second time that week. I found myself looking up at Charlie's face, sweaty and red from dancing but with his blue eyes looking at me with a kind of wounded, fearful worry that I recognized from most of the kids on the streets. I have to admit, I jumped.

Then I scowled, barking at him before I knew I meant to.

"Cut that out!" I said. "It's not funny, Charlie! Jesus."

"You do know my name," he said, smirking a little.

"I know you're a kid, and I'm not into that. So cut it out!"

He smiled, but that more scared, wounded look never left those large eyes of his. He did back off though, like I'd asked, and I exhaled once he had, realizing only then that my whole body tensed once I knew who was pressed against me, and that I'd held my breath and clenched my fists.

"We should talk," I told him, once I'd relaxed.

"Are you going to kill me?" he asked, speaking loud over the music.

I flinched again, staring at him. Then I realized I hadn't been the only one making inquiries. He obviously knew who I was.

I shook my head, hoping I looked reassuring. "No," I said.

"What, then?" he said.

"How do you feel about San Francisco?" I asked, speaking loud, like him, to be heard over the music and clinking glasses.

He frowned, but I saw him thinking. He looked back at me, a few seconds later.

"Won't that get you in trouble?" he said.

I shrugged off his words, smiling. "Does it matter?"

"Yeah," he said. "Maybe. Maybe it does."

I only looked at him, not sure if I should laugh or be touched, or see it as another smooth con by one spooky smart and way-too-jaded kid. I decided to do neither, and just shrugged.

He was right, though. I knew he was right.

The Family might kill me, if I let him go.

I tried not to let that fact touch my expression, though, or my voice.

"No choice, kid," I began. "In fact, I really think you'll have to get out of here tonight—"

I was going to go on, to say more about that, but then the lights came on.

I heard voices I didn't know, giving a speech I more than recognized.

"Police!" a loud voice shouted. "We're taking the place!"

The raid had come early.

Which meant I was too late to pull Charlie out of the fryer, too.

* * *

No one wanted to cooperate.

Especially the trannies, and they were kicking up a real stink for once, too, refusing to go to the ladies' room and stand in the smell of piss and vomit while a female pig inspected their man-parts, declaring them perverts.

I can't say I blamed them.

I'd never seen them balk outright like that, though.

Eventually, the plain-clothers gave up and took them to the back room. That left the rest of us standing like guilty schoolchildren by the bar, waiting our turn to be harassed. Maybe in solidarity with the queens, a number of the 'norms' also refused to produce ID, even though those who did mostly got released.

I stood in the line with the rest of them.

I should have known I wouldn't get away with that.

I frowned at a couple of those pigs feeling over a dyke wearing a man's suit jacket, watching her elbow and slap away hands on her breasts and rear, when another voice jerked my chin and then my eyes to the other end of the line, where cops still argued with a few of the fag suits, trying to bully them into handing over their IDs.

My adrenaline was up already.

Maybe like an animal, I could smell that something was different.

I watched as another suit glared at a cop before he stalked towards the front door instead of scurrying out in shame, like normal. When he opened that same door to exit, I heard voices outside, too…more than a few. Enough to make me wonder, even that early on, if only in the periphery of my awareness.

Then I saw him. Franklin.

He grinned at me, like seeing me was some kind of present, wrapped up especially for him. I met those rodent-like, washed-out brown eyes right as he flicked his fingers in my direction, doing a bad impression of a local tough.

"Chief," he said. "You here working?"

I didn't answer.

Franklin only grinned wider. "He's one of them," he said, his voice dismissive, but holding an underlying note of glee. At the blond, twenty-something rook's vacant stare, Franklin clarified. "The tall guy. He works for the Micks. Put him in the truck with the others…"

I stiffened.

That wasn't how things were done, either.

Something must have shown on my face.

"You here on Family business, Chief?" Franklin asked again.

I glanced at Charlie, who remained next to me.

Despite the weirdness of the Friday night raid, I thought they'd follow the usual script, at least on the surface. When Franklin said those words, though, it hit me that if they dragged me in now, Charlie was dead.

It also hit me that I wasn't ready to see that happen, even now.

I'd committed, I guess. Some part of me couldn't let it go.

I reached casually for the envelope tucked behind my belt at the small of my back, but Franklin saw that, too. He held up a hand, his voice sharp, no-bullshit that time. Almost a real cop voice.

"Whoa, Chief! Hold it! Hands where I can see them!"

I hesitated, giving him a hard stare, then did as he asked, raising my palms slowly to either side of my head. Without looking over, I muttered to Charlie under my breath, teeth gritted.

"Envelope. Back of my belt."

Charlie looked up. That time, I glanced at him, meeting his blue eyes which had gone bright under the harsh lights. For the first time, I saw a scared kid there, under the tough street con.

Franklin was walking towards us, though.

I didn't have much time.

"Kid?" I prodded. "Last chance. Ticket to paradise."

Something in that seemed to wake him up.

He pressed his body up against mine, like he was scared, or maybe like we were together, which made me tense up all over again. But I kept my hands in the air, watching Franklin head my way, glancing at the cops stacking crates of booze by the door, readying them for the paddy wagon. Ignoring Charlie's sweated clothes against mine, I watched as Franklin broke into another of those stupid smiles, even as I felt Charlie's deft fingers relieve my belt of the envelope.

"I heard you were a limp-wrist, Chief," Franklin said. "But I didn't know you were a cradle-robber, too…"

I felt my jaw harden, seeing Franklin's eyes on Charlie.

"Yeah," Franklin said, giving me a knowing wink. "I think we got a case of moral corruption of a minor here…no question."

I didn't answer that either.

Robbie always thought this piece of shit was the one who turned him in on the racketeering. Looking at him now, I found myself thinking Robbie was right. Franklin had that paradoxical mixture I'd seen in a lot of government types, meaning dumb as a stump coupled with an inhuman knack for targeted ass-kissing. He would rat out a fellow cop without blinking an eye.

I just stood there while the rookie cop cuffed me.

And yeah, I felt something by then, sure…but I can't pretend that I expected what actually happened.

It was more like the smell of ozone crackling the air, right before lightning strikes the ground, burning a whole new pattern into the earth.

* * *

The sheer size of the crowd shocked me when they dragged me out into the street. I stiffened, too, I admit.

Fear, I guess.

Crowds make me nervous, and tension was high in this one; that much was obvious the second they shoved me out that door. A few of the more theatrical type queers yelled at the cops, jeering at them while the others laughed.

Out of habit, I scanned faces, ignoring the cheers when they saw me and the other Family types being hauled into the one and only police van standing at the curb on Christopher Street. I counted maybe one-eighty faces in that rough scan. A big enough number to have my adrenaline going. Locals, mostly. A lot of street kids, only the rougher and angrier variety than the Charlies of the world.

I was already being shoved inside the van when I heard the crowd start to sing, what sounded like "We Shall Overcome." I heard more laughter, too, but it sounded pretty tense.

By then, the hairs were standing up on my arms.

I've always had a good instinct for sensing trouble. Robbie used to joke it was my "sixth sense," and really, it truly was the only reason either of us was still alive, given some of the dumb-ass jobs we took in those early years. Right then, I found myself wishing like hell that I wasn't wearing cuffs, especially when they uncuffed one of my wrists only to re-cuff both to the van's metal bench.

I sat there, my back stiff as a poker, glancing at Charlie who now sat across from me, his own wrists only cuffed together, since they clearly didn't see him as a threat. They'd even taken my church key by then after they frisked me, but I hadn't seen them take the money off Charlie, not yet. It would only be a matter of time, though, I knew.

As they shoved the bartender into the back of the van, I found myself thinking the Family would hear about it once they did, that they would put one and one together and know where the kid got it.

Either way, I was screwed.

Either way, Charlie would still be dead.

I heard a commotion outside then and craned my neck in time to see a queen hit a uniform in the face with a woman's purse. I flinched, feeling myself tense as the crowd seethed, muttering and shifting like an angry swarm. I heard boos from a few bystanders, but more than anything, I could feel the tide of anger rising, the restlessness of feet on the pavement, the sharper tension in the air.

I found myself looking at one of the cops as he shoved that same street tranny in to sit on the bench a few people down from me.

"This is going bad," I told him. "Call it a night."

"Shut your trap, queer," he shot back.

He didn't even look at me.

Glancing around at the other faces in the van, most of them either pale and scared or as angry as the faces I saw outside those open doors, I felt that tension in my limbs worsen. Outside, I heard another commotion break out, heard female screams, then glimpsed the butch from inside the bar with her face contorted in anger or pain…or maybe both. She was fighting the cops, trying to get free. A sharp, pinging, ricochet sound hit the outside of the van then, and I realized some in the crowd were throwing things at the police van now, too.

This was going bad.

"Hey," I said, louder. The cop standing just outside the doors looked at me that time, his face taut. "Don't be stupid. Get us out of here!"

He pointed at my face. "Shut it. Now."

I looked at Charlie, who had also gone pale and silent on the bench across from me. He stared back with those shocking blue eyes, and I saw both the adult man he would be and the child he still was all in the same breath.

He felt it, too, that charge crackling through the air…but that made sense, too. No one survived on the street, not without developing that sense, not in the Village, not in New York, so he probably felt it more keenly than I did.

I don't know when things clicked over exactly.

I don't know what that final spark was, what made things explode from suppressed tension into something new, but as the baby butch was yelling for help and they slammed her against the van door, the crowd went totally berserk.

I watched bodies surge towards us like a tidal wave on a beach, knowing only that it was too late to get out of the way.

Then people were running out the back of the van, and the van was being rocked, the crowd outside shouting as they tried to tip it over.

I stared down at my wrists cuffed to the bench, feeling helpless.

Then I found myself staring at Charlie.

"Run," I told him. "Why are you still here? Run, Charlie!"

"What about you?" he said.

I stared at him, uncomprehending.

"Don't worry about me!" I snapped. "Go! Now, damn it!"

He hesitated, just looking at me. Feeling my adrenaline spike, I stared out the back of the van, my muscles tensing as I saw the cops beating back the crowd with batons, pennies and other coins and rocks and even bricks pelting into them and into the side of the van. I heard the engine start up on the van and half stood from the bench, stopped only by the chain on the cuffs.

"Charlie!" I snapped. "Go! Now! Or I'll kill you myself, I swear it!"

Charlie stood that time, fluid as a cat. Hesitating the barest second, he leaned toward me, shocking me by kissing me on the cheek.

"Thanks, Chief," he said.

I barely blinked away my surprise.

Then he was gone.

* * *

The van took off a few seconds later.

Those few seconds took a lifetime, it seemed.

I saw batons swing, queers yell and shove and fight back, the crowd surge and reconfigure. I heard objects slam into the van, chanting, screams.

I heard about the rest in the clink, of course.

How in a weird twist of irony, the cops locked themselves in the Stonewall to get away from the crowd, how the crowd broke in, doused the place in lighter fluid and tried to send the whole thing up in flames. About the bricks and garbage cans thrown through the boarded up windows of the Stonewall itself, about paper set on fire and shoved through the holes and cracks. About cops' bleeding heads and bruised faces…a parking meter that got used as a battering ram against the doors of the Stonewall itself, and cops pulling their guns when the crowd finally broke through those boarded windows.

Stories came at me all night, pictures painted in words from cells full of bruised and bloodied queers, most of them laughing, in high spirits, cursing out the cops with barely suppressed glee to anyone who would listen.

It was like a fire got lit that night, a fire that couldn't be extinguished, not even by threat of death…not even after the cops got really pissed off and were truly out for blood.

Everyone knows about Stonewall now, of course.

The very first homosexual riots—ever, as far as I know— erupted with me and Charlie right in the middle of it, and right in the middle of me making a decision that should have gotten me killed, and for a kid I barely knew.

Still, a few images stick with me.

Seeing that crowd rush the van. The coins and bricks pelting the cops even as the van pulled away from the curb. Charlie's blue eyes staring at me right before he kissed me. And later, in the jail cell, trading cigarettes with a queen with a bloody face who told me about kneeling on the chest of a boy in blue, beating him with her high-heeled shoe, laughing as she put the cigarette to her cut lip.

It was hard to feel much sympathy for the pigs.

They'd been pushing buttons and shaking us down and beating us up for years. That night, the Village queers weren't having it anymore, I guess.

I never heard anything about Charlie, though.

Not once, ever again.

When I asked later, a few of the old queens who looked out for him said he'd been hauled off with some of the trannies, stuck in a second police van before he could escape. But he never made it to the jail that night, either.

Believe me, I looked.

I had to hope that he ended up on that bus.

I had to hope he found his way to paradise.

Acknowledgements

Thank you to the following wonderful people who supported the *Fiction River* Kickstarter Subscription Drive:

A Fan
Karen Alcorn
Cora Anderson
Jeffrey A. Ballard
Clayton Bassett
DiAnne Berry
Elizabeth Bourne
Marla Bracken
Alexandra Brandt & Erik Kort
Valerie Brook
Linda Bruno
M.L. Buchman
Cheryl Bunn
Michael A. Burstein
Brenda Carre
Stephen Couch
Jamie Curierre
Leah Cutter
dafaolta
Steven B. Davis
John Devenny
Diana Deverell
Simon Donohoe
Dragon Mom
Robert Early
Eric Kent Edstrom
Darren Eggett
Bonnie Elizabeth
Ferran
Felicia Fredlund
Denise Gaskins
Gavran
Marian Goldeen
Lotus Goldstein

Jaq Greenspon
Carol J. Guess
Michael Harbour
Pat Hayes
Chuck Heintzelman
Judith Herman
Sandra Hofsommer
Neil Hume
Wendy Ice & David Delamare
Jim Johnson
Sharon Joss
Francesca Jourdan
Everett Kaser
B G Knighton
Brian D Lambert
Frédéric Lambert
Michele Lang
Anthea Lawrence
AJ Lemke
Mark Leslie
Li
Sara Litt
Margaret Ann Long
John Lorentz & Ruth Sachter
Robert J. McCarter
Meyari McFarland
Jason McGee
Big Ed Magusson
Susan Miller
Shirley J Mitchell
Deirdre M. Murphy
naleta
Maralee Nelder
Shyam Nunley

Lisa Owen
Irette Y. Patterson
Steve Perry
Brian Pettera
Lauren Quick
Mary Jo Rabe
Paula Richards
Theresa Rogers
Risa Scranton
Bryan Thomas Schmidt
Margaret St. John
Colleen M. Story
Mike Skolnik
Vaughan W. Smith
Ruth Stuart
Raphael Sutton
Michelle Tatam
Andrew Timson
Tasha Turner
Laura Ware
Thomas Werner
Keith West
Ryan M. Williams
Kristyn Willson
Chrissy Wissler
Kari J. Wolfe
Stephanie Wood Franklin
Lyn Worthen
Mandy Wultsch
B. Zingmark

and

The Bijou Theatre
Lincoln City OR

About the Editor

USA Today bestselling author Kristine Kathryn Rusch writes in almost every genre. Generally, she uses her real name (Rusch) for most of her writing. Under that name, she publishes bestselling science fiction and fantasy, award-winning mysteries, acclaimed mainstream fiction, controversial nonfiction, and the occasional romance. Her novels have made bestseller lists around the world and her short fiction has appeared in eighteen best of the year collections. She has won more than twenty-five awards for her fiction, including the Hugo, *Le Prix Imaginales,* the *Asimov's* Readers Choice award, and the *Ellery Queen Mystery Magazine* Readers Choice Award.

She also edits. Beginning with work at the innovative publishing company, Pulphouse, followed by her award-winning tenure at *The Magazine of Fantasy & Science Fiction,* she took fifteen years off before returning to editing with *Fiction River.* She acts as series editor with her husband, writer Dean Wesley Smith, and edits at least two anthologies in the series per year on her own.

To keep up with everything she does, go to kriswrites.com.

FICTION RIVER: YEAR TWO

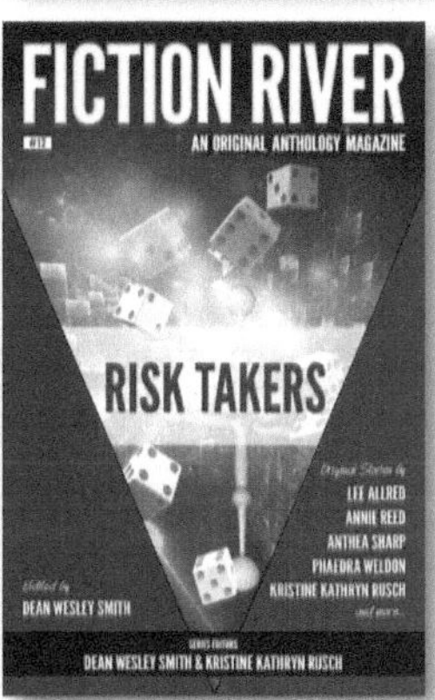

A subscription to Fiction River saves you money and ensures you receive the very best short fiction from some of today's best authors. Subscriptions are available in electronic and trade paper formats and begin with the very next volume.

Don't wait!
Subscribe today at www.FictionRiver.com.

FICTION RIVER: YEAR ONE

Missed a volume from Fiction River's first year?

No problem. Buy individual volumes anytime from your favorite bookseller.

See why *Adventures Fantastic* calls *Fiction River* "one of the best and most exciting publications in the field today."